HER DUCHESS
TO DESIRE

What Reviewers Say About Jane Walsh's Work

Her Lady to Love

"If you are looking for a sweet, cozy romance with grounded leads, this is for you. The author's dedication to the little cultural details do help flesh out the setting so much more. I also loved how buttery smooth everything tied together. Nothing seemed to be out of place, and the romance had some stakes. ...Highly recommended."
—Colleen Corgel, Librarian, Queens Public Library

"Walsh debuts with a charming if flawed Regency romance. ...Though Honora's shift from shy curiosity to boldly stated interest feels a bit abrupt, her relationship with Jacquie is sweet, sensual, and believable. Subplots about a group of bluestockings and a society of LGBTQ Londoners add depth..."—*Publishers Weekly*

"What a delightful queer Regency era romance. ...*Her Lady to Love* was a beautiful addition to the romance genre, and a much appreciated queer involvement. I'll definitely be looking into more of Walsh's works!"—Dylan Miller, Librarian, Baltimore County Public Library

"...it's the perfect novel to read over the holidays if you love gorgeous writing, beautiful settings, and literal bodice ripping! I had such a brilliant time with this book. Walsh's novel has such an excellent sense of the time period she's writing in and her specificity and interest in the historical aspects of her plot really allow the characters to shine. The inclusion of details, specifically related to women's behaviour or dress, made for a vivid and exciting setting. This novel reminded me a lot of something like Vanity Fair (1847) (but with lesbians!) because of its gorgeous setting and intriguing plot."—*The Lesbrary*

By the Author

Her Lady to Love

Her Countess to Cherish

Her Duchess to Desire

HER DUCHESS TO DESIRE

by

Jane Walsh

2022

ISBN 13: 978-1-63679-065-7

This Trade Paperback Original Is Published By
Bold Strokes Books, Inc.
P.O. Box 249
Valley Falls, NY 12185

First Edition: March 2022

_____

Credits
Editor: Cindy Cresap
Production Design: Susan Ramundo
Cover Design By Tammy Seidick

Acknowledgments

Thank you so much to the fantastic team at Bold Strokes Books—I deeply appreciate everyone's hard work and dedication to making our books shine.

Many thanks to my wonderful wife, Mag, who is the world's best listener. You are an endless source of support and encouragement and I appreciate your love more than I can ever express. Thanks for the hugs, the balloons, and for encouraging me to order chocolate mousse on the night the book was due.

This book was written during a time when so many of us were working from home, and it's probably no surprise that so much of it revolves around a house and what it means to its inhabitants. I hope you enjoy the historical HGTV!

I am indebted to David Watkin's meticulous research on Thomas Hope, particularly to the designs for his Duchess Street estate, in his book *Thomas Hope: Regency Designer* (Yale University Press, 2008). Hope's work and ideas strongly influenced Letty's philosophy of design and the choices she makes for the renovation of Hawthorne House.

My Regency romances not only have queer main characters, but they also feature a community of LGBTQ people whose lives are threatened by the social and political prejudices of the time. Unfortunately, more than two centuries later, difficult and dangerous times persist for queer people in many countries.

Please, please always exercise your right to vote. Let's make sure that love, dignity, and human rights will always win.

Dedication

For Mag, because your love makes our house a home

CHAPTER ONE

London, 1813

Anne, the Duchess of Hawthorne, had often wished her husband to go to the devil. Today was the first time in ten years of marriage that she felt the urge to personally aid him on his journey there. She eyed the letter opener on her desk. Efficient, quick, and quid pro quo for the knife that he had long ago stabbed into her back.

The Duke of Hawthorne leaned a shoulder against the ornate mantel. The rich velvet of his coat gleamed in the firelight, and so did the jewels that studded his fingers. His dark hooded eyes gazed at her, inscrutable as always.

Once, he had been her lighthouse in stormy seas. Now he was the sea itself, intent on sinking her.

How dare he crash upon the shores of her drawing room?

"It wouldn't be immediate, if you don't wish it." His voice was always deep, but she suspected he had pitched it even lower in an attempt to soothe. Instead, it aggravated.

"I don't wish it to happen at all," she snapped, rising from her chair and leaving the letter opener on the desk and out of her line of sight. Less tempting that way. "Why on earth do you wish to establish your lover in *my house*?"

"I would naturally accompany him. May I remind you that this is *our* house?"

"You said you were content to keep your bachelor apartment at the Albany. You certainly aren't the only husband there who is estranged from his wife."

"Things change."

She sucked in a breath. "But we had settled this when you returned from France in May. We would live apart so that your scandalous ways do not touch the duchy—or sully my good name."

"Is it not the privilege of this title to change the rules as I please? Have I been mistaken all these years in thinking that a duke's power is limitless?"

"*Now* you lay claim to the power of the title?" There was no one on the face of this earth who could rile her the way that he did. He seemed unaffected, lazily twisting his signet ring on his finger. Seeing the emblem of the House of Hawthorne winking at her enraged her further. "Who has been the face of this duchy for the past decade, Hawthorne? Who presided over countless decisions on behalf of your name? And what have you done instead while you gallivanted in France?"

"My legacy will be known to my kind of people."

"From the wild parties you used to throw?" Anne shook her head and sat again, glaring at the stack of letters that had arrived for her from the estate managers. She had a meeting with her secretary in an hour to draft her replies. Every day, she worked to maintain the dukedom, and suddenly Hawthorne had a vested interest in it? Did he expect her to hand everything over to him just because he was a man?

Over her dead body. She glanced again at the letter opener. Or better yet, *his*.

When she looked up, she saw the twitch at Hawthorne's right eye that told her, even after all these years apart, how upset he was. "You may not understand the work that I have done through the years, Annie. But I assure you—I have toiled to help people who needed it."

"I think we are rather far from returning to given names, are we not? In case you somehow failed to notice, I am not your *Annie* anymore."

The tic jerked at his eye again and he pushed himself away from the mantel and into a low bow. It was meant to be insulting, she knew, because he scraped to the extent that would have better suited the Queen.

"My humblest apologies, Your Grace." By the time he straightened, the bored look had returned to his face. "Yet I am indeed the Duke of Hawthorne, and your husband. I kept away for six months after my return to England out of respect to you, to give you time to adjust. I came today to extend an olive branch, which you can snap and throw away if you wish. However, you must accept that I will take back the reins of the dukedom. I will return to my birthright—this house. And where I go, I take Phin with me."

Anne narrowed her eyes. "Must you carry on with a mere *sir*? Sir Phineas is nowhere near our rank."

Hawthorne laughed. "Is that what you care about? You believe he isn't good enough for this house? How wrong you are. He is a man valued above rubies. He stays with me. I shall postpone our moving date until after the start of the new year, when you will be back at Hawthorne Towers and our presence here won't bother you. But that is the best I can offer."

After Hawthorne left, there was nothing but the stolid ticktock of the grandfather clock in the hallway for company. Usually she enjoyed being alone. Life was much easier when she could focus on what must be done, without the emotion and tension and complications that another person brought into the equation.

Especially when that person was her husband.

Anne took a deep breath, then rang the bell for a housemaid to add more coals to the fire and to bring a cup of tea. It was never warm enough in this room, and it was only October. God help her if she had to stay here through the winter.

She was in London to handle pressing business, but usually by now she would be ensconced in Hawthorne Towers in Kent, where her custom was to stay through the winter. Summer and autumn were always spent touring the dukedom's vast country holdings, managing the land and its tenants, and hosting events for the elite social circle into which she had been both born and wedded. In the spring, she kept a careful eye on the duchy's business from London. She had rarely been in the capital as late as October.

But she couldn't bear to think of staying in Kent while her husband took up residence in the London townhouse after ten years away. Who knew what changes he would try to implement at Hawthorne House? Who could predict the staff's reaction if he instituted his lover in his own bedchamber? What if he threw scandalous parties from the ballroom? Only her presence could prevent gossip. It was her duty to avoid even the hint of scandal.

Anne had spent too long establishing a sterling reputation to see it chipped under the weight of Hawthorne's indiscretions.

He couldn't expect to roll up his sleeves one day and start signing his signature again. He might wear the family signet ring on his finger with the full weight of the dukedom behind it, but the heavy gold seal carved with strawberry leaves and an ornate *H* on its tip belonged on her desk, not his. That seal had become the mark of approval from the duchy during Hawthorne's absence. Maybe she should move it to her bedchamber, or start carrying it on her person—but no. That was taking things too far.

On the other hand, she only held power through the Hawthorne name. She managed households and business affairs, and by God, she was good at it. If the duke returned, did it mean that his duchess would have nothing left of her own?

Anne gripped her teacup and willed the warmth to seep into her ice-cold fingers. There was no choice. It was going to be a long, bitter winter in the heart of London. But she had endured worse for duty. If Hawthorne was staying, then so would she. The fire burned brightly with the added coals, and she moved closer to its flames.

If the duke wished to wage war, then he could have chosen no better enemy than the woman he had abandoned.

Hawthorne was sorely mistaken if he thought that his wife would be biddable.

Miss Letitia Barrow fixed the merchant with a gimlet eye. "You *lost* my marbles?"

"I wouldn't say that they've been lost, exactly. The ship sank—and all the cargo aboard was destroyed. It's a sad state of affairs." Mr. Bridge gave a deep sigh and raised his eyes heavenward.

She thought of the Italian marble tiles, deep veins of gold and pink swirled into eggshell white stone, meant to grace the front hall of Judge Peterson's quarters. Now they were scattered in the deep silt of the Thames, visible to the fish instead of the judge's dinner guests. She could well imagine the judge's face when she told him the news. It wasn't the first time that something had not gone according to plan on his renovation.

But this wasn't adding up. "I didn't hear of any cargo ships sinking."

"Miss Barrow, a woman such as yourself cannot be expected to know all the comings and goings at the ports." He smiled at her. Placatingly.

Letty didn't return the smile. "I do, in fact, keep abreast of them. I order so many goods from the Continent that I am quite aware of everything related to importing. Customs documentations. Tariffs and fees. I even arrange the wagons to pick up the cargo and move it to the establishments that I renovate. No, Mr. Bridge. This is too smoky by half."

He blinked. "I beg your pardon, madam, but this changes nothing. The marble is gone."

"Gone? Or resold to a higher bidder?"

"We would never do such a thing," he spluttered. "This is a reputable firm. We provide marble, granite, and limestone to all the best establishments."

"Except to women who pay up-front, and thus allow you to get away with fraud?"

Too late, Letty saw her mistake. Hell and the devil, she should have made a down payment instead of risking the money from the start. But the marble was the crowning touch for the foyer's design. She had bargained and begged this man three months ago to sell it to her—and now she wondered if the tiles had always been promised elsewhere, and *she* had been the one to pay the merchant twice for the same goods?

She stood and rapped her silver-tipped walking stick on the floor. "You will be hearing from my solicitor, sir. Good day."

She inhaled the crisp scent of autumn leaves as she crossed the street to hail a hackney cab, the air fresh on her face. The work for the judge was almost complete. All she needed to do was arrange workers to lay the tiles, and she already had a crew lined up for the days that she needed them. Then the new furniture would be placed and polished, the room would be scoured clean, and the job would be done.

But if she didn't have the marble, she would have to cancel the job with the tilers. She would owe at least partial wages to the crew, as they wouldn't be able to find other work on short notice. Letty winced. The budget she had been given to finish the job was fast dwindling. More importantly, she couldn't risk this blow to her reputation. It was already difficult for a woman to succeed in any sort of design work. It would be disastrous if she became known for canceling work, or for being unreliable with product that she had promised to provide.

Or if merchants thought that she was easy to fool. She clenched her fingers around her walking stick as if it were Mr. Bridge's scrawny neck.

Letty shoved her key into the door beside the entrance of a furniture shop and went up the narrow stairs. She marched into her suite of rented rooms and hung up her hat and stick on the hooks by the door. She slapped her hand onto the wood table by the front window, where her solicitor-in-training son was making himself a sandwich.

"Robert Barrow, is that the ham that ought to be for dinner?"

He grinned with all the impishness of a twenty-two-year-old man who was still half a boy in his mother's eyes. "I just took a little piece, Mum. Growing lad and all that, right?" He ducked as she tried to rumple his hair. "Hey now, I've an appointment in twenty minutes and it took me twice that to fix my hair." He darted to the corner of the kitchen and took a hearty bite of his sandwich.

"After your appointment, I have another that you must tend to." Letty glowered. "A marble merchant is trying to cheat me. It's for the job I have for Judge Peterson. I told him he would be hearing from you."

Robert's mouth screwed to one side. "Mum, I've told you. No one is going to listen to a lowly clerk like me. Besides, I must stay late at the office to prepare documents for Mr. Selkirk. If I am to have any hope of apprenticing with him, I must be above reproach. And so must *you*. He is such a stickler that any transgression would be reason for him to choose another man as apprentice. Neither of us can get involved in petty squabbles, much less for the judge's office!" He looked stricken.

"There are other solicitors, Robert. You act as if Mr. Selkirk holds the keys to the kingdom, yet he is but one professional man. In all of London, I might add. Look around at our own neighborhood. Holborn is teeming with opportunities for a bright, responsible boy such as yourself. Any of the men in Chancery should be delighted to have you under their wing."

"It doesn't work like that, Mum." He rolled his eyes up to the rafters. "Mr. Selkirk is one of the few willing to overlook the circumstances of my birth. To make up for that flaw, I must be impeccable in every other way."

"That isn't fair," Letty said, but she knew it was the truth.

"I wish you had told people that you and my father had been married." His voice was quiet, and he shoved another bite of ham in his mouth as if to prevent himself from speaking further.

She thought of Robert's father. "That wasn't possible. Besides, I am not ashamed of what happened. Not when it gave me the gift of you."

Letty gazed at his thick chestnut brown hair, so like her own, though hers had been streaked with gray for years. His hair was his only resemblance to her. Everything else—his high forehead, his sturdy chin, his hazel eyes—was his father all over again. Especially his godforsaken sense of misplaced propriety.

There was no denying that Robert was every inch a lord's by-blow.

He blew out a sigh. "I know I should not be ashamed, Mum. But it dogs my feet everywhere I go. If I cannot secure myself a profession, how am I to live? This is my opportunity to advance myself. I cannot waste it. I *will* not."

"Is your illegitimacy the only thing Mr. Selkirk finds objectionable?"

Robert averted his eyes. "He has mentioned his dislike of women in professions."

"Women such as myself?" Mr. Selkirk sounded like a pompous ass who would do better to keep his opinions to himself.

"Well. I suppose so. Yes. You know, Mum, I was wondering if I could beg a favor from you, until the apprenticeship is chosen." His eyes beseeched her.

"What exactly do you need?"

"You take so many jobs for the professional men in Holborn, but it means you are always working near where my offices are. I almost had to accost Mr. Selkirk to prevent him from seeing you the other day. I—well—I haven't told him that you still *work*."

"But everyone knows I work. Robert, we have lived in this neighborhood your whole life. People know us."

"Well. I may have let him believe that you had given it up and had settled into a respectable living. At home."

She was too shocked to feel hurt. "You are ashamed of me? Your own mother?"

"Never that. But maybe after the judge's quarters, you could consider not taking another job?" He cast his eyes down and Letty thought he might be a moment away from scuffing his shoe like a schoolboy. "He should choose among the clerks soon."

"How soon?"

"Maybe Yuletide," he muttered without meeting her eye.

"I can't be without work for months, Robert! We're stretched tight enough as it is. This is a fool's hope that you're nurturing. What if Mr. Selkirk doesn't even choose you?"

His face mottled. "The one thing I ask of you!" he cried. "And you deny me."

Letty willed herself to be patient. "Robert, Holborn is where I work. The men who hire me recommend me to their friends and colleagues, and yes—they may well be in the same area. That's how it is."

"Then I am forever twice damned, both in birth and in consequence."

Robert's bitter words hung in the air after he stormed out of the apartment. The four whitewashed walls of their sitting room felt like they were closing in on her.

Letty had spent her adult life in this neighborhood, cheek to jowl among barristers and artisans and their apprentices. Granted, she used to have the lease on a grander house a few streets over, but it was no use remembering better times.

How could she find a job outside of her network? Her reputation wasn't impressive enough for people to find her on the strength of her name. It was difficult when so few people understood the value that she could give them. People were accustomed to architects furnishing their homes and offices when they were built and hiring craftsmen directly to provide any necessary refurnishing. It had taken time and effort for her to convince the neighborhood that although she produced nothing with her own hands, she could facilitate things by coordinating with all the necessary people on a project and could design rooms that were suited to the individual's needs of the moment, instead of merely following the initial architect's plans.

Yet if Robert was asking for help, how could she refuse it? There was a pit in her stomach when she thought of Robert's angry face. It reminded her of her father, screaming at her to leave Lincolnshire after she had found herself in a delicate condition.

Robert was all she had now. She couldn't bear to lose him, too.

She drummed her fingers on the table, then sighed as she swept the crumbs from Robert's sandwich into her palm and dusted them into the empty fireplace. It would do her no good to stay here for the afternoon, not with the memory of Robert's words as company.

After the work for the judge, she had nothing lined up. She had no reason to go downstairs to her tiny workroom with her sketchbook, much as she would like to lose herself for a while in dreams.

Judge Peterson wouldn't be inclined to recommend her services now that she couldn't deliver the marble, so maybe Robert didn't have to worry about her being employed in the same area after all.

But perhaps one of her usual suppliers would have good news for her. Maybe someone knew of an opportunity. Ideally someone with a snug little house far away, in desperate need of repair. As long as its owner wasn't cursed with a noble title, or more money than sense.

Letty drew on her thick wool cloak again and left the apartment, determined to find something.

Anything.

After all, either her own livelihood or Robert's depended on it.

CHAPTER TWO

As it was unfashionable to stay in London at this time of year, Anne spent every afternoon that week with no visitors and nothing to look forward to. There were no calling cards these days. Even her secretary's briefing this morning had been quick compared to the usual hours that they spent working together.

Being without something to occupy her time was most unusual for her. But since Hawthorne's return to England, she had felt unusual. Unsettled. Unmoored.

It was raining outside, with a misty swirl of fog on the ground that made her glad to be indoors despite the draughts that seeped in. Hawthorne Towers was much warmer, and she pulled her thick shawl closer and thought of how nice it would be to be in the cozy morning room *there*, instead of the frigid one *here*.

There was one event on her evening agenda tonight—a dinner, hosted by Hawthorne's nephew, Edward, who was also his heir. One did not turn one's back on family despite the inclement weather. Besides, if there was war to be waged against her husband, it would be best to make sure that his relatives were aligned with *her*. He had been out of the country for ten years—surely, the family's relationship with her would be stronger than his own? She had been to every baptism, every wedding, every funeral. She had curried favor with the Prince Regent for them.

It wouldn't hurt to show up and remind them.

Five hours later, after a team of maids had primped and prepared her and she was dressed in finery that her modiste promised would make women of lesser means weep with envy, Anne sat in a towering fury. She stared down at the first course of a meal that already promised to feel like it would last an eternity.

Hawthorne had stolen the advantage and won the very first battle. How had he secured an invitation? No one had told her that *he* would be in attendance.

Anne clutched her soup spoon and glared down the table. Edward was hanging on Hawthorne's every word. There was a sourness in her stomach, and she pushed her bowl away a fraction of an inch, enough for the footman to remove it in an instant. She wished they could as easily remove the fatted calf that had been hauled out before her husband.

Edward was twenty-one, having barely gained the age of his majority. Since he was a lad of eleven, she had taken a firm hand in his education and his social introductions. He would be the next Duke of Hawthorne, and she took her responsibility to him and to the title seriously. Why, the Queen herself had commended Anne on the fine job she had done to raise a young man of such good character.

Was her influence gone now? Was Hawthorne regaling him with tales of his exploits in Paris? Was that why Edward was laughing so hard, in a way that he never laughed with her?

Anne realized she was still holding her soup spoon, even though the bowl had long been removed. What a horror. She set it down, and a footman picked it up and placed a new course in front of her. Thin slices of roast pheasant were piled in an artful way with a few spears of asparagus on the gold-rimmed plate. Though she had lost her appetite, she took a requisite bite and then busied herself in talking to her neighbor, while keeping an eye on the betrayal that was playing out at the end of the table.

Florence, Hawthorne's sister, fussed over her after dinner. "Let me seat you by the fire. The place of honor." She handed Anne a glass of warm spiced wine and hovered over her until she sat, carefully shielding her from the drafty room by a painted screen. It was well-known how little she liked the cold.

Just like a dowager. Why, Hawthorne's great-aunt was nodding herself to sleep in the chair next to hers. She gripped the crystal stem of the wineglass hard enough that she feared breaking it. This was not to be borne. She was far from her dotage.

Anne spied Hawthorne next to the bay windows, laughing with his cousins like he had never been away. He slapped them on their backs, his manners easy and warm, and for a moment she hated him for all the charm that he possessed. Granted, his cousins seemed far more reserved. They didn't reciprocate his smiles as widely, and one of them kept glancing around as if looking for escape. Perhaps Hawthorne was going to have to work for their affections after all.

If she were to lose her consequence among his family, then Anne had no one. And if Hawthorne took back the work of the dukedom, she would have nothing. What had all her hard work been for if she was to be forgotten, even while she stood among them? Would generations to come know her only as a scrawl in the family Bible or a footnote in Debrett's? Anne, eldest daughter of the Earl of Clydon, childless wife of the Duke of Hawthorne. What was her legacy, if not the work that she put into the dukedom?

She ought not to have raised a finger on the Hawthorne family's behalf if this was to be her reward.

Anne managed through a few well-placed stares to be seated next to Edward when tea was being served in the drawing room.

"Aunt Anne, thank you for being here tonight. Mother told me that I really ought to start having more gatherings, and I daresay she is right. It makes it easier when there are people I like in attendance."

Anne didn't miss his sidelong glance at Hawthorne as he delivered his last remark. "I am always happy to be with family," she said. "You know you can count on me." She patted his knee a little awkwardly. She wasn't one to touch people, as a rule, but Hawthorne seemed so natural at it. Maybe it was part of the key to his success.

"It's smashing that Hawthorne is back in town, isn't it? He has ever so many stories. Well, you must have heard all of them by now, I suppose."

"Of course."

In fact, Anne had heard none of them. At least, not from Hawthorne. There had been plenty of people over the years who had been only too pleased to drop the latest *on-dits* in her ear. In the guise of concern for her situation, of course.

As if the mere mention of his name had the power to conjure him, Hawthorne ambled up to them and sat beside Anne. The sofa was narrow, and his thigh pressed against her own, radiating heat like it was a brand. She eyed his leg. Maybe he truly did have infernal powers.

This was the closest they had been since their wedding night. She wondered if he was thinking the same thing.

"Well, here we are all together at last," he said. "Edward, my lad—or I suppose you would prefer the title now that you are no longer a stripling, wouldn't you? My apologies, Kensworth. You should come by the house more often. One day, I expect that it should be your own. You might as well be familiar with it."

His ears turned red. "Oh, I am quite often at Hawthorne House. I also spend time at Hawthorne Towers every summer as Aunt Anne's guest. She has been ever so insistent on it."

"I have long considered it important to encourage Kensworth to consider the Hawthorne properties as his own." The name felt odd on her tongue. She never called Edward by his title, though he had been Marquess of Kensworth for years, and would be until he became the Duke of Hawthorne himself someday.

Hawthorne gazed at her for a moment, then turned to Edward. "I should bring you round my club, introduce you to some very fine people. Call on me at my apartments and I should be glad to take you anytime you wish."

Anne stiffened. The gentlemen's clubs were purviews that she could not enter, and Hawthorne knew it. She hated how his influence could reach further than her own because he was a man and the duke.

Why could he not have stayed in Paris?

"That sounds like a good deal of fun." Edward grinned. "I say, might I ask why I need to send word to the Albany? Why are you not both at Hawthorne House?"

Hawthorne's expression didn't change. "Renovations."

Anne shot a look at him. *Renovations?* That was the reason he was giving for having a separate address? She wondered how many people believed it. To give him credit, it wasn't a bad decoy if it prevented polite society from thinking about his illicit love affairs despite all the rumors that had floated across the Channel.

Hawthorne and Edward fell into an easy conversation about the theater, as Anne sat beside them. Was this to be her fate now—to act for all the world like a good wife?

Quiet. Invisible. Entirely proper.

Entirely *boring*.

She stood no chance against the force of her husband's charm. She had never predicted that Hawthorne would return, or that he would want to integrate himself back into the *ton*. Everything that she had built was now at risk.

As their voices droned on around her, she thought about what Hawthorne said. *Renovations*. What if it became more than an excuse?

Maybe this could be the perfect plan to keep things exactly as she wished them to be.

It was a short walk from Letty's house to Swann's Ale Rooms and Eatery. Her apartment had a fireplace in the main room, and she had a handful of pots and dried goods that her housekeeper could use to cook in a pinch. These days, however, she most often had her main meal with friends, and Robert likewise. He worked so late that it was unusual to see him until long after nightfall, stumbling in bleary-eyed and rumpled from hours spent toiling over his books and writing up case notes for the solicitors he clerked for.

Two years ago, her smart townhouse had a proper kitchen, and she had employed a full staff instead of a housekeeper and one maid-of-all-work. She spared a thought for the life she once had, then shook her head and picked up her pace. Life had moved on, and so must she.

It was a company mostly of men at Swann's, but Letty was used to it. She fit herself into life as she wanted instead of how society dictated, and people were long accustomed to her ways.

Independent was how the kinder neighbors described her. *Mannish* and *cocky* was how others thought of her, and she knew it because enough of them had felt the need to spit the words in her face.

Two dozen booths, with room for four to six diners apiece, lined the walls under graceful arches and a high ceiling. The paintings that adorned the rooms featured hunting scenes and battlefields, which Letty had helped the owner purchase at auction. When she had been living on the stipend provided by Robert's father, she had dabbled in decorating for friends and family and local businesses, talking to them about what they needed, and then piecing all the arrangements together like a puzzle. It had been a passion for her, long before it had turned into necessity.

It was early enough in the evening that one of the smaller booths was still unoccupied, so Letty snagged it and sank onto the padded bench. She leaned her walking stick against the wall. The past few days had been difficult. Although she had found replacement tiles for the judge's foyer, they weren't as nice as the marble and it had meant going over the budget. Again. She had a feeling that the untimely budget adjustments would be deducted from the total payment that she had negotiated for her work.

Fraser MacDougal slipped into the seat across from her. "You look exhausted, Letty lass."

"Not words any woman wishes to hear, not even from a dear friend."

As far as friends went, Fraser was one of the very dearest. He was a short Black man whose cropped hair and neat goatee glittered with gray, but she would bet that his coat and trousers were the same size as they had been when she had met him at twenty years of age.

"The privilege of friendship is the permission to make uncomfortable observations without incurring rancor from the other party," he told her. He slipped his quizzing glass out of his brocade vest and held it to his eye, peering at her. "I observe that you look like you've not slept a wink in a week." His gentle Scottish brogue was a balm to her tired ears.

"You don't need your fancy affectation to observe that."

"No, but there is a gentleman at the table behind you whom I am trying to impress." He grinned at her and tucked the glass on its gold chain back into his vest, then nodded in the direction of the man.

"You are enough all by yourself to impress anyone," she said.

"Thank you, lass, but I will take any help I can get these days. I haven't had companionship in two months, you know. Not since Marcus and I broke things off. Again."

"Two months? That's nothing, Fraser. It's been six for me," she said, remembering the journalist that she had taken up with for a few months in the spring.

"Men are different. We have *needs*, Letty."

She threw her hands up. "Are we back to this nonsense? Women have *needs* too, you wretched man. You sound like you've been too long among the gentry, filling your head with fluff about doe-eyed girls who don't know the first thing about the ways of the natural world."

"Wynn has been trying to arrange a marriage between myself and his daughter," he admitted. "It's getting difficult to say no when it would strengthen our business connection."

Fraser ran a furniture shop with his partner, Mr. Wynn. An expert woodworker specializing in luxury furniture, Fraser spent half his days now in the workshop and the rest of it managing the team of craftsmen while Wynn oversaw the sales and finances. Their showroom was on the ground floor of the building where she and Fraser both kept apartments.

"You would be content to be a husband in name only?"

"I could do the deed and perhaps beget a child," he said thoughtfully. "But it wouldn't be my first choice."

They were joined by more friends as they sat together. Mr. George Smith was a ne'er-do-well gentleman, redheaded with a startling number of freckles, who was friendly with near about everyone in London. He dropped in on their dinners every few weeks or so. Mr. Marcus Thomson was tall and stocky with a cheerful disposition and tousled sandy brown hair that topped his pale face. He ran a stationary shop on Chancery Lane, which was always bustling due to the reams of paper and dozens of quills that the solicitors and barristers seemed to run through every month. Letty spent plenty of coin at his shop on Robert's behalf, though she bartered with fresh paint and new upholstery every now and again.

Platters of food soon arrived as they caught up on each other's news. Roast chicken dripping in gravy, pickled vegetables, thick beef pasties with golden crusts, mock turtle soup, and a basket of hot buttery buns were scattered in platters across the table. Coffee was poured, comforting and warm on a cold day.

"I don't know what I'm going to do," Letty said, propping her elbows on the table. "I've been losing sleep, as Fraser not-so-kindly pointed out to me. Robert has been pressuring me to find work outside of Holborn. It would be best for his potential career endeavors, he says."

"That's not Robert's decision to make," George said, frowning.

"I know." She fiddled with her spoon, then stirred more sugar into her coffee to cover the evidence of her nerves. "But he's so close to being successful."

"Young people often think they have only one chance to get it right, don't they?" Marcus mused. "Yet look at all of us here. None of us are the same people we were at his age. The young must learn that they must adapt to life, no matter what those circumstances are." He glanced at Fraser, then frowned down at his plate.

"It's easier to say that when it's not your child. Anyway, I have no jobs lined up in this neighborhood or any other, so things are looking precarious for me."

Fraser ran a thumb over his beard. "If you wish to aim high, I heard talk from Wynn that the Duchess of Hawthorne is looking for an architect. We supplied the dukedom with an oak table a few years ago, and the same architect has been in touch with us in case they get the job."

"Is that so?" George asked. "I heard nothing from Hawthorne about it, and we're thick as thieves." He had run in the same circles as the duke when both men had lived in Paris. "Not that Hawthorne would be up to date with what the duchess chooses to do. You could be a good fit, Letty. You're too talented to be only designing for the shops around here."

She almost spit her coffee out. "Me? Work for a *duchess*? You know I avoid the nobility like the plague. They all say one thing, but they mean quite another. It's not worth the investment. Besides," she added with a roll of her eyes, "a duchess would expect to hire a *man*, with wealth of his own as well as a wealth of experience furnishing great estates. No, I am quite out of the running."

Marcus laughed. "It's easy, Letty. Invent yourself a title and a pedigree and then waltz into the house like you own it. Perhaps she will be impressed by your nerve. In business, you must take risks now and then to get ahead."

"Lies aren't the way to get ahead," Fraser snapped, his eyes flashing at Marcus.

"I won't even pretend to be married, let alone pretend to be nobility. I'm not ashamed to be Miss Letitia Barrow."

Fraser leaned in and stabbed at the table with his index finger. "Haven't you often said that you wanted to build your name? Working for the Hawthornes would put it on the map. In great big letters. George is right. You're talented enough to move on from the opportunities that you have had so far."

She saw it in her mind's eye. Her name, on lists of illustrious designers. Her name, bandied about during conversations of who to consult for the latest trends or timeless fashions. Her name, coupled with the phrase, "I simply *must* have a room by Barrow."

"How do you think you're going to get ahead without patronage?" Marcus waved a bite of pasty for emphasis. "Everyone does such things for business. I certainly have."

"The duchess wouldn't be my patron," Letty said. "It would be one job. If I were interested. Which I am not."

"One very lucrative job," Marcus pointed out. "Haven't you heard that the Hawthornes are as rich as Croesus?"

"That's even worse," she protested. "Fraser, you have worked with plenty of clients who are richer than they are sensible. You can't agree with such nonsense."

Fraser winked at a waiter through his quizzing glass, then let out an *oof* when Marcus elbowed him in the ribs with a bland apology. "I don't recall there being any problems with the job. But it was only one table that we built for the duchess."

"What about Robert, then?" George asked. "Couldn't you use a windfall and help him on his feet?"

"He needs to learn that not everything is handed out for free," Letty said.

"There's nothing wrong with helping when you can," Fraser said. "Wouldn't it be nice to gift him the nest egg that his father should have laid for him, if he hadn't been such a thoughtless prick?"

She *could* provide that, couldn't she? The Wilson family might have cut them off, but she could make it right. She could make Robert forget the hurt of being abandoned, like she had been by her own father. She wanted him to work and earn a living, but it would be sweet revenge indeed on the Wilsons if she could be the one to give him everything he deserved without a ha'penny of their help.

Her friends were right. This is what she had wanted. What she had dreamed of. What she had worked for. "George, would you be willing to talk to the duke?"

George hesitated. "I can always put in a word with the duke, but his word won't hold water with the duchess. She despises him these days."

"My calling card would end up in the butler's dustbin before the duchess could ever clap eyes on it." Her hopes dashed, she slumped back against the booth.

Fraser looked thoughtful. "George, couldn't you see if Hawthorne would be willing to give word to the duchess's secretary to include Letty in the interviews, instead of speaking to the duchess? I've heard that Hawthorne is always willing to help out people like us." He patted her hand. "Look around you, Letty lass. You are surrounded by friends, and we will find something for you even if this doesn't work out."

Finally, she thought, her heart full. Maybe luck was going to turn her way after all.

Chapter Three

Hawthorne House was a stately townhouse in Mayfair that soared four stories high. Tall wrought-iron gates guarded it from the street, and bare-branched trees marched alongside the path cut into the front lawn to the door. The chance to see the inside of a ducal mansion was an opportunity that Letty might never have again, and she felt a rush of excitement as she strode up to the door with its imposing lion's head knocker.

The butler who enquired after her business looked almost ducal himself with his nose in the air. Letty was accustomed to such looks from people who considered themselves her betters, eying her style of dress with displeasure. It didn't change her affinity for cravats and a smart beaver top hat with her velvet skirts.

She gave the butler her hat and her cloak. She wished she could keep her walking stick with her as she had a habit of tapping it whilst thinking, but she relinquished it after the barest of hesitations.

Letty gazed around the drawing room in which the butler had deposited her. It was easily twice the size of her entire apartment. White marble columns carved with leaves and fruit were everywhere, and heavy gold curtains hung from the windows. If she shouted, she rather fancied that she would hear an echo.

She doubted the pair of dour-faced footmen stationed at the doorway would be amused if she attempted such a thing.

Hawthorne House was by far the most elegant building that she had ever set foot in. Her friends' encouragement last week, nursed along with a pint or two, had bolstered her confidence. But now, looking at the sheer scale of the estate, she wondered if she actually had a chance. She didn't often feel nervous, but her palms felt sweaty inside her leather gloves.

If Letty considered the house to be the height of elegance, it was nothing compared to the woman who glided into the room. She was tall, slender, and commanding, with sharp cheekbones and a firm chin and lips that looked like their natural state was to be pressed together into a mild frown. Not a strand of her pale blond hair dared to stray from its swept-up coiffure studded with emerald-tipped pins. Letty's hair would never look like that, not even if she had an army of maids to fuss over her every morning.

She supposed the woman's dress might be considered plain by her peers, unadorned with embroidery or jewels. But to her it represented months of good salary—the heavy satin was rich and shiny, and the tailoring was impeccable. Letty knew that simple things done to perfection were often pricier than showpieces.

The showpiece before her in the pricy dress could only be the Duchess of Hawthorne.

"Miss Barrow, I presume?" the duchess asked, with a slight incline of her head as she took a seat by the fire, the full skirt of her dress falling into place around her like Letty supposed everything was wont to do.

She curtsied. "Yes, Your Grace. Thank you for agreeing to see me."

"I will tell you up-front, Miss Barrow, that everyone that I have interviewed thus far has more extensive experience than you have." Her voice was cool and light.

Letty thought about the wealthy men who would be vying for the same job. But she couldn't change the circumstances of her birth any more than Richard could change his, and she had not been born into fortune. "Good taste does not always come from experience. I consider my work to be the equal of any that you may have already reviewed."

"Equal? I have a duchy to uphold, Miss Barrow. It demands a *superior* touch."

Letty wanted to roll her eyes. How had she forgotten the snobbery of the nobility? It had been too long since she had been before anyone with a title, preferring to avoid them altogether. Maybe she should let the job go to one of the architects who felt the same way as the duchess. Then she felt the itch of her ambition, coupled with the thought of her empty coffers. "I can assure you, Your Grace, that I can provide better service than anyone else you are considering."

The duchess gazed at her. "Yet you have no prestigious credentials. You are no architect, I presume?"

"Is it so laughable that a woman could be an architect, if she wanted?" Her temper flared, and she struggled to leash it. This was no way to win the job. She found it within herself to smile. "You are correct. I build nothing. But I guarantee that I can satisfy you. I can give you exactly what you need." There was a little tingle in her abdomen as she realized what she said. The duchess was an attractive woman, and under other circumstances, she would very much like to satisfy her. Was she mistaken, or did the duchess's eyes widen slightly? Interesting indeed. She cleared her throat. "Along with letters of reference, I brought sketches of my recent designs."

The duchess nodded, and Letty spread open her black leather portfolio. She flipped each page, pointing out details and discussing materials that she had used in each renovation, her enthusiasm growing the more she spoke. The duchess let her explain without interruption, a thoughtful look on her face, but those lips were still turned down at the corners.

"What was it that you were thinking of having done here at Hawthorne House, Your Grace?" Every room that she had glimpsed on her way to the drawing room had been flawless. Perhaps they were planning an addition. Or maybe there was water damage somewhere, and a room or two needed to be repaired.

"Everything must be redone," the duchess announced. Although she was smiling now, the intensity in her eyes was frightening.

"Everything?" Letty blinked, and then glanced around at a fortune's worth of furniture that showed no obvious signs of use. The antique Aubusson was as vibrant as if the carpet had been woven that very morning.

"I do not make a habit of repeating myself, Miss Barrow."

Letty was on fire to know more, but the look on the duchess's face made it clear that she would brook no questions. "Of course. I quite understand."

But she didn't at all. This would be a massive undertaking. Whatever could be improved in this room, for instance, where a Ming vase gleamed atop an Italian mantelpiece?

It would take months, if not an entire year or more, if the duchess truly meant to change every detail in every room of the vast mansion. The amount of work to be done was staggering.

And expensive.

And—best of all—*private.*

A thrill went through her. A duchess's recommendation could establish her career for the rest of her life. She could leave behind the lawyer's chambers and eating houses and dressmaker's shops forever. Plenty of rich people wanting nice things would find a letter from the Hawthornes to be persuasive indeed.

"I can do it," she promised, but what she meant deep in her soul was that she *wanted* it. Whatever it took.

The duchess picked up her portfolio and looked again through some of the pages. "I have been considering consulting with Thomas Hope," she said. "Or John Soane."

Of course she was. They were some of the greatest names in Britain for such work, and the duchess was wealthy enough to afford them both if she chose to. John Soane designed architecture for no less than the Prince Regent, after all, and Thomas Hope had brilliantly and painstakingly furnished his house on Duchess Street into a thing of wonder. Letty felt sick thinking of them as her competition, because if they were under consideration, then there was no hope for her at all. "They are men of great talent."

"But there is one issue. They are men," the duchess said, closing the portfolio and looking into Letty's eyes. She sucked in a breath. Those eyes were large, sapphire blue, and magnetic. "I don't know where my secretary found your name, but I agreed to meet with you because you are the only woman who applied for this opportunity."

Letty narrowed her eyes. "My talent stands up against any of the work that you have seen, by a woman or a man. I have a network of architects and furniture makers and textile artisans that I work with, and I can facilitate the work and streamline it so everything is furnished according to your exacting standards. I am efficient, and hardworking, and I can make anything you need happen." Maybe it was pure bravado, but she would worry about filling those expectations later.

The duchess stiffened, which was remarkable because she already exhibited an admirable posture. "You have made your living working on the businesses of professional men, with the occasional home design for their wives. Hawthorne House was built over eighty years ago and is the very epitome of the dukedom. It would be most unlike anything you have ever done before."

Letty steeled herself for the inevitable disappointment.

"But I want you for the job."

The words hit her like a brick. Unexpected, and jarring. It was good news. Wasn't it? With the duchess still boring holes into her with her eyes, she was no longer quite sure. It was no matter how she *felt*, she told herself. It was time to seize opportunity. "I will endeavor to deliver satisfaction, Your Grace."

What the duchess couldn't realize was that it was far more difficult to convey something with design besides wealth. A judge's reputation for fair ruling could be represented with a painting of Libra on the wall, but it was heightened if everything was balanced in his chambers, one side exactly reflecting the other, down to the dried flowers in the matching vases placed along each wall. Eateries were a study in charm, practicality, and efficiency—plenty of space for the waiters, enough tables to maximize profits, pastoral paintings to aid digestion. A doctor's office and his sitting room needed to soothe patients' nerves and persuade them to have confidence in his work, as well as requiring any number of clever pieces of furniture that she designed, and Fraser built, to hide the intimidating tools of his trade.

Any of the designs that she had presented in her portfolio had taken more effort and creativity than Hawthorne House would. If the drawing room that she was sitting in was any indication, then the rich simply wanted décor to showcase how rich and powerful they were. Any Ming vase would do to fill these shelves. Any Rembrandt that she could find at auction would look fine on those walls.

This was going to be the easiest job she ever had.

The duchess handed her the portfolio, and Letty remembered to curtsy before striding out of the room.

Yes, indeed. Luck was finally on her side.

Anne marched to her bedchamber. Hiring Miss Barrow was the first step toward taking control of her problem with the duke. The designer was an engaging woman, and there was something about her that inspired confidence. Her hair had been a bustling mess piled on top of her head, silver and brown and haphazardly braided. But her dress had been neat enough, a velvet frogged spencer jacket with a high collar and a neat cravat, and a full velvet skirt with buttoned-up ankle boots peeking out beneath it. It looked quite smart on her, flattering her generous proportions. The cravat was a masculine affectation that she had to admit made her pulse beat a little faster.

Anne hadn't missed how Miss Barrow's eyes had darted all over the room, taking in every detail. They had taken in every inch of *her*, too, and she didn't want to admit to the desire that had wakened in her. Those deep brown eyes had almost dared her to hire her, dancing with passion as she had talked about her designs.

She wondered what it was like to have that sort of fire, burning one up inside. Imagine spending days on end indulging in one's interests. It was quite marvelous. Although Anne was endlessly busy, she never forgot that her work was driven by duty. Never passion.

Yet as talented as Miss Barrow was, her lack of experience was what made the decision easy.

It hadn't crossed her mind until she saw the portfolio that *inexperience* was the very thing she was searching for. The designs had been well done—but catered to a middle-class taste level. Her plan had been to hire men at the top of their professional careers with experience on houses like hers. She had been prepared to give them carte blanche and a bottomless purse and assumed it would take them months to dither over decisions when faced with unlimited potential at their fingertips.

It had been a surprise to see Miss Barrow's name, unknown to her, among the illustrious list that her secretary had presented to her. She didn't quite understand how her secretary had thought that someone who arranged furniture for doctor's offices and eating houses would be a good fit for Hawthorne House.

But the more Anne thought about it, the more sense it made to hire someone that couldn't have any real idea what they were doing in an estate this size. If the renovations were poorly done, or slated to continue for years because Miss Barrow would need to learn everything there was to know about even the most minor of ducal parlors—it was even more likely to prevent Hawthorne from *ever* moving in, wasn't it?

Hawthorne House had been the same forever. Once she had thought it a matter of pride to enshrine it as it had been passed to her, to uphold tradition. But she was starting to wonder if the very house was mired in stagnancy instead.

Anne trailed one hand along the bifurcated staircase that curved against the walls on each side of the grand hallway. There was a glass ceiling that soared four stories above that let in enough light to feel like the heavens themselves smiled on Hawthorne House. She had walked down these stairs during her debutante ball, which the duchess had insisted on throwing for her after Hawthorne had made it clear to his parents that he would consider no other woman to be his bride. His mother had drilled the values of the dukedom into her from that very moment. She could still recite them on her fingers.

Proper comportment above all else.

Unblemished virtue.

Modesty.

Kindness to those less fortunate.

Condemnation on all others below their rank.

Every action was a reflection on the Hawthorne name, which must be upheld with honor, dignity, and pride. After all, no scandal had touched their name in years.

Her husband had changed all of that.

Hawthorne had been a severe disappointment to his parents after his marriage to Anne. They blamed her, of course, for what they claimed were his unnatural tendencies, and she became skilled at biting her tongue in her anger at their callousness. It had taken years of patient toadying to win them over to her, as she spent hours demonstrating for them the qualities they loved. It was only natural that she was just as careful at every Society function, and soon she gained a reputation for impeccable behavior and formidable censure.

At the top of the second floor, the duke's and duchess's suites were the first rooms to the left. Anne had always found her bedchamber to be far too big for one woman. If it wouldn't cause a lifetime of disapproving stares from the staff, she would have chosen another suite after moving into the house. Something far less grand. Instead, there was a four-poster bed that could likely sleep six people in it, more sofas and chairs than she knew what to do with in a room only meant for sleeping, and the room was overstuffed with bric-a-brac.

And all of it was gold. Gold leaf, gold curtains, gold paint, gilt trim, shining at her from every angle. Anne hated it, but her mother-in-law had loved its pomp and circumstance. She remembered when the dowager duchess had put a hand on her shoulder and told her that all of this would be hers, and to sleep among such riches meant that they were blessed indeed.

Anne supposed she had the power all along to change what she didn't like, but she had been told over and over that it was her duty to maintain the building as it was. A symbol of their power, and their prestige. Eternal and everlasting. This building, which had been graced by monarchs, was the heart of their ducal status.

Could someone like Miss Barrow, who from her accent and manners appeared to have been born to the gentry but who had no experience among the *haut ton*, ever really understand how to imprint the importance of the duchy onto her work?

Anne sat on the edge of the bed and looked around again at the room that didn't suit her in the least. Since the duke's proclamation that he was returning to Hawthorne House and taking back control of the dukedom, and since the disastrous dinner party at Edward's, Anne had come to the realization that the endless work she had poured into the dukedom had only ever benefited Hawthorne and his vision. Or his father's vision and outdated values.

Her own suggestions for improving the estates had fallen on barren ground time and time again, with no possibility of planting even the seeds of ideas that could eventually grow.

Maybe it was time to change all that.

It felt like treason—going against her husband, his family, and everything she had been raised to stand for. Perhaps this renovation was an excuse to prevent Hawthorne from moving in, but she was awash in petty delight to think of erasing the heart of the dukedom in the same way that she herself felt erased.

It would feel *good* to disrupt the duchy, she realized, and that was a strange feeling indeed for she had always intended to uphold it.

Anne smiled. She couldn't wait to begin.

CHAPTER FOUR

Robert stomped around the sitting room, scowling into every corner as he sought his hat from its hook and then retreated to his bedchamber, muttering to himself along the way. He wasn't often in foul tempers, and Letty's heart sank as she watched him stalk about the rooms from the corner of her eye. There was only one thing they argued about these days, and it was clear Robert was spoiling to start it up again.

Best to get it over with, then. She leaned against the doorjamb. "Robert, is there something the matter?"

He was staring into his meager collection of cravats and starched collars. "I have been invited to take dinner with Mr. Selkirk after work is finished. It is a mark of high favor."

"That's marvelous news." But that didn't explain his pallor, or the crease between his eyebrows.

He cleared his throat. "Could you loan me a guinea or two?"

Letty was glad she was leaning against the door or she would have been at risk of falling on the floor. "Guineas? What kind of dinner are you attending? It shouldn't be more than a *shilling* or two."

Robert's hands tightened on the edge of the dresser as he stared into the drawer. "I don't have a choice of the location, Mum. I can't very well suggest something less expensive, when I may be beholden to this man for my education."

"Is the opportunity worth the cost? You are under constant stress these days. You know, Fraser always has need of apprentice carpenters."

He swung around to face her, his eyes bright. "Do you think I am good enough to work with my hands, but not with my mind?"

"I am surprised to hear such snobbery from you. I thought I had raised you better than that. Fraser and his employees make a good wage."

"Oh, what a choice you present me!" he cried. "To give up my dreams, so I can apprentice for your friend. I want a *profession*. Woodwork would get me no more than I earn now, and my future would be much more precarious as I develop a hunchback and sore eyes with no chance to earn my way up unless I open my own shop."

Letty crossed her arms over her chest. "Then you could choose something else that suits you better."

"It's not fair that my father provided for us for so long, only for us to be cast aside now." Robert laughed, the sound low and bitter. "But maybe I should thank him for passing when he did. At least I am still young enough to join the clerks without much notice. It should have been more difficult indeed to have continued to be brought up in some fashion as a gentleman's by-blow, without enough education to ape my betters and without any training to earn my own bread."

Letty frowned. "That wasn't the plan."

It had been a shock when her stipend was cut off two years ago upon John's death, with no bequest to last through Robert's own lifetime. Had she failed to prepare Robert for the realities of working life? Had she led him to believe he would have a life of leisure forever? Her chest tightened. Of course she had. That's what she had believed herself.

"Why didn't you ask my father for the funds for me to go to university?" he asked.

"I had no control over what John provided."

"Surely an education would have been a natural enough provision, had you but reminded him of his duty! If I had been to university, at least I could train to be a barrister and I would still be considered a gentleman, instead of a lowly solicitor. This may be the best paying career I can think of," he said, "but I shall never now be a gentleman." There was a sneer on his face that she didn't recognize. She hadn't realized that he harbored social ambition like that.

"There are worse things, Robert. After all, I am no lady, and I am happy with my lot in life."

"How can you compare us!" he cried. "My grandfather was an army captain, and you were born into the gentry, to wedded parents. You chose to fall from grace with my father, yet it is I who has to reap what *you* have sown!"

She felt as if she had been struck. "I gave you the best life I could under the circumstances in which I found myself," she said, struggling to keep her temper reined in. "Many are born into less. You still have plenty more than most, Robert Barrow. Your father was generous enough to provide what he did. We should be grateful for that." It was what she always reminded him. "After his death, the Wilsons had every right to make the decision that they did."

Robert didn't reply.

Letty went to her bedchamber. From the deepest corner of the last drawer of her dresser, she drew out a sack of coins that she kept on hand. Over the last year, the pile had dwindled at an alarming rate. Thank the Lord that she had been given this opportunity with the Hawthornes, she thought. All she had to do was wait until the end of the month to start being paid.

Robert brightened as she came back to his room and pressed the coins into his palm. "Thanks, Mum. You won't regret this. Someday I will find my fortune as a solicitor and I will have our futures secured. You understand, don't you? I don't ever wish either of us to worry about money again."

Letty wanted to reassure him that she could provide for him. The job with the duchess should secure her fortune and her reputation, and she would be able to give him what he needed. But deep down, she wasn't sure. She had learned long ago not to trust the sweet words of the nobility.

"Your worries are better spent about looking your best for dinner tonight. Maybe fuss with your hair again before you go," Letty added with a laugh, hoping to move past their quarrel.

Robert scowled as he buttoned his cuff. "Nothing wrong with wanting to look proper anyhow," he grumbled. "The fellows at the office prefer a neat appearance."

A rap on the door revealed a smartly dressed footman. "Miss Barrow? A carriage is here to take you to Hawthorne House, ma'am, if you would."

"Now?"

"The duchess appreciates efficiency and expediency, ma'am. A word to the wise—if you have taken employment with the duchess, you should expect to be available whenever she has need of you."

"Thank you for your advice. I shall be down in a moment."

Robert stared at her. "Now who is worried about appearances? Hobnobbing with the fancy folk? Why has a duchess asked you to call?"

"I have a new job, far away from the streets of Holborn and deep into Mayfair," she said coolly. "I am renovating for the Duchess of Hawthorne."

The tips of his ears reddened. "You had the gall to reproach me for my ambition? All I want is to secure a livelihood, but I suppose it's all well and fine for you to reach to the very top of the upper crust."

Could nothing she do ever be right in his eyes these days? "Robert, you asked me to stay away from your offices on my next job or two. I've done exactly that. What right do you have to complain about where I earn my coin, when I've done my best to accommodate you?"

He grumbled as he shoved his hat on his head and banged his way out the door.

Letty re-braided her hair and straightened her skirts before she went in search of the carriage. It wasn't hard to miss on their quiet street, bereft as it was of any other crested conveyances. The inside was much nicer than any other she'd been in. The seats were lined with buttery soft leather, and the padding was marvelously thick. The novelty of the experience made her forget her annoyance that she had been summoned without more than a by-your-leave.

She willed herself to forget the argument with Robert, but he was right in one regard. She may have told him that he had more than most, but as she passed larger houses and greener pastures in the streets of Mayfair, she had to admit that there were many who had more than they did. Where was the fairness of it all? She counted herself lucky enough to work for the Duchess of Hawthorne, but how much luckier was the duchess to have been born into wealth and leisure?

The itch of her ambition turned into a howling ache. She wanted this power and prestige for herself, but she wanted to earn it through her work and reputation.

When the duchess swept into the drawing room, her lips were curved down and her chin was high, and Letty was struck again by her beauty. No doubt she bathed in milk every night or some such frivolous nonsense. Her navy wool gown was buttoned up to the throat, and Letty didn't need the measuring tape from her toolbox to notice that the dress followed her sleek frame within an eighth of an inch.

"Thank you for being available on such short notice, Miss Barrow. I am most anxious to begin."

"I understand, Your Grace. I am grateful I didn't have another appointment when your footman arrived."

She wanted to add that she didn't appreciate the duchess taking her availability for granted. But a shilling saved by not paying a hackney helped pay for Robert's dinner tonight. The imposition rankled, but it was part and parcel of working for the nobility.

"I thought I would give you a tour this morning, and you could give me your thoughts."

Although Letty had expected to be shown the estate, she never thought that the duchess herself would guide her. Shouldn't she be in the company of a housekeeper, or a secretary?

She followed the duchess down a long hallway. "It is a beautiful house, Your Grace." She judged the paintings on the wall to be at least three hundred years old. Impressive indeed.

"It is *magnificent*."

Curiously, the duchess's voice was flat. Perhaps she was so accustomed to the treasures that surrounded her that she was bored with them.

"Although I wish to transform everything, I decided to start with the private rooms first."

Letty was disappointed that she wouldn't have the opportunity yet to work on something more public, where guests would see her talents. But she had to admit it would be easier to start with a sitting room compared to a ballroom. It would give her the time to understand what was expected for the rest of this enormous house.

"I suppose you have no need of a constitutional stroll outdoors when you traverse such distances every day?" Letty asked.

She knew it wasn't considered good manners to speak first in a duchess's presence. But the staircase was devoid of any member of the *haut ton*, wasn't it? Besides, the duchess might belong on another social echelon, but she was no better than Letty herself.

The duchess blinked. "In truth, I haven't taken a walk outside for pleasure since September, when the weather was nicer," she admitted.

"But we haven't had any poor weather."

"I beg to differ, Miss Barrow. There is a decided chill in the air these days. I am not inclined to dwell in it lest I catch a cold."

"Perhaps it is unwise for the elderly, or the unwell," Letty allowed. "But a good bit of fresh air can do no harm when one is young and healthy, Your Grace."

"Are we so young?" she asked, her lips twitching as if to suppress a smile. "I am indeed glad to hear it. My nephew is all of twenty-one, and I think in his eyes I might as well be a crone, though I have only just past my thirty-fourth year."

Letty chuckled. "My son is much the same age, and I am afraid he has much the same opinion of me at forty-two."

"Young people think they know everything, don't they?"

"And what they don't know surely can't be of any importance at all."

The duchess laughed. The sound was airy and charming, and to Letty's surprise, it transformed her. Instead of an untouchable statue, the duchess came to life beside her. It was a subtle difference. Her posture relaxed by a fraction, and her lips curved up by a hairsbreadth. But Letty had trained herself to notice the minute differences in measurements, and to her it was a startling change.

"I suppose we must resign ourselves to being old and old-fashioned."

"Now, that's a bold-faced lie if I ever heard one. Neither of us are old in the least, and no one could accuse you of being unfashionable," Letty said. "Your Grace," she added.

"My mother-in-law would consider me sadly lacking in proper ducal fashion today. I believe her opinion is that one should wear the diadems as often as one can. Or at the very least, carry a scepter more than once in a great while."

"I have always wondered what occasions might require a scepter," Letty said with a smile. "Do feel free to wave one about, if only for my benefit."

After the argument with Robert this morning, the easy conversation soothed her. The duchess hadn't censured her for speaking out of turn. Perhaps she wasn't quite like the rest of the nobility.

Letty followed the duchess into a cavernous room at the top of the stairs, filled with ornate furniture and gloomy colors.

"This is the duke's suite," she announced. "Now that Hawthorne has returned to England, no stone must be left unturned to welcome our dear duke back to these hallowed halls. You are to take as much time as you need." The duchess's hands clenched into fists, and her jaw was set as hard as granite.

Letty nodded. If the duke had inherited the title while he was away, then presumably these rooms had not been touched since his father's time. It was natural that Hawthorne would wish to change things to avoid painful memories. The hint of strain on the duchess's face must reflect her sympathy for her husband's needs.

Starting in the duke's bedchamber must be symbolic. Letty glanced at the bed. Most likely the duke had returned to beget himself an heir.

"Is there anything specific that the duke would like to see in these rooms?"

"I would not know."

"Perhaps I could review with the duke himself, if he would be so kind to be available for a meeting?"

"Under no circumstances is the duke to be bothered."

First she had been fetched out of her house by the estate's footman, now she was tasked with deciphering the whims of the wealthy. The allure of this job was dimming slightly. "Is there anything at all that you would like me to keep in mind?"

"Are *you* not the designer, Miss Barrow? Can you not make these decisions on your own?" She paused. "Did you not assure me that I would be satisfied?"

There was that word again. *Satisfied.* Letty eyed the duchess. For all her froideur, there was something about her that was appealing. She was commanding, intelligent, and confident, all traits that Letty warmed to. The duchess also had magnificent deep blue eyes that snapped with fire when she was busy looking down her nose at her. Too bad there was no passion behind them, only irritation.

"You shall be satisfied," Letty promised, her voice low. "But a designer is not a magician, Your Grace. I cannot conjure paper and fabric and wood from thin air. It would be best to know what I am working with here, if I am to make something exceptional for the duke."

The duchess was still for a long moment. The only movement was in her eyes, scrutinizing the room in such a way that Letty wondered if she had ever truly looked at it before. Given the rumors one heard about her husband, maybe she hadn't. "It is just a room, Miss Barrow. I am sure you can find something to fill it."

Ah. Here was the side of the nobility that she was familiar with. John had been much the same—in one breath, he had been charming, in the next, frivolous and capricious. Letty would bet her best drafting pencil that the duchess would change her mind tomorrow and have her start on another room instead.

But it didn't matter, she reminded herself. At least she would be well compensated for whatever work she could get out of it.

"I accepted the job in good faith, Your Grace. I will show you what I can do."

❖

For a cold November night, Lady Taylor's soiree was well enough attended to boast an evening of dancing as well as an elegant supper. Scores of flames danced atop the chandeliers, magnified by mirrors that lined the walls. The light that bounced off the pearls and emeralds and rubies on necks and fingers and gowns turned the room into a glittering marvel.

Anne's own dress sparkled like starlight when she glanced down at it, tiny diamonds nestled deep within thick black velvet. She had only been half in jest earlier when she had told Miss Barrow that the dowager duchess preferred her to overdress for all occasions, though she herself preferred clean tailoring in her wardrobe. With all the other values of the dukedom, the dowager had instilled in her head that the rank demanded heaps of jewels and ornamentation. Thus she bore the weight of a dazzling tiara on her head tonight, and to save herself neck strain, she balanced it with small pearl earbobs.

Anne nodded at an acquaintance and considered the refreshment table. A little wine would be nice. She picked up a glass of pink champagne.

Lord knew that her nerves needed it today after speaking with Miss Barrow and putting her plan in motion to ruin Hawthorne's rooms. Miss Barrow was an interesting sort of woman. She was bold. Unconventional. Anne liked that she had spoken to her as if she were an equal. She oughtn't have liked it, of course. Her mother-in-law would be shocked at the insolence. But it was so rare that anyone *talked* with her. And more than that, *disagreed* with her. It was refreshing.

Those full lips of hers seemed always ready to smile, the little lines at the corner of her eyes crinkling as if she were perpetually amused. But she shouldn't be noticing Miss Barrow's eyes. Even if they were a marvelous deep brown, with flecks of gold. That way led to distraction.

It also hinted at *satisfaction*.

She shook her head clear.

There were dozens of people that she mingled with every week who were respectable, distinguished, elegant, and well-spoken. But for all the conversations she had, there was not a single person who she talked to like she had talked with Miss Barrow today.

On the other hand, there were plenty of people that Anne could hear talking tonight, and none were words that they would dare speak to her face. It was about her husband, of course. A constant source of amusement and derision to the *ton*.

Hawthorne's actions had never touched hers before. There was no reason to believe that they would touch her now. If she could keep him out of her house and at a distance, then everything should be fine. She didn't know why tonight the gossip rankled her, when she had grown accustomed to it over the years.

Anne tried to relax with the knowledge that she was exactly where she belonged. This was a typical soiree, and she was fulfilling her typical role. It was well known that she seldom bestowed her favor upon any man for a dance. The royal dukes, of course, could never be turned down, no matter how clammy their hands were. She had spun around a ballroom with Prince George several times this past summer, which was never a highlight of her evenings though she was duty-bound to act as if it were. Mere misters knew better than to even consider asking their hostess if they had a chance to approach her.

While she drank her champagne, she debated with herself whether or not she would drop a word of advice in the ears of a debutante who looked too eager to escape to the gardens on the arm of a besotted friend.

Anne was known to be something of a stickler.

She spied a flirtation or two, and a pair of ladies who might be giggling a trifle too enthusiastically together, but nothing beyond the pale. Perhaps it was time for her to move on from analyzing others, and to seek what she herself might want.

A warm hand settled on her shoulder, and Anne jerked away.

But before she turned, she knew that only one person would dare lay a hand on a duchess.

Her duke.

Chapter Five

Hawthorne's white teeth gleamed in a grin as he snatched Anne's hand and kissed her gloved knuckles. "My dear duchess, would you spare a dance for me?"

How could she dance when every inch of her was stiff with shock? Anger soon loosened her voice, but not before he cupped a hand under her elbow and guided her to the dancing. "What are you doing here, Hawthorne?"

"I came to dance with my beautiful wife."

"Surely not to try to sweep me off my feet?"

As they stood waiting for the music to begin, she heard the swell of murmurs. The people closest to him inched away. Hawthorne didn't react, the same sardonic look on his face as always. He looked expensive, exquisite, and bored, as if he were a million miles from the crowd and they were the only two in the room.

A rush of anger on his behalf flooded through her.

The music started and they started to dance. "How can you bear it?" she asked in low tones, sending a scathing look at those around her. She may be ready to throttle Hawthorne herself, but the man was a *duke*. Didn't that incur any respect anymore? What was the point of ducal power without societal influence?

"I would bear much more if necessary," he told her, and she saw a flash of emotion in his eyes. "But this, you see, is why I have need of you."

Anne allowed herself to be lifted, then twirled. "Oh?"

"I need that pristine reputation of yours."

"Even my good name is not my own, but is merely another appendage of the duchy?" Her stomach twisted at the thought of losing her reputation by proxy. By dancing with him, did it appear as if she accepted his return?

"When was it ever your own, after you linked it to mine in matrimony? Your reputation as a Hawthorne is unparalleled. What is it I heard them call you after I arrived tonight?" He grinned. "Ah, yes. The Discerning Duchess. The Stickler of Society."

"No doubt from dandified Corinthians with more fashion than sense. Your monikers are far less kind," she snapped. "The Duke of Misrule is the one currently in fashion."

"Indeed, I heard it muttered under some wag's breath as I passed him in White's the other day."

Her lips thinned. "You brought it on yourself." But she felt unconvinced, uncomfortable with the way people were staring at him.

"I did it for love," he said softly, his deep-set eyes full of emotion.

"You didn't have to be so public about it," she whispered, her fingers tightening on his arm. "No one would have raised a brow if you had kept things discreet. Instead, you drew attention to the scandal and allowed it to grow."

"And has your love of secrecy resulted in such a difference here in London?" Hawthorne laughed. "Are you still cautioning ladies from standing too close to each other, or berating a young miss when she refuses to dance in preference to gossiping with a jaunty widow?"

Anne's face burned. "It is my duty to protect them! I swore to myself to shield all those that I could find, to guide them away from such public displays. We all risk danger when people act imprudently. Public action draws attention to us all." She looked around. "Which is exactly what you have done, and you see the result before you now. Social ostracization."

"Which brings me back to my need of you. I wish to be reputable again."

"Do not use me for your own gains," she warned him.

"No one is being used," he said. "But you and I were meant to be together, you know."

Anne laughed, clutching his arm as they spun and whirled. "Tell that to your lover, Sir Phineas."

"We were meant to *rule*, not to love. Unparalleled wealth. Limitless power. Look at these people around us, laughing and sniggering at me, for something so simple and so basic as love. We could have had it all, you and I."

"Are you seriously disregarding the fact that ten years ago, *you left me*?"

"I can't change the past. I can only do things differently now."

"I trusted you," she choked out, her heart hammering in her chest with anger and hurt. She could blame her flushed face on the dancing, but it would be harder to hide the welling tears that threatened to spill. She was horrified, as she prided herself on showing as little emotion as possible in public. These feelings had lain dormant in her for so many years, and now it felt as if they choked her. "You betrayed me, leaving me here all alone with the gossip and your *mother* and the responsibility of hundreds of people who rely on the duchy. You should have stayed."

"I know. And I am sorrier than I can say." Hawthorne gazed down at her, his eyes intense, so close that their breath mingled. She inhaled his smoky amber cologne and was swamped with memory. "We could still have it all. If you make me respectable again, I could rule by your side."

She wanted to believe it. "You are full of nonsense," Anne said, blinking back the tears. "I want nothing to do with you, or your plans."

When the dance ended and the music faded, she could still hear the whispers swirling around them. Hawthorne grinned at her. "Think about it, Annie," he said. "I'll be in touch."

It might be possible to rehabilitate him, she thought later that night as she tried to puzzle it all together. If she could convince everyone that the scandal was left far behind in France, then maybe she had a chance. It would mean that Hawthorne would need to give up his lover. He couldn't risk being seen with Sir Phineas if he wanted her to convince High Society of his newly respectable ways.

But she suspected that he would never agree to end his liaison, so why should she put herself and her reputation in jeopardy because he wanted the impossible? Reputations were fragile. If Hawthorne refused to change his ways, and if he insisted on seeking her out in ballrooms and soirees, then soon the rumors would damn her as well and soon she would wield no social currency whatsoever.

Anne lay down in the bed and stared at the gold glinting at her from every angle. She hadn't liked the attitude of the people at the ball tonight. She didn't like their judgmental sneers, or their condescension toward Hawthorne. But wasn't that what the dukedom itself represented? Prestige, virtue, and superiority?

Tonight, those ideals didn't sit well with her. She might be opposed to the duke, but her reasons were personal.

It was going to feel so good to rip out every board from the ducal bedroom. Maybe she could cast every stick of furniture into a bonfire, for good measure, and throw away the hypocrisy of the dukedom along with it.

She wondered how soon Miss Barrow would start to arrange things, and for the first time all evening, she felt the tension in her neck lessen. She relaxed into the mattress.

She was so tired of being used in some way or another by Hawthorne's plans for himself, always acting in reaction to his scandals.

She wanted something for herself.

A lover.

Someone of her own class, someone discreet. Someone who understood the rules and the risks. Someone who could maybe hold her, so she didn't feel quite so alone. The more Anne thought about it, the better it sounded. She didn't want to stand at the outskirts of the ballroom any longer. She wanted to be in someone's arms.

Once she thought she had found the perfect partner in Hawthorne, but it had all proved to be a web of lies.

She wanted someone she could rely on.

For once.

❖

Anne gazed down at the piles of letters that required her attention. It was the same routine every day, whether she was in London or in the country. The letters were in stacks of dyed leather portfolios related to subject matter, which had been the first improvement that she had made after taking the role. Crimson red leather encased urgent matters, navy blue surrounded business deals and queries, and leaf green was for daily affairs.

The steaming coffeepot was always the same, too. Silver, with an illustration of Hawthorne Towers etched into it. A teacup sat to the right, the handle pointed at a precise ninety-degree angle. Two biscuits fanned across a plate with a white linen napkin tucked beside them.

Predictable.

Like herself.

Feelings didn't matter much when managing a complex network of estates and the villages associated with them, and all of the business dealings that underpinned it all. Anne cleared her mind, poured a cup of coffee, and set herself to work.

As she made a notation about the thatched roofs scheduled for repair in the village bordering Hawthorne Towers, she thought about all the ideas she had raised over the years that had been blocked by estate managers, the dowager duchess, or the bankers. Investing in railroads and coal mines. Removing enclosures from the estates. Purchasing different breeds of sheep and cows to introduce better quality wool and meat.

Anne had spent enough time perusing the papers and listening to lectures over the years that it frustrated her not to make the changes that could improve things drastically for the people in the dukedom. But even though the Hawthorne seal beckoned at her from the desktop and she yearned to press it into her own service, it couldn't grant her the one thing that the estate insisted on for any major change—the mark of the Duke of Hawthorne's signet ring.

By noon, she had finished the most pressing paperwork, and held a meeting with her secretary. She closed the portfolios and restacked them on the desk. For all Hawthorne's talk last night at the ball about ruling together, he had shown no interest yet in handling anything himself. She wondered how long her luck would hold out.

Being a duchess meant being the chair of many a charitable organization, and today a committee dedicated to helping the orphans of London were soon due to arrive for their quarterly meeting. On a whim, Anne decided to check with the housekeeper if they had any of the cake from the previous day to serve with tea.

The housekeeper, however, was already deep in discussion with Miss Barrow in her sitting room. Anne paused in the doorway, watching them pore over sketches and notes that were spread out on the table. Her fingers twitched as she thought of picking them up and looking over what Miss Barrow had envisioned.

"Mrs. MacInnes, I do apologize for interrupting."

She sprang to her feet into a curtsy. "Your Grace, I did not see you enter. Are the bell pulls in order?"

It wasn't usual behavior for Anne to seek out the servants in their quarters, and she felt a twinge of embarrassment that she hadn't stuck to convention. "Everything is in fine working condition. I thought to stretch my legs before the committee arrives, and to enquire on a point of pure indulgence—whether or not there was any lemon cake to have with tea."

Anne inclined her head at Miss Barrow to acknowledge her presence. She was wearing a green and black plaid gown, snugly encasing her full waist and hips before flaring into a bias-cut skirt. Her dress was short enough to show her narrow-heeled black boots with their thin line of buttons that disappeared beneath the ruffles of her crisp linen petticoat. Her snowy cravat was tucked into the bodice of her dress, and most distressingly it drew Anne's gaze to the swell of her bosom. She flicked her eyes back up to the safer territory of Miss Barrow's smiling face. Her hair was as haphazard as ever—a nest of chestnut braids piled on the crown of her head, brilliant silver streaks racing from her temples.

When Miss Barrow straightened from her curtsy, she could have sworn that she winked at her. Did she dare to be so familiar?

Her legs trembled, and she swallowed. Such insolence had no right to be so appealing.

"We do have lemon cake, Your Grace. I will instruct the maid to serve it with tea, at the usual time." Mrs. MacInnes nodded.

Anne hesitated. Miss Barrow was clearly of the gentry, and though she wasn't a guest, she also wasn't a servant. She was a businesswoman, and her purpose here was to work. And yet…it felt rather rude to discuss refreshment and to offer nothing.

For a moment she felt most unlike a duchess, here in the housekeeper's parlor with a framed catechism on the wall and a vase with dried flowers on the crocheted doily by the door. All she wanted was to sit at the narrow table and *talk*. The very idea should be appalling to her sensibilities. When did a duchess ever socialize in the servant's quarters?

But hadn't she told herself last night that she was going to start taking what she wanted? Was this not some small rebellion that she could have for herself?

Anne smiled. "Miss Barrow, may we offer you refreshment?"

Mrs. MacInnes drew herself up. "We were indeed planning on refreshing ourselves. *After* our meeting." Anne knew her well enough to recognize those injured tones, however faint they may be.

"Of course you were," she soothed. "I know I am acting out of place, interrupting your meeting for such a frivolous reason as cake."

"Cake is never frivolous," Miss Barrow said with an easy smile that made Anne want to sink into a chair and gaze at her full lips forever. "Lemon is my favorite, Your Grace."

"Shall we all have a slice and a cup of tea, then?"

Mrs. MacInnes looked even more affronted. This was unusual indeed, but, oh—how she wanted to stay.

Miss Barrow seemed to know what she was thinking, for she had that look in her eye again that Anne remembered from the house tour—a twinkle of merriment that creased the skin around her eyes, a little half-smile which spoke of repressed laughter. She didn't seem the type of woman to repress herself in general. Anne liked that about her. Miss Barrow picked up a chair and placed it at the table beside her own.

"Please join us, Your Grace."

That *voice*. Low, smooth. Seductive. No, it would never do to think of Miss Barrow this way. Anne stepped in front of the chair, and Miss Barrow slid it under her as she sat. The hair on her neck rose as Anne felt the heat from her hands on the chair, inches from her waist.

"Thank you, Miss Barrow. I am intrigued by your ideas for Hawthorne House."

Miss Barrow gathered up her sketches to clear the table. "Still early days yet, Your Grace. Mrs. MacInnes was kind enough to give me another tour of the house yesterday, and I was scribbling some loose ideas last night. I was showing her potential concepts so we could discuss how many additional workmen we may need, as even your impressively large staff will not be able to handle certain tasks."

"You work fast," she said. "Those drawings don't look loose in the least." She spied the columns of the grand hall on the top sketch, with furniture drawn in intricate detail.

"I have a knack for drawing," Miss Barrow said with a shrug. "It is useful in such a trade. But my etchings must pale in comparison to what you could accomplish with brush and canvas. I assume you had the best of painting masters when you were younger?"

"I can accomplish a pretty enough watercolor," Anne admitted. "I have a certain fondness for pastoral scenes and have one or two of my paintings hanging in my dressing room."

"I should very much love to see them in their natural element someday, Your Grace."

Anne blinked at the thought of Miss Barrow in her dressing room, where she disrobed every night and spritzed perfume on her naked skin and...Oh, this was going too far. That half smile was back, and Anne couldn't be confident that she knew what it was meant to convey. The words from anyone else could be interpreted as disrespectful.

But instead of insolence, could that warm look in her eyes be meant to imply something intimate?

To flirt with a duchess was risky business. She wouldn't *dare*. Would she?

And yet, what was the harm in a little light conversation, or a covert glance or two? They were in the privacy of her own home. They weren't moon-eyed misses gazing at each other across a ballroom in full view of the *haut ton* and their sharp tongues. There was no danger of discovery here except from Mrs. MacInnes, but Anne could handle a housekeeper's ire. She relaxed in her chair.

Anne stared down at the slice of poppyseed lemon cake in front of her, its white icing piped in intricate flowers. She had a weakness for sweets, which her cook indulged in. Her slice had a few extra pink icing roses tucked into the corner, which she knew had been added specially for her. Cook often put such embellishments on her plate, believing that a duchess deserved the best.

Miss Barrow took a bite and sighed. "This is delicious."

"It's an old recipe. The dowager duchess had a taste for lemon when she was with child, and we served this cake many times during that joyous occasion." Mrs. MacInnes smiled. "Nothing could be sour enough for her, so Cook would serve it with a little lemon glaze for her."

Miss Barrow laughed. "I had less refined tastes when I was in an interesting condition. I'm afraid to admit that I wanted nothing but pickles."

"How many children do you have?" Anne asked.

"Only one. Robert. He has become a fine young man." Her voice was bursting with pride.

"And what does Mr. Barrow do?" Mrs. MacInnes asked. "Is your son following in his footsteps?"

Miss Barrow's smile held, but her body tensed. "There was never a Mr. Barrow," she said and took another bite of cake.

Mrs. MacInnes gasped, then looked at Anne. "No Mr. Barrow? No husband to speak of? But you have a son? Oh no. No indeed. This is beyond the pale. Why—"

Anne was also taken aback, but part of being a duchess meant that she never showed shock before a guest. Miss Barrow might not be a guest of the estate, but she was a guest at this table and deserved to be treated with kindness and dignity. "Your son is lucky to have you as both mother and father," she said firmly. "What a difficult and rewarding thing it must have been to rear him by yourself. Well done, Miss Barrow. I applaud you."

"Thank you, Your Grace."

Anne quelled Mrs. MacInnes's disagreement with a cool stare, and she spluttered herself into silence. Miss Barrow smiled at her, a little ruefully, and Anne wondered how often she had to disclose and defend her situation.

It didn't seem fair.

Miss Barrow was indeed an unusual woman with unusual ideals. Her life was so very different from her own. It was *free*. Free of the heavy mantle of Society's strictures, if she was so unbothered about her son's parentage.

Anne indulged herself for a while longer, listening to Mrs. MacInnes unbend under Miss Barrow's charm and start talking again about favorite cake recipes.

"I am sorry to break up this gathering, but I must meet with the committee now for our meeting."

Mrs. MacInnes rose. "Of course, Your Grace. I shall send up another dessert with the tea when they arrive, shall I? We have petit fours, and chocolate biscuits—"

Anne met Miss Barrow's eyes. "I definitely want more cake," she said, but she meant she wanted more of *this*. More of these moments, outside of her real life and responsibilities, precious parcels of stolen time for her. Like extra icing on the cake.

Miss Barrow grinned at her, and Anne knew that somehow, she understood.

CHAPTER SIX

It had taken a full day of work, but finally the footmen grunted their way out the door with the last mahogany chair, and Letty stood alone. It had been an exhausting chore to map out where all the furniture would go after Mrs. MacInnes told her there was no room in the attics, and she had helped with her fair share of the moving as well. She had never thought that she would be anywhere near a duke's bedchamber in her life, and she wanted to take a moment to appreciate the opportunity.

It gleamed now, the scent of lye and lemon thick in the air. Her back ached and her feet were sore, but Letty reveled in the feeling of a job well started. This was one of her favorite parts of the process, when the space was fresh and charged with potential.

It was beautiful. Soaring ceilings, wood floors that lacked a single nick or scuff, windows so large and so numerous that the tax on them alone must cost a fortune. It was a dream come true to have an opportunity like this.

It was dark outside, but she itched to continue. It might tack an extra hour or two to her day, but it was efficient to finish the job now so that tomorrow she could start sourcing furniture, paint, and trims, instead of wasting time going first to Hawthorne House and out again to the shops.

Letty fetched a chair and table from the guest room that she had stuffed earlier with ducal accoutrements. She propped her toolbox of tapes and rulers and pencils on the table, pleased to see her humble working tools on top of a Hepplewhite table. It didn't look like it had ever held anything more useful than a vase of flowers.

Everything was ornamental in this house. Of course, functional furniture would have its place in the servant's domain. She snapped her tape along the baseboard and took note of the measurement. Had the duchess considered the servants' quarters to be part of her decree to change everything? Probably not. She likely wasn't thinking of the people who worked there, despite all that Letty could do to improve the lives of the servants. She had noticed that Mrs. MacInnes's parlor could use fresh paint. Kitchens often had a need for new ironing boards, better ovens. Maybe even something newfangled, like a furnace.

Letty looked down at her sketchbook. Everything was laid out now on the page, with most of the important measurements noted. She needed one more for the fireplace, and then she would be done.

As she slid her tape over the carved marble, she was suddenly aware that she was no longer alone.

The Duchess of Hawthorne was several inches shorter than Letty, but when she looked down her nose it gave the illusion of much greater height. "Miss Barrow, it is good to see you again in Hawthorne House."

Her accent was so refined, her voice clear and high as a bell. She loved hearing the duchess talk. Letty knew she still had the tones of Lincolnshire in her own voice, tempered by the London accents that she had grown accustomed to over the decades of living here.

She straightened, the tape dangling from her hand. "Your Grace, I was finishing up a few measurements."

The duchess inclined her head a regal quarter inch. Had she practiced such precision before marrying the duke, or did such manners come with the experience of the position? She longed to ask, though surely the duchess would merely continue to gaze at her with thoughtful gravity.

"I didn't think you kept such long hours." The duchess went to the window, bereft now of curtains. The night sky was gray with cloud and smoke and fog, and bare tree branches waved in the wind.

"It's been so long that I was in this room that I have quite forgotten the view."

"The view is exceptional," Letty said, but her eyes had strayed to the duchess's bottom.

She was all covered up as usual, firmly buttoned from throat to wrist to ankle in an emerald day dress that set off her pale hair. Letty thought it a shame that she would never see the duchess in the first stare of elegance. It was her sad lot in life to never be lucky enough to be seated across from her at dinner, allowing her eyes to linger over her chest in a low-cut sparkling silk evening gown.

The very idea of dining with a duchess was absurd. Nothing more than a Banbury tale—and everyone knew such fairy stories never came true.

Letty cleared her throat. "The work is progressing smoothly, Your Grace. Tomorrow, I had thought to start looking at furnishings."

The duchess frowned. "So soon?"

Letty blinked. "Well, yes. Now that we have cleared out the room, and I have measured everything, I would expect to start painting as soon as we have reviewed the plans for color and furniture." She winced. "Not *we*. I meant I would review with Mrs. MacInnes, of course. I would never dream of imposing upon your time, Your Grace."

"Have you given no thought to ripping up the floorboards?" The duchess glanced around. "Or perhaps replacing the windows? Maybe expanding the size of the room? I expect to be *astonished*, Miss Barrow."

Her mind reeled. This would set her schedule back weeks if the duchess insisted upon any of it. "I hadn't considered changing the structure of the house. I would need to review with an architect to see what is possible. Professional workers would have to come in and give estimates on the time and budget. These arrangements, even if you choose not to pursue the change, would take much longer than I planned."

The duchess waved a hand. "As I told you, time is no object. I want the job to be done right. If you have other obligations, cancel them and you can discuss with Mrs. MacInnes about any issues with the wage."

Letty stared. The duchess seemed almost…giddy.

More evidence of the frivolity that one could expect from the nobility. Well, it was no more or less than she had expected. It was only disappointing because she had been lost in the duchess's sapphire eyes, and in her own dreams for the design. It wasn't her own house, she reminded herself. The client had a right to make changes.

"I can begin to arrange such meetings this week," Letty said.

"Thank you. I shall keep you no longer, Miss Barrow. I understand the demands on your time must not permit you to dally."

"Wait," she said, and the duchess's eyebrows flew upward in an almost comical expression. Too late, she realized that no one outside of the royal family told a woman of this station to *wait.* "That is, if you have a moment." That wasn't the right thing to say either. But she wanted to prolong the conversation. She wanted to go back to the easy back-and-forth that they had enjoyed over cake. She wanted…oh, she *wanted.*

But most of all, she wanted to know if she was right in her assumptions.

"I wanted to ask your opinion on finials."

"Finials?"

"Yes, Your Grace. Naturally, we will replace the bed here, and I wanted your opinion on the topping for the bed posts. I'm rather partial to decorative finials, myself. Smooth, carved, and fanciful." She couldn't help herself, even though the duchess was the least likely of any woman she had ever met to respond to something like this. "Pretty, like a woman's curves." She winked. Perhaps she would have needed Fraser's quizzing glass to see it, but was that the barest hint of a smile on the duchess's lips? Encouraged, she pressed on. "Finials. Would you be interested in discussing them further?"

The smile, if it indeed had ever been there, was quickly no more than a memory. "I don't think my preferences are relevant here. If you find you cannot accomplish the job with your own decisions—"

"No, Your Grace. I can manage quite well. I had hoped to have your opinion—"

"I am not inclined to provide one."

"Of course. Then I shall take my leave."

The duchess frowned and looked out the window once more. "You must take the carriage. I insist. You are working far too late tonight, and it isn't safe."

Letty was touched by her concern. She hadn't been escorted in the ducal carriage since the first house tour, and she relied on hackneys of varying degrees of comfort to bring her to and from the estate if she couldn't spare the hour it took to walk. The Hawthorne carriage, if memory served, had a thick fur bundled in the corner, ideal for one's lap on a late night. "I am accustomed to making my way in the world without such means, but I admit that it is cold and I am tired. I would very much welcome a ride."

"Excellent. Please speak to Mrs. MacInnes and she shall arrange it. I would never expect you to work such hours, Miss Barrow. I am perfectly content for this job to take as long as it needs to. You must have a care for your health."

"I suppose it is risky to stay," she said and met the duchess's eyes.

The duchess took a deep breath. And a step back. Was that a wash of palest pink across those ivory cheeks? "Risk is always best avoided."

"Then we miss the best parts of life, don't we? I cannot condone it, Your Grace. I will always embrace the chance of risk."

"I wish you a good evening, Miss Barrow."

With a sweep of her gown, she was gone.

Interesting. So, the duchess did have feelings somewhere in there. Maybe she was fixated on the ducal bed to beget an heir, but she didn't seem immune to Letty's casual flirtation. She had been right after all. The duchess was more like her husband than people thought.

Letty tucked that fact away like the rulers in her toolbox as she went in search of the housekeeper before she left Hawthorne House for the night.

Chapter Seven

There was nothing so pretty as dawn in December, Letty thought as she peered out the window at the weak amber light glinting off the quarter inch of snow that had fallen overnight.

When the kettle came to a boil, she lifted it out of the fire and prepared two sturdy mugs of strong coffee. She tucked a cloth around a basket of buns and went down the stairs at the back of the house, unlatching the door to the first floor and inhaling the familiar scent of fresh wood shavings and linseed oil varnish.

Fraser stretched and scratched his goatee. "How did you know I was down here, Letty lass? There's still time for me to be abed with a pretty lad, you know."

"I know how much you enjoy your Saturday mornings to yourself in the workroom. And you've been complaining all autumn about the lack of lads in your life. I think you're still pining over Marcus."

"Aye, but he's a damn fool who needs to come to his senses. You thought to raise my spirits with breakfast? If you were not my favorite friend before, then surely you are now." He took a mug and pressed a quick kiss to her cheek.

"Yesterday's Chelsea buns, from the pastry shop up the street. Robert and I are at outs again, and this was meant to be a reconciliation but of course he's turned up his nose at it."

"First time in that boy's life that he's refused sweets." Fraser shook his head and took a hearty bite, then licked excess sugar and spice from his thumb. "He's another one acting the fool these days, if you ask me."

Letty plopped herself down onto a rocking chair. "You seemed happy enough in the summer with Marcus. Why are you on the outs again?"

"Because he thinks with his prick, that one does."

Letty laughed. "And you don't? I saw the way you were winking at those waiters at Swann's. You were acting like your eye was in danger of falling out."

"Sometimes a man wants more than a twist in the sheets." He scowled at his coffee. "Marcus needs to come to his bloody senses and realize we could have something good together if he could stop tupping other men."

"Neither of you ever stopped and thought twice before pursuing a pretty face before." Letty was surprised. In all the time she had known them, Fraser and Marcus had been involved in a casual way, always circling their way back to each other.

"I want more these days, I suppose. We're not young anymore, carousing around the molly houses until dawn, foxed until we fall down in any bed we could find."

"I didn't think you were considering settling down."

He shrugged. "I suppose I'm not, if Marcus refuses to hear a word about it."

Fraser's face was still dark as a thundercloud, so she decided a change of subject was in order. She ran her hands over the satiny smooth arms of the chair. "This is nice work. Is it a new piece?"

He glanced up at her from where he had gone back to work on sanding down a table leg. "That is more than *nice work*," he said in injured tones. "Do you not see all the detail I put into the Renaissance revival carvings? Did you not notice the painted panel upon which your derriere now rests?"

She grinned and propped an elbow on the chair arm. "I admit, I did not. But I trust that it is in impeccable taste, as always."

Fraser snorted. "It's a custom piece for one of our more aggravating customers. We have an architect who chooses to do business with people who have the worst taste. This one is for a shipping magnate who has insisted on having dragons carved into the chair legs. And fruit. And flowers. The more, the better, in their opinion. Looks atrocious, but worth a mint of my time at least."

Letty laughed. She loved spending time with Fraser in his workroom, tucked at the back half of the first floor. The front half was the showroom and shop, and the second and third floors were split between her and Fraser's apartments. Fraser's business partner, Wynn, had originally lived above the shop but had moved upon his marriage. When John had died, the lease on Letty's townhouse expired with him, and Letty had been happy to move here, eager to be close to friends and to stay in the same neighborhood. Fraser and Wynn even allowed her the use of the smallest room at the back as her own workroom.

"There is certainly no accounting for taste," Letty said with feeling. "The renovations at Hawthorne House are still stalled as I await the duchess's final verdict on the floors."

Fraser took a sip of coffee. "Haven't you been working there for over a month now?"

"Yes. And every day, it's something different. First she wanted to consider replacing the floors, but when I had someone come in to take a look at them, she changed her mind. Then she thought maybe we should put down tiles. In a duke's *bedroom*. I could not quite condone it, but one doesn't say no to a duchess, so I went and brought back tile samples and a work estimate. She has now decided that the original floors are fine, but wishes to be presented with carpet samples on my next visit." She blew out a breath. "Do not get me started talking about the paint options for the walls."

"She sounds like a pain in the rear. I'll stick with the shipping magnate, dragons and all."

"The housekeeper says she isn't acting like herself. Apparently, the duchess is usually very decisive. The butler has started to give me sympathetic looks every time I arrive at the estate. Probably because he sees the frustration on my face when I leave at night."

"It must be difficult for the duchess to have her husband come back to England after so much time away."

Letty frowned. "I know that George told us that the duke and duchess are at cross ends, but that isn't what the duchess conveys. She appears intent on perfecting the duke's bedroom for his triumphant return."

"Married life is a mystery, Letty lass." Fraser set the sanding aside and picked up his whittling knife, using it with more force than necessary on the table leg as he scowled at it. "It's one that we may never know ourselves."

"Fraser, you've never seen such a mess. I have excess furniture crammed into almost every available bedroom, and there are makeshift shelves of samples and fabrics and papers lining the entire hallway, because Her Indecisive Grace cannot choose among any of them. Why, a whole floor of the estate is in total disarray. It's professionally embarrassing. If anyone saw, I should be disgraced and would never work again."

"You work for the highest of the high now. A duchess has every right to be as picky as she chooses. She can well afford it, after all. Is she cruel?"

"Far from it. She's the epitome of serenity. If she wasn't so aggravating, I'd like her."

The issue was that there seemed to be two Annes—the duchess, and the woman. The duchess was aggravating and arrogant. But the woman looked at a slice of lemon cake like it was a lover. The woman had stood up for her against the housekeeper when Letty had revealed that she had an illegitimate child, which would spare her any difficulties with the rest of the staff. The woman was concerned about late hours and carriage rides.

Fraser glanced at her slyly. "I think you like her anyway, lass."

"All right, I do like her," she admitted. "But it's almost as if she doesn't want the renovation to be *started*, much less completed. Beyond endless consultations and meetings, I have done nothing concrete except move items out of one room. It could all be put back as it had been before, with nothing changed except for a month of my time wasted."

"But you're getting paid. What's the harm?"

Letty glowered. "How will it help establish my name if I am known as the designer lucky enough to be hired by the Duchess of Hawthorne, only to accomplish *nothing*? I will be judged as incompetent. It will be said that a woman designer can only dither and delay, not create. My work crew wasn't happy from the marble tile fiasco for the judge, and I can't have them thinking that these delays for the duchess are my fault. I have to finish something, and I have to do it fast."

Fraser held up a hand. "I know that look, Letty. Think about what you're doing. You have rushed into things before, and things have not always turned out well for you."

Letty barely heard him. "The Duchess of Hawthorne hired me for a renovation, not a demolition. Maybe she doesn't trust that I can do it. I'll have to prove to her my worth." She took a deep breath. "I need to take a risk."

For the first time since starting work on Hawthorne House, she felt passion stirring in her. She grinned. "Fraser, do be a dear and show me all your unsold pieces, will you? Especially anything that you think might suit a duke."

Letty could hardly contain her excitement as she strode up the stairs to Hawthorne House two weeks later. She had been here so often now that she had developed an inordinate fondness for the lion's head knocker bolted to the front door, for the butler and his dour demeaner that thawed a little every time she saw him, and for the shiny black and white tiles that lined the grand hallway.

There was nothing better than a reveal day.

Although this was the first time in her career that the reveal would be a total surprise to the client.

She grinned at Mrs. MacInnes as she passed her in the hallway and received an encouraging look in return. The housekeeper had been instrumental in helping with the organizational work involved over the past week, and Letty was looking forward to working with her more closely on the rest of the house.

Letty slipped into the duke's dressing room. She pressed her thumb against a painting to straighten it, fussed for a moment with the curtains, and then took one final look around. It looked good. *Really* good.

She heard the clacking of the duchess's shoes as she approached the room before she saw her. Letty took a deep breath as the duchess appeared, the final crowning element of any room she entered.

Letty beamed. "Surprise."

But the duchess's face was pinched and white with rage. "Miss Barrow, you have overstepped."

Letty whipped her head around, worried there was something out of place after all. But everything was as she had designed it. The mirror in the mahogany frame that Fraser had delivered yesterday looked wonderful. So did the set of armchairs in the corner. The walls were pristine, papered with navy and cream stripes.

The effect was masculine and dark and powerful, with black leather and deep bronze stud accents, and pops of gold as she had noticed that the rest of the house was full of it. The hammered bronze washstand glittered in the sunlight. A trio of white handkerchiefs embroidered with a fanciful *H* were fanned out on the satinwood dresser.

"Overstepped?" she asked slowly.

The duchess skimmed a hand over the slick surface of the dresser, which Letty had polished within an inch of its life. "What gave you the right to refurnish this room? You were meant to be still planning the designs for the bedchamber, not working in the dressing room."

"*Everything* was the charge you gave to me during our interview, Your Grace," Letty said stiffly. "I believe I covered every detail in this room. However, if you do not care for it, then *everything* can be removed and replaced as it was. The wallpaper could be torn down by tomorrow."

"The paper is not the issue, Miss Barrow." She appeared to be struggling for words, which surprised Letty. The duchess was always composed. "*You* are the issue."

"Me?" Her heart started to hammer. This wasn't going according to plan at all.

"To tell you the truth, Miss Barrow, when I hired you, I didn't know if you could do it."

That stung. Deeply. "Excuse me?"

"I thought you inexperienced. Incapable of doing what would need to be done in such an estate. I didn't think you had the knowledge, or the expertise."

"I told you I could give satisfaction, Your Grace," Letty snapped. She wasn't going to give up without fighting on behalf of her work. "I may have never designed for the nobility, but I know exactly what I'm doing. Those are fleur-de-lis on the drawer pulls, and French lavender pressed among the towels. Forgive me, but I have heard the talk about the Duke of Hawthorne. I hear that he is an extravagant man who loves to socialize. The shelves in the dresser are extra deep to fit his considerable wardrobe, and there are chairs and a chaise lounge to entertain friends."

The public rooms downstairs would be redone to focus on wealth and power and prestige, with as much marble and gold as she could fit into them. But the upstairs rooms would never be on display, so she had personalized the dressing room to suit the man as much as the duke. The bedchamber was meant for the duke and duchess and their duty. But she rather thought that the duke would appreciate the privacy in the dressing room to do what he liked.

"To entertain…friends." The duchess gave a hollow laugh.

Letty frowned. Surely the duchess knew of the duke's affairs with other men? But perhaps it had been too familiar of her to have drawn attention to it. Maybe that was what offended her.

"The room is perfect," she said flatly. "Hawthorne would doubtlessly love it. You have more than proven that you are capable beyond my expectations. But the point is that you didn't *listen*, Miss Barrow. You were to start nothing, let alone finish a room so quickly."

Quickly? She had been employed for over a month. She had worked her fingers to the bone merely to earn a lecture? She tried to think of the money as incentive to bite her tongue. Sour words would win her no repeat customers. Not that she necessarily wanted to continue to work for the duchess anyway, or anyone else from the nobility if this was how they showed their appreciation—or lack thereof.

"Most clients appreciate when a job comes in under budget and ahead of time, Your Grace." Were time and money considered only by the middle class and lower? Letty couldn't fathom it. "I was not hired to take things apart. What I love about my job is the opportunity to create—to build something beautiful and serviceable and meaningful. I wanted to prove to you that if you leave the decisions to me, as you seem to have a great deal of trouble making any yourself, then you can have a finished product that exceeds your expectations."

"This is what you do not understand, Miss Barrow. I don't wish the project to finish."

Chapter Eight

The duchess sank into one of the upholstered chairs in the corner of the duke's dressing room, her posture still impeccable. She didn't look angry anymore. Now she looked exhausted.

Letty tamped down her irritation and took the chair next to the duchess. She had arranged the seating close together to encourage intimacy, and their knees almost brushed. "You are correct that I do not understand. The delay to start the renovation is causing frustration and confusion among both your staff and my crew and is costing you a small fortune."

"The money is going to good places. People must work, after all. Artisans must be paid, whether the pieces we commission are displayed in my husband's room or consigned to the attics. Isn't it our noble duty to provide work?"

"Not like that," Letty said with a frown. "Artists don't want their wares to be stored away. They want them displayed. And you're causing double work for everyone by changing your mind all the time. What do you really want, Your Grace?"

The duchess's eyes glittered. "I don't want the duke to return to Hawthorne House. If the renovation is unfinished, then he cannot come home."

Letty was shocked. The duchess had been so solicitous of the duke's comfort—or so she had thought. "Did you ever intend to have me finish anything?" The duchess's hesitation was all the answer she needed. "You may not value my time or my expertise, but I assure you that I can find good work elsewhere, where I can actually build my portfolio."

But the truth was that she was no further along than she had been before she started. In fact, she would be in a worse situation as the crew would lose faith in her capabilities to keep a job. What if the duchess refused payment for the past month's wages? Letty had been docked more for overstepping far less. She felt sick as she thought of the money she had given Robert last week for the new books that he insisted he needed.

"What do you expect from me now, Your Grace?"

"I don't quite know. All that I am certain of is that I have grown to hate this house." The words rushed out, and the duchess looked startled, as if she hadn't meant to say such a thing at all.

This was more emotion than Letty had ever seen cross the duchess's face. "I can help you with that," she said. "What do you hate about it?"

She gave her a sidelong look. "My own suite, for one."

Letty's interest sparked. "What if I abandoned the work in the duke's chambers, and shifted my focus to renovating yours?"

She rose to her feet. "Come with me, Miss Barrow."

As soon as she saw it, Letty hated the duchess's bedchamber too. It was enormous but crowded to a dizzying degree, from clocks to figurines to settees to footstools and more. *Much* more. "This is a lot of gold." She eyed a set of gilt candlestick holders crowding the mantel. "Very…intimidating."

"The dowager duchess is an intimidating woman. I have changed nothing about the suite since I moved into it."

Watching the duchess move through her most private rooms gave Letty a strange feeling. It wasn't simply desire, though she felt it surging through her blood with an insistence that was hard to ignore, especially when a truly enormous bed was right there in front of her.

But she also felt something a good deal more tender. She wanted to tear apart this room and give the duchess something lovely and peaceful and gracious, something that reflected the new opportunity that she felt so grateful for, something that showed her that Letty didn't just see a duchess. She saw the woman.

But those words were difficult to express and felt far too intimate to be comfortable. Desire was easier, and that bed was beckoning.

"I told you during our interview that I would satisfy you," Letty said in low tones. "And satisfy you I will, Your Grace."

There was a long, heated moment where she was perfectly sure they understood each other, though she doubted the duchess would act on it.

"What exactly would you do to this room, if you had carte blanche to…satisfy me?"

Letty blinked. Perhaps she had been wrong. She licked her lips. "I would examine every inch. Look at every angle. Then I would strip the room bare and cover it with whatever came into my imagination."

The duchess sucked in a breath. "Oh?"

"I was thinking of the lemon cake," Letty said, watching her. The duchess didn't tend to show much on her face, but she could see her nostrils flare and her pupils widen. Her chest was moving fast with shallow breaths. All very interesting indeed. "Light and frosted and pristine and elegant. Delicious. Like you."

The duchess blinked.

Letty bit her lip. Too far. "Those are décor ideas for the room, of course. I didn't mean that you were—"

"You don't think I am elegant? My dressmaker would have a fit of the vapors if she heard it."

The air felt different somehow. The bedchamber felt sunnier and warmer than it had a minute ago. "You are always elegant, Your Grace."

The duchess's eyes seemed to measure her, spanning her wrist to wrist, and crown to toes. A prickle of awareness followed the path of those eyes.

"I would like to create a space as ethereal as you are. A room befitting the Duchess of Hawthorne."

❖

Anne struggled to keep her composure. Miss Barrow was bold as brass, standing there with a hand on her hip and lust in those dark brown eyes. Had her own desires been so obvious? Outside of the bedchamber, flirtation had seemed a harmless game, but she hadn't thought it through to its obvious conclusion.

Miss Barrow had.

And now there was naught but a bed between them.

This was too much. Anne took a step back, then another.

Miss Barrow seemed to understand, and her smile turned bright instead of sensual. "I thought Hawthorne House would be like any other in Mayfair and renovating it would be easy. Any old gold and silver would do to grace its hallowed halls. But I am wondering if perhaps there is more to it," she said. "Give over your suite to me. One more chance."

Anne hesitated.

"I understand better now. You don't know what you want, because you don't know what you *could* want. I can figure that out—if I know *you*."

"I don't think that will be necessary. It's unbecoming." Flirtation was one thing, and desire was another, but getting to know each other was quite out of the question. The very idea. Anne tried to convince herself to feel affronted, instead of this unwelcome frisson of delight. Oh, the very *idea*.

"If you want me to give you something personal that suits you, and not your rank, then I will need to spend time with you."

"Maybe I could work a few appointments into my schedule," Anne said, astonished at the words. Usually, she had no trouble at all saying no. She said it all the time. Why was she opening herself to *yes*?

Trusting in someone was tempting after doing everything alone for so long. After all, she was paying Miss Barrow. Was it such a risk to put her faith in someone who had such a vested reason to stay?

Miss Barrow laughed. "You needn't look as if you are about to have a tooth pulled, Your Grace. If you could grant me several hours a week, that would be ideal. More would be better, but I do not wish to presume too much upon your time."

She managed a nod.

"Then it's all settled. I shall redesign your suite and leave the duke's in disarray. We are to be co-conspirators to prevent your husband from coming home."

"Conspirators? I dislike that word. A duchess has no thought of revolution." Faint alarm pulsed through her at the lie. She indeed wanted to uproot the dukedom's values, but she didn't think she could share that with Miss Barrow.

"You're taking a stand against your lord and master. Is that not revolt?"

"Hawthorne is hardly my master." She thought for a minute. "More like an absentee landlord."

"A tenant overthrowing his landlord is upheaval at its finest. What if your own tenants ever did such a thing?"

The idea rankled. "They wouldn't," she muttered. Or at least they wouldn't if she could convince the estate managers to allow her to put her ideas into action to improve the tenants' lives.

There was a look of mischief in Miss Barrow's eyes.

Maybe—just maybe—this could be *fun*.

Chapter Nine

At quarter after two in the afternoon, Anne closed her portfolios and stoppered her inkwell. Penciling in time for insubordination had been remarkably easy despite her busy schedule, given how keen she had become on the topic. It was about time she focused on herself instead of the duchy.

It was thrilling to think of having a partner in thwarting her husband.

Miss Barrow entered the room behind a footman at half past, her face full of its usual good cheer and amusement. "Your Grace, you are not dressed!"

Anne looked down at herself. "My clothing begs to differ."

"For our *walk*. That is not a promenade dress."

This sounded more alarming by the moment. She took in Miss Barrow's dark blue pelisse, thick gloves, and leather boots. They looked more than sturdy enough to venture through any manner of unpleasant outdoor elements. "I thought you meant we would walk about the estate."

"We have done that already, haven't we? No, I meant a proper walk."

"In *December*?"

"It is neither raining nor snowing."

"It is *cold*. We have a nice fire in here, and I can ring for tea." Inspiration struck. "Maybe lemon cake?"

"We know these four walls too well now, and they have nothing more to tell us. Come with me, Your Grace, and let's begin to know each other so I can give you the bedroom of your dreams."

Anne remembered the feelings that Miss Barrow had stirred in her the last time they stayed inside the house, and hastily agreed to go outdoors.

After she changed into her warmest walking dress, two footmen followed her and Miss Barrow out of the house and trailed them at a respectful distance. The first hint of wind on Anne's cheek had her snuggling deep into her fur-lined cloak and shoving her gloved hands into her matching muff. It was a damp sort of cold, the kind that crept into one's boots and beneath one's hood. She would be shivering and sniveling before long.

She told herself that was a good thing. There was nothing less appealing, after all, and shouldn't she wish to be at her least attractive to quell this desire between them?

"This is a rapid pace for a stroll," she said, trying not to huff. Miss Barrow had a long stride.

She slowed. "I apologize, Your Grace. I walk most everywhere. It's wonderful outside at this time of year."

Her breath came in little puffs of white, contrasting with the redness of her cheeks and the tip of her nose. She swung her walking stick by her side. It was no wonder that she liked to be outdoors. Miss Barrow was a handsome woman, but never more so than with a healthy flush on her face.

She gestured with her stick at the houses that they passed. "I love being around people, and buildings. Buildings *last*. It's one of the reasons I love my trade—creating something inside that gives pleasure for either a minute or a lifetime, but housed in something that could last forever. It's a nice balance."

Anne hadn't considered it like that before. "I have endeavored to preserve what is already in place, enshrining it for the next generation."

"Perhaps I am overstepping, Your Grace, but I must admit to being curious about why you don't want the duke to return to the estate."

When was the last time anyone besides Miss Barrow had spoken to her so casually? It felt shocking. And intimate. And yet, she liked it. Questions that would have seemed rude or prying from someone else seemed like nothing more than simple curiosity from her. "I'm sure you understand the type of man that Hawthorne is."

"Was this news to you?" Miss Barrow asked. "Forgive me, but the rumors have been running amok for years. Do you despise his inclinations so much?" Her tone had cooled.

"It's not that," Anne said, lowering her voice. "I knew who I married."

"Then what difference is it if he is in France or in your house?"

It was always easy to talk with Miss Barrow, but it was even easier out here in the open air. It felt different. Exciting, somehow, even though a stroll across Grosvenor Square and into the streets of Mayfair was hardly a clandestine meeting. She stole a look at Miss Barrow. Maybe it wasn't the walking that was having such an effect on her. Maybe it was the *woman*. Who was the last person to whom she had spoken so freely, without the pressure of Society rules and propriety influencing what passed her lips?

"When the duke is not in residence, I am the de facto duke," she confessed. "I can't make all the decisions that I would like, but I am in control of a great many things regardless. Now that he has returned, he wants to wrest control of the dukedom back—but I find I am loath to give it up."

"Could he not choose to run things from his apartments?"

"He could, but he hasn't done so." She struggled to find the words. "Hawthorne House is more than a building. It represents the power itself, and that is what I think he is after. A duke issuing edicts from his own estate is a force to be reckoned with, more so than a mere man writing letters from his apartment. I believe his pride would be too wounded to return and stay in a lesser room, if his own chambers are not available."

Miss Barrow tapped her stick against the sidewalk. "Has he said why the power is suddenly so important to him?"

"No. But Hawthorne is forty years of age now, and I am wondering if he feels that it is past time for him to settle down into his responsibilities."

"You said you wanted everything redone. But it is only his suite that you were looking to destroy? I wonder if it's too conspicuous if his is the sole room in shambles."

"It is the most important room of the house, after all, as he is the lord and master of us all," Anne said piously. She stole a look at Miss Barrow and saw a mischievous smile on her lips.

"The duke's empty chamber is a message, I suppose. It represents his authority, but if it's all undone, then it exposes his impotence as a figurehead."

"You understand." Relief flooded her.

"I spend a great deal of time thinking of the symbolism of the rooms I work in."

"I admit to a great satisfaction to seeing the empty room, as if there is no duke at all. But I am also eager to see every mark of the Hawthorne legacy in the entire house struck from the record and rebuilt, at *my* word."

"Everything needs a refresh now and again, lest it become stagnant."

Like me, Anne thought. She felt stagnant. Maybe it was time for a change, and not for the house.

"Does your son also have an interest in interior design?" Anne asked.

"No, my Robert is in training to be a solicitor." Miss Barrow's voice warmed with pride, but a shadow crossed her face. "He was recently accepted as an apprentice to a well-to-do man who works in the courts of Chancery."

"It is wonderful to see the younger generation take the reins of their lives. I am impressed every day with my nephew since he reached his majority. He is Hawthorne's heir, and I can think of no one better to inherit the title."

"You never had children, Your Grace?"

Anne stiffened. She spoke of this to no one for fear of seeming unnatural. A lady's most important role was to bear an heir. How could she ever explain why she—the Stickler of Society—had failed to execute her primary duty?

Yet there was something so open and encouraging about Miss Barrow, and Anne thought she would understand.

"I suppose people think that the duke's absence made things challenging in that regard," she said. "But the simple truth is that neither of us wanted children." Saying the words was a relief.

"I thought at first that you wanted me to work on the duke's bedchambers so you could resume your marital duties in hopes of an heir."

"Oh!" The idea startled a laugh from her. "No. Certainly not."

"I only had one child," Miss Barrow said. "I was never with any man after Robert's father."

Anne was shocked to hear her speak so casually.

She leaned close. "I have only lain with women."

"Use your *discretion*, Miss Barrow!" Anne gasped. She whipped her head around and was relieved to see the footmen still far behind. The admission wasn't a shock to her—she hadn't missed the way that Miss Barrow's eyes lingered on her or the sparks that sizzled the air between them—but to say such a thing out in the open!

"Oh, I hide nothing from anyone," she said, a little smile on her lips. "I am not afraid of who I am."

"It's too dangerous," Anne hissed. "Do not think me unsympathetic, but you risk everything to speak so boldly. I cannot condone this." She shoved her hands deeper into the muff, clasping them together so hard she was worried she would crack the bone.

"I merely thought, knowing of your husband—"

"You *must* stop, Miss Barrow. No more."

"I apologize for offending you, Your Grace." Her voice held a note of scorn.

Anne struggled not to flush. "It is not—offensive," she said, pitching her voice as low as she could. "But it is not safe to say these things in public, where anyone could overhear."

She shrugged. "I think natural needs and desires are entirely appropriate for conversation, but I suppose that is but one more difference between a duchess and a lowly miss such as myself. It matters not anyway. I am here to know more about *you*, after all, and *your* needs. For your renovation, of course."

It was easy to pretend that those words meant more than they did. Those moments in the bedchamber rushed back to her, bringing not only a much-needed warmth to her wind-chapped cheeks but also a most inconvenient warmth between her legs.

That was dangerous indeed.

But oh, so tempting.

"What else would you like to know?" she asked.

Miss Barrow thought for a moment. "What is your happiest memory, Your Grace?"

"My wedding night," Anne said without hesitation and in perfect truth.

"I must admit I am surprised."

"You go too far, Miss Barrow. I thought perhaps we would be admiring the neighbor's houses and envying their windows."

Miss Barrow grinned. Anne was annoyed that she found it as charming as ever. "Do you often feel envy, Your Grace? Shall we get to know each other through examining the seven deadly sins?"

Anne couldn't help it. She laughed. "Wherever did you learn your manners, Miss Barrow? No one speaks so familiarly to me. *Ever.*"

"I think maybe you like it." She smiled. "Maybe you are beginning to like it outside, too, where it's different from what you're used to. Different company. Different ideas."

The cold had seized her fingers, and her toes were curled in her boots, but the breeze now felt fresh instead of freezing, and the light flashing off the snow dazzled her eyes. She felt invigorated and alive, every sense heightened.

It was beautiful out here.

Anne stole another look at Miss Barrow. Beautiful, indeed.

Letty had been sorely mistaken in her assumption that winning the apprenticeship would cool Robert's recent tempers. It was as if his grievances had multiplied when they should have lessened. He wasn't home often, but when he was, he was peevish in a way that he had never been before, not even when he had been a recalcitrant youth begging her for shillings to drink at any tavern he could find with his friends.

She couldn't solve his issues for him. Her heart still hurt after his most recent outburst, and she suspected it would hurt more if she dwelled on it. Best to turn her thoughts to work. She brewed herself a cup of tea and brought it down to her workroom.

Letty thought of Hawthorne House, its rooms so familiar to her now. She wanted to change this house. Not simply for the money, or to secure her reputation. But she liked the bones of the building, the shape of its walls and stairs, its archways and windows. Fully decorated though the house already was, barring the duke's bedchamber, the estate was starting to look like a blank canvas. What it lacked was *personality*.

She wanted to stamp hers all over it.

Letty frowned into the tea. This wouldn't do at all. The house wasn't hers, and it was dangerous to think about it with such arrogance. She had lost jobs over such things before, rushing in and thinking she knew better than the client. She had almost lost *this* job by doing exactly that with the duke's dressing room.

But there was no harm in dreams, was there?

As she opened her sketchbook to a blank page, Letty let her thoughts wander to her favorite room of the house. She had seen it when Mrs. MacInnes had given her a detailed tour and history lesson about the estate, and though she had only spent a few minutes there, she had been captivated by its potential. It was a small parlor that opened into a smaller terrace. A haven of privacy.

Slowly, Letty started to sketch out the lines of the room, then tapped the pencil tip a few times against the paper as she thought of how she yearned to fill it. The room should reflect the peace and quiet of nature, with the theme being rest and respite. There would be oversized plants in big copper tubs, and trails of flowers hanging from chains hooked to miniature ceiling rosettes. Perhaps an ornamental tree or a fern in the corner. She penciled in a chaise lounge and a pair of deep-set chairs facing the opening to the terrace, which she would transform into French doors covered with graceful gauzy curtains. Rosewood tables with thin legs and the slimmest of tabletops would be set between the chairs, perfect for a cup of tea and the newest books from the lending library.

She tapped her pencil against the page again. The duchess wouldn't use a lending library, not when she had her own library and a staff who doubtlessly purchased books for it as soon as they were published.

No, this was purely Letty's fantasy. It wasn't for the duchess at all.

She tried not to look up too much while she worked. It was easier to lose herself in thoughts of luxury when she wasn't gazing at the whitewashed walls of her workroom, and the scraps of fabric and trims that she could never afford for herself. She was grateful to live next to Fraser. It afforded her a sense of security. But though it was practical, it was also impersonal. Impermanent. Mrs. MacInnes's parlor had more decoration in it than she had in her own rooms, even though Letty was the one calling herself a designer.

The townhouse that Letty had lived in for twenty years had been leased furnished with beautiful things, which she had naively considered to be hers for her lifetime. Curse the Wilsons for being heartless. But she didn't like thoughts of them to intrude on her day, so she bent her attention back to her drawing.

She spent some time inking in the details of her sketch, and layering watercolor onto the page. Pale yellow walls, bright white chairs, deep green leaves, warm brown wood. While the paint was still damp, she scribbled her name in the corner. *Letitia's Parlor.*

After all, the design was too fanciful for the duchess. It didn't have the clean lines that she thought the duchess more likely to favor. She also thought the duchess would prefer greenery to be kept where it belonged, either out of doors or contained to a greenhouse. When it was time to focus on the rooms on the first floor, she would have to redesign the parlor from scratch. But for now, it gave her a little glow of satisfaction deep in her chest to look at it.

Letty thought again of the Duchess of Hawthorne. She needed to start piecing together what she knew of her so far and start thinking about potential design elements for her bedchamber and dressing room.

She knew that the duchess had a sweet tooth. She knew she liked being outside, even if she protested it. She knew the sound of her laugh now. High trilling notes, like birdsong. Letty felt a thrill at the thought that she had been the one to make her laugh, to shake her out of her polite mask and reveal something of who she really was. She knew the staccato clack of her heeled shoes and thought she could recognize her by rhythm alone at this point.

She knew the downward curve of her lip that seemed to be most often on her face even when relaxed, and the polite smiles that she wore from time to time, but what she yearned to see was a full smile, wide and genuine and delighted instead of decorous. Surely there was passion to be coaxed from those lips.

The duchess was uptight and reserved, but every conversation intrigued Letty further. She was eager to see her again and to explore what it was that this woman wanted from her life, instead of what the duchess wanted for her station.

Letty had always been attracted to unconventional women. Her lovers had ranged from business owners to artists to writers, and what they all had in common was a sense of disquiet. They were ambitious, like herself, and they wanted more for themselves, and for others like them.

She had never expected the Duchess of Hawthorne to be anything except a taskmaster to tradition or filled with whims and careless indecision. But instead she had proved herself to be unconventional indeed. She was uptight but hadn't been judgmental about Robert being born on the wrong side of the blanket. She was hell-bent on rebelling against her husband. She wasn't indecisive or frivolous at all—that had been a pretense to prevent her from progressing too far on the duke's suite.

Despite the chasm of rank between them, she had been surprised to discover their compatibility. Most importantly, the duchess didn't mind if she spoke to her as an equal.

It had been impulsive to be so straightforward about her romantic preferences during their walk, but she hated hiding herself and she was tired of hinting at it. Ever since her family had disowned her upon discovering her pregnancy, she had sworn to be honest in who she was. Nothing had ever hurt her more than her father's disappointment when she hadn't lived up to his expectations. It was easier to be up-front from the beginning, and let people judge her accordingly. That way, there was no opportunity for disappointment or betrayal.

It was folly to risk a flirtation with the duchess, though. It risked blurring the lines between what she could offer the woman in bed, and the duchess she yearned to impress with her design skills. She needed this job, and she needed the references to be dependent on her work. Not on her back. It was too much to risk.

A friendship was one thing, but flirtation had to remain out of the question. It was too bad that she yearned so much to tease smiles from that pretty mouth.

The duchess didn't seem the type to indulge anyway. She was too straightlaced for Letty. She liked it when a woman knew her mind, and the duchess couldn't even bring herself to talk about desire when it was clear no one could hear them. No, this was a one-sided yearning, and best to lock it away.

Feelings and desires aside, Letty was starting to understand the duchess, and she thought maybe the duchess was beginning to understand her too. Could she design something that suited her? She grinned. She thought she just might have some ideas.

CHAPTER TEN

At Christmas, Anne decided to give herself a gift. Earlier, she had distributed bolts of cloth to the servants, and presided over a dinner and dance for them with mistletoe strung up on the chandeliers and boughs of pine on the mantels. Snow coated the ground outside, and there was plenty of good cheer inside with roaring fires and mince pies. She had made merry with the staff and enjoyed her share of the milk punch that she suspected the kitchen staff had made stronger than the recipe book recommended.

Bleary-eyed after the late supper and dancing, she stifled a yawn and stole down into the morning room where she worked. It was dark and quiet. A shiver ran up her spine as she remembered the ghost stories that the butler had told earlier with glee. There was sure to be a host of chambermaids giggling and whispering all night with fancies of creaks and groans to entertain them.

Anne set her candle holder on the desk and slid open the top drawer where the stationary was kept. She had been putting off the task for weeks now. She stared down at the blank paper and the black inkwell, waiting for her to fill the page with recriminations.

It seemed out of charity with the season to tell Hawthorne that he couldn't move back to the estate. But the plan was in action. Not only was his room dismantled, but the entire second floor was in chaos, stuffed with fabrics and furniture. There were a few bedchambers left on the third floor, but none satisfactory enough to suit a duke.

She picked up the pen, and then set it back down. How many times had they danced together when they were young, before they married? Hawthorne would murmur witticisms and *on-dits* in her ear, his worldly humor making her laugh for ages after they left the floor. It had not all been bad between them.

Marriage was meant to be a partnership. It was unfortunate that her partner had abandoned the ship so soon. She was long accustomed to doing everything by herself now, but she longed sometimes for a shoulder to lean on. Or a lover to comfort her.

As wealthy as she was, Anne couldn't afford regret. She had been born the daughter of an earl, and she had ambitions to marry higher, and she had achieved her goals. It was nonsense to cry over what she had sown with such meticulous care. It must be the punch that was making her maudlin. Cook had tipped in the brandy with a generous hand indeed.

Anne focused on every letter of every word, carving her decision in black and white. The duke was not to return, as the estate was in sad state and not ready for guests. She sprinkled sand across the page to soak up the extra ink before blowing it off and folding it into neat fourths. She tipped her candle to splash hot wax across the fold and picked up the heavy Hawthorne seal. For a moment she studied it, studded with rubies and carved with strawberry leaves, then pressed its ornate *H* into the wax, grinding it in so that every line would stand stark against the scarlet wax.

She set it aside on top of her other letters as if it were any other business correspondence.

It was difficult to sleep after that. She tossed and turned, her thoughts flipping from Hawthorne's dark hooded eyes to Miss Barrow's warm brown ones.

Her desire wasn't appropriate. Miss Barrow was gently bred, but she worked for her living—and not as something quite respectable, like a governess. Anne had no issues with a woman making her way in the world. In fact, the more she knew about Miss Barrow, the more interested she was.

But she wouldn't do for a *lover*. It would be difficult enough to find a woman from within the *ton* to understand her. As rarified as the lives of nobility were, there was nothing to compare to the rigors and expectations and duties of a duchy, outside the royal family. To even think that a working woman could begin to understand her life seemed like a dream.

Also, there was that disconcerting honesty that Miss Barrow wielded as comfortably as her pencil. Someone who was so calm about disclosing her unmarried state with a grown child would never be as discreet as Anne needed a lover to be. She admired it, after the shock wore off, but it could never be for her. She had been devastated when Hawthorne had left her and started flaunting his lovers from across the Channel. She needed someone who understood discretion. Someone who understood the parameters of her life—strict adherence to Society in the streets, indulgence when concealed within the bedsheets.

It didn't matter if she ached for Miss Barrow's touch or wondered what her lips would feel like against hers. She was long accustomed to denying herself, and this would be no different.

There must be someone else that she could consider. All those times she had spent with her eyes peeled for sapphic indiscretions should have netted her a host of names to consider, but all she could think of were several lonely wives and widows who were wintering at their estates.

Who among the denizens of London could warm her through the long cold winter?

Miss Barrow's mischievous smile came to mind again, and Anne buried her head into her pillow. Maybe she wouldn't be a suitable lover for the long term. But would it be so risky to give in to temptation while the house was being renovated? Their liaison would be private by its very nature, given that Miss Barrow needed to frequent the house to do her work. No one would ever guess at what else might be going on in the private rooms of Hawthorne House.

The most compelling reason was that Anne *yearned*.

It wasn't because it had been years since she had taken a lover to bed. It was because of Miss Barrow's low sultry voice when she had promised her satisfaction. When she said she would give her what she needed.

Anne twisted in the bed, far too warm.

Could she have what she wanted, if the only thing that stood in her way was being brave enough to take it?

Her decision made, she fell into a fitful sleep.

❖

Letty drank deeply. "I don't think I can hide the truth any longer."

Swann's Ale Rooms and Eatery was crowded tonight, and she was pressed cheek to jowl in a booth between Fraser and Marcus and across from George and the proprietor, Sam Swann. It was loud tonight, and no one except her friends could hear her even if she shouted. But still she thought it best to be prudent, especially as she had downed two Burton ales already in quick succession and could no longer be sure how loud she was talking under the best of circumstances. Her thigh pressed against Fraser's, and she threw her arm around his shoulders to wedge herself closer and whisper in his ear. "I fancy her."

Fraser laughed. "Letty Barrow, you're no lass to be turned by a duchess."

"It's a passing fancy, nothing more. There is no rhyme or reason behind it."

Marcus nudged her. "Hey now, am I to be left out of all the fun and gossip?"

She lifted her other arm around him and leaned her head against his heavyset frame, solid and comforting. "There is no fun to be had for me, alas. I pine for the unreachable, a twinkling star of which us lowly creatures dare not dream. I am again to a lonely bed tonight."

Fraser gave a little two-fingered wave at a fine-faced fellow with fashionable sideburns and a natty coat and ducked as Marcus leaned over Letty to cuff his ear. "It's not hard to find company. Let yourself be open to the moment."

This might be the problem, she thought. Not that she wasn't open to encounters. But that she spent a good deal of time with men, in abodes where they liked to flirt with other men. How was she to find companionship for *herself* with such company as she kept?

Swann chortled. "You two ought to work out your tensions elsewhere, Marcus and Fraser. Might I suggest a bout upstairs for you both?" He was a big man with a bushy beard and a wolfish look in his eye.

"I think not," Fraser said. "He knows what he's done."

Marcus snorted. "I'd gladly go up with *you* if you're in the mood, Swann."

Fraser stiffened. "George, how about you? Would you care to join *me* upstairs?"

"Am I to be left alone for supper?" Letty asked. "What a shameful lack of camaraderie tonight."

George smiled. "I'll stay with you, Letty. These days, I'm a taken man. I shan't be available tonight or any other."

This distracted Marcus and Fraser enough to forget their quarrel and to start ribbing him, but he would say no more of it, claiming a lady's name was at stake and he was too much a gentleman to ever compromise it.

When their meal arrived, Swann got up to take his turn at pulling drinks at the back of the eatery. "Sort yourselves out or I'll crack your sodding heads together the next time I come round, lads."

Fraser took a bite of pigeon pie. "Well then, Letty lass, let's get back to your tale of woe as you're the only one willing to talk about your love life tonight."

"I may be willing to talk of it, but the problem is that the lovely duchess refuses to hear even a hint of such conversation." She told them about their walk through Mayfair, then sighed. "At least we seem to be forging a friendship, of sorts."

"Perhaps then it's time to take another job if this one is giving you trouble."

"You know I can't." She poked Fraser's rib with her elbow. "I need this job, and I need her to review my services highly. This is important for my future."

Marcus snorted. "I know which of your services you *wish* she was reviewing."

"That's all you think about," Fraser muttered.

She gasped in mock outrage. "You are far too much." She tore off a piece of crust from Fraser's pie and popped it in her mouth. "This is business only."

"Why not *sex* only?" Marcus said, leaning back. "Nothing to it. I'm sure we've all had thoughts of getting beneath the skirts or trousers of the upper class and being on top for once." He laughed. "Don't you want to know what it's like with a duchess? Maybe her quim is covered in diamond dust."

"Don't talk about her that way," Letty snapped. "I can't imagine it." She could, of course. She *did*. All too vividly. "I swore I would never be involved with the nobility. It was bad enough with John, sneaking away our indiscretions, for the reward of being cast out of my own family. The last thing I want is to be someone's secret again. Especially not for someone who can't even voice her own desires."

"There are far less complicated women in far closer proximity," Fraser broke in. "With so many people like me willing to overlook a woman's attractions, there should be a whole host of opportunity if you look hard enough."

"Maybe I'll have time after the job is done." She frowned and took another bite of crust.

He pushed the plate at her. "Eat the damned pie, Letty, and I'll order something else. When is the job projected to be done?"

"Forever from now. Months. Maybe a year."

A whole year of pining would test her limits, Letty thought. Fraser was right. There were other women, and she needed to find one.

The door opened and a chill wind swept three night watchmen into the eatery. It was a neighborhood of solicitors and barristers and lawmakers, many of whom jostled about here and sneaked upstairs like the rest of them for a spot of fun now and again, knowing it was an establishment generally friendly to men like themselves. It wasn't often that they saw the watchmen in these parts.

The noise level dropped like a tide retreating to the ocean, leaving ripples instead of crashing waves of conversation. With heavy-booted steps, the men marched to a counter at the back of the restaurant where the drinks were pulled. On their way, an errant nightstick poking out smacked someone in the back of the head, who bore it without a murmur, not looking for trouble.

Letty eyed her walking stick. But a ruckus was what they all wanted to avoid. It was much better to exist peaceably with the law, paying exorbitant fees as protection when necessary, confining their attraction to arenas like this where they were accepted among their own, and not out in public where they faced persecution.

Or the hangman's noose.

George glowered at their backs. "Someday, things will not always be so uneven," he vowed. "We will not always have to hide in the darkness or suffer the consequences."

The watchmen stayed long enough to enjoy a tankard at the bar, then to gather up a stack of meat pasties and rolls and stroll back out. On their way, the nightstick cracked against another head and an elbow.

After the men left, the diners' voices were loud and angry. The wounded were tended to, and glasses raised in their name.

Swann sent out a round of mulled wine and gingerbread to everyone, on the house. He clattered a plate down in front of Letty. "They come in here wanting to make a show," he spat. "Make me pull their beers, wait on them, and then let us know by their presence that they've an eye on us. That they have the power to do what they've done to poor Tom over there, and Anthony, and that they could do worse if they felt a hankering."

George's face was grim. "Something must be done to protect the community, or to help shelter it."

Letty thought of Anne's reluctance to discuss it when she had brought up her affairs with women. Ugliness like this was at the root of that need for secrecy and sowed the seeds of fear in all of their hearts.

The eyes of her neighbors were on Letty. But the eyes of the King himself were on Anne and Hawthorne. Would she be risking more than Anne's reputation if she flirted with her?

It was best if she didn't act on her desires for the duchess. Even if it went against every grain of her being.

Chapter Eleven

Letty poked her head in the door of the duchess's morning room. She was writing letters at her desk, the light streaming in from the window behind her. Letty's breath caught for a moment. The light turned the duchess's pale hair almost white, and her face was animated as she wrote, her lips parted slightly.

This was a look of interest, and passion, and Letty wanted quite desperately to have it turned on her instead of the page on the desk.

She tapped on the doorframe and the duchess looked up.

"Did we have a meeting scheduled, Miss Barrow? I apologize, I was lost in my letter to the estate manager at Hawthorne Towers."

"We had no meeting, but I wonder if you would care to accompany me? I am far from completing the bedchamber, but I do have one room ready for you, Your Grace." She smiled. "I thought you might be envious that the duke had his dressing room completed, so I finished yours as fast as I could." She leaned forward and lowered her voice in an exaggerated whisper. "Worry not—I made yours much nicer."

The corners of the duchess's lips twitched. "I hadn't thought you were too far along, but again you surprise me with your efficiency."

Letty couldn't help herself for all that she had convinced herself that flirtation between them was a bad idea. "I think the pleasure is all the better for being prolonged," she said. "This is a taste and will whet your appetite for the main room."

They made their way to the empty bedchamber, which the duchess had sworn not to enter until Letty deemed it time and was pleased to hear her gasp as they entered.

"It's smaller!"

"This is the first time in my career that I thought someone might wish for a *smaller* bedchamber, instead of a larger one. I thought it would be easier to keep warm. Though it's still large enough for three of my own bedrooms in here," she added with a laugh.

The new wall was plastered but not yet painted, but Letty could see how it would look in her mind's eye and was pleased.

"Is this what you wished to show me?"

"Not exactly."

Letty led the duchess to the unfinished doorway that had been cut into the wall and gestured for her to go inside. "*This* is what I wanted to show you."

"Oh. Oh, Miss Barrow!"

The look of wonder on her face with her hand clasped to her mouth told Letty volumes, but she was anxious to know if she saw all the effort that had been put into the space. Did the duchess notice the color gradient of the thick Turkish towels, stacked from palest seafoam to cerulean and finally to royal purple? Did she see the golden fish painted onto the tiny tiles on the floor around the bathtub, which had come all the way from Greece?

The duchess tugged off her gloves and trailed her finger over the towels, then along the rim of the copper bathtub and down its hammered sides. "It's wonderful."

The mirror was set into an airy wooden frame that Fraser had carved, with hundreds of wooden vines and tiny leaves weaving around it, creating depth and movement. There was a deep-set chair near the bathtub with a blanket draped over its back, with plenty of shelves next to it for her cosmetics and creams.

The dressing room was twice as large as it had been, having taken space from the bedroom. The top row of the mullioned windowpanes had been replaced with stained glass in shades of blue.

"I love it," the duchess announced, circling back to rest her hands against the bathtub again.

"It suits you," Letty said softly, looking at her sleek hair and the sharp contours of her face and the little blunt edge to her chin that she yearned to touch. She had designed the room with linear planes and smooth curves, spare but elegant, wanting it to suit her vision of the duchess.

"Does it?" she asked, and she sounded almost shy.

Letty took a deep breath. "It is functional and pretty."

"You think I am pretty?"

"Beautiful." The light in her eyes warmed Letty. "I haven't shown you the best part yet."

She leaned over and turned on the faucet with a flick of her wrist.

The duchess's mouth dropped open. "Why, it's almost automatic."

"Wait for it," Letty urged her and watched for the instant that the duchess realized that the water was not only portable, but steam was billowing from it.

"It's *hot!*" Delighted, she stuck a finger into the stream but drew it back with a gasp and brought it to her mouth to blow cool air onto it.

The bathtub had been a mistake, Letty thought now, looking at it. Large enough for two or even three, it was roomy and romantic. Watching the duchess blow gently on her finger made her think very illicit thoughts indeed.

Despite her best intentions, she didn't know if she would be able to keep her hands to herself. Not when the duchess looked as pleased as punch at what Letty had designed. It made Letty want to give her everything for the reward of that smile.

This was playing with fire. It was too bad that her good intentions were lodged so firmly in her head, when it was other parts of her that were at risk of going up in flames. Flirting to ease the heat was self-preservation.

She managed a cocky grin. "Now you've seen miracles and wonders. The workmen tell me this is the very first hot water installation in all of London, and you have the very first water closet as well, over there." She pointed to a discreet alcove tucked in the corner. "The privilege of working on behalf of a duchess is that there have been no shortages of people petitioning me to show their innovations to you."

A shadow crossed over her face. "It's endless."

"I'm sure it is. But this invention is useful. Think of how amazing it would be, if you supported them and they were able to bring their wares to more households. Imagine—anyone having the power to have hot water on command!"

Letty would like it for her own home. One nice thing about working on Hawthorne House was that she could cram it full of her wildest fantasies and then live vicariously through the duchess's experience of them.

She stole a look at the duchess, who was testing out the water faucets again.

Wildest fantasies, indeed.

The carriage turned down a street lined with narrow townhouses and tradesmen's shops, and Anne resisted the urge to press her face against the window to see the neighborhood where Miss Barrow spent her time.

The driver rapped on the door next to the entrance to a furniture shop, and soon enough the bright winter sun sparkled on Miss Barrow's silver-shot brown braids. Anne waved and was pleased to see Miss Barrow smile before she hurried into the carriage.

"Have you come all this way to drive with me back to the estate?" she asked. "I should run back inside and fetch my sketchbook."

"I thought to do things out of the ordinary today. You like to encourage me to be away from the house, so I wondered if I might come to yours and we could talk."

Talking was all she meant. But when she saw Miss Barrow's pink tongue lick her lower lip, she knew it to be a lie. Talking wasn't all she wanted.

Miss Barrow smiled. "Please do come in." She leapt down the steps that the driver put at the door of the carriage and held out an ungloved hand to support Anne. Anne clasped it harder than the situation warranted, but she wanted that hand on her anywhere she could get it, even if it was only offered in such innocent circumstances.

She followed Miss Barrow up a flight of stairs, then into a small parlor where embers glowed from the remnants of a fire. Anne was reluctant to shed the warmth of her pelisse, but there was no other option if she wished to be polite. Her reward was immediate when Miss Barrow stepped behind her and eased the pelisse from her shoulders, the ghost of her breath on her neck as she drew it down her arms and away from her body.

Anne shivered a little, but not so much from the chill as from the look in Miss Barrow's eyes. It was an all-knowing sort of look, one corner of her mouth raised in that little half smile that she was starting to adore.

"I wanted to speak with you in private," Anne said, sitting down in a comfortable but worn armchair. "I wrote to Hawthorne last week and told him about the renovation. I said he was not to return."

Miss Barrow's eyes widened. "Well done, Your Grace! There is no turning back now."

"I feel changed," she said. She felt bold and breathless. "I didn't expect to."

"Articulating something can give it power," Miss Barrow said.

"I also wanted to give you something. A belated token for Christmas. It has helped to know that I am not alone in this." Anne fumbled with her reticule and drew out a paper-wrapped parcel.

"Thank you, Your Grace. Or should I say, my co-conspirator."

Anne laughed. "You know I don't like to hear that." But it was true. They were in this together.

Miss Barrow slid her thumb under the edge of the paper and unfolded it from the gift. It was a wooden box that opened to reveal a pair of slim metal cylinders. She lifted one out of the box, her face puzzled.

Anne took it from her. "It's a pencil, but without wood. There's a mechanism here that propels the lead forward. The shopkeeper informed me that there is no need to sharpen such a tool."

Miss Barrow's face cleared. "How ingenious. This will be marvellously helpful while I work." She beamed at her. "I don't suppose you would wish to see it in its proper place—my workroom?"

"I would be delighted."

Miss Barrow led her downstairs and unlocked a door to a small room that seemed to be more storage than anything else. A table in the center took up most of the space, covered in bits and scraps. Boxes bulged with fabrics along one wall, and shelves held examples of decorative wood and metal samples.

Miss Barrow flipped open a book and thrust it at Anne. "This fabric would be perfect to cover the armchair that I have planned for the corner of your room."

"It is a pretty enough shade of green."

"Go on, touch it," she urged her.

She tugged off her glove and stroked it. The thick downy surface was like touching a kitten, and a sense of pleasure welled up inside her. "Indeed, it is perfect."

There was a light in Miss Barrow's eyes as she seemed to study her more closely than the fabric. "Then you must feel this piece of elmwood for the finials that I am designing for the bedposts."

Anne blinked. The whole point of a bed was the mattress and coverings, so why should she bother with touching the posts as long as they *looked* suitable? But Miss Barrow was already pressing it into her hand, and the satiny gloss finish under her fingertips was lovely. She shucked off her other glove and gripped the wood in both hands. "It's so smooth."

She remembered what Miss Barrow had said once about finials being curved like a woman's body and she bit her lip.

Miss Barrow leaned in behind her, slipping a sample of wallpaper before her. There was a chill in the room, and Anne yearned to press her backside against Miss Barrow's generous front.

Unlike the furnishings, she could well enough imagine how she would feel. Warm. Secure. Those strong arms would wrap around her waist, those clever hands would steal up to squeeze her bosom.

She shivered.

"Cold?" Miss Barrow asked. "I could stoke the fire."

But the fire was already stoked, deep within her. It needed no encouragement. She cleared her throat. "Please do not trouble yourself on my account."

"It would be no trouble at all, Your Grace." That low voice was like a bellows, fanning her flames as she felt the warmth of her breath on her cheek.

"I feel as if I have new eyes," she said. "I never thought about the details so closely."

Miss Barrow gave a sharp nod. "Then I will concentrate on textures for your bedchamber if you find that you enjoy them. Now come back upstairs and let us have a cup of tea before your carriage returns to take you home."

Anne followed her back up the stairs.

"I daresay none of the houses on this street have entertained a duchess before," Miss Barrow said with a laugh as she settled tea and biscuits between them. "I shall be the talk of Holborn."

Anne gripped her teacup. "No one can know that I visited," she said.

"Trust me, the neighbors would have noticed that carriage already, and they would remember that it's not the first time it's been down this street."

"What are you saying to them?"

"The truth. There is no shame in the work that I do. These are good honest people who understand a woman's need for good honest work." Miss Barrow raised a brow. "Are you concerned for your reputation, being around someone like me?"

"And what would that mean?" she managed to say.

"I am no stranger to this neighborhood. If a woman leaves my chambers in the evening with a flush on her cheeks, no one thinks it merely from too much wine," she said dryly.

"No one would think such a thing of me," Anne said with more confidence than she felt, given that she very much wanted Miss Barrow to put a flush on her cheeks. "I am here on business."

"Would it bother you if they wonder if business turned to pleasure?"

"Of course. I have a reputation."

"My reputation hasn't suffered."

"When you don't care, there isn't much to suffer."

"Of course I care. My name means everything to me," Miss Barrow snapped. "*My* name, not the name of my father, or my son. I have no patron of the arts to support me, no man financing my goals. Letitia Barrow stands on her own. And that means something." Her lips were thin and her eyes narrowed.

Anne took a breath. "It is I who has overstepped now. My apologies, Miss Barrow. I won't take more of your time today."

She got up from the chair, and was caught between it and Miss Barrow, who rose at the same time. She was so close that Anne could smell her spiced vanilla perfume, so close that there was no mistaking the fire in those gold-flecked brown eyes.

"This is a mistake," Anne breathed, but she knew it wasn't a warning she heard in her own ears. It was *anticipation*.

"If it's a mistake, Your Grace, then we should make it well worth it."

Those words should have scared Anne from moving, so surely this was some other woman leaning in, someone else's hands caressing Miss Barrow's strong forearms and sliding up to her shoulders, some other pair of lips that sought sweet purchase.

But no, those lips were very much Anne's own, desire heating her body where it came up flush against Miss Barrow's. Her lips were so soft, her hands gentle on Anne's waist. Anne ran her hands over her braids, learning their texture the way she had learned that of velvet and brocade and gloss polish downstairs, and then held onto her shoulders to draw her closer as she deepened the kiss.

Miss Barrow bumped her up against the tea table with a clatter of cups. Anne hoped they hadn't broken, but thought escaped her as

Miss Barrow's warm lips moved over her chin and down her throat and pressed against a sensitive spot above her collar that weakened her knees. To hell with the teacups. She could always buy more. She arched up against her, shifting so her bottom was on the table, allowing her thighs to part enough for Miss Barrow to press closer between them.

This was all the heat she could ask for, packaged up in rather too much wool and petticoat and lace, but glorious under her hands as she wrapped her arms tight around Miss Barrow's back.

The door was thrown open.

CHAPTER TWELVE

Robert stood there, his mouth agape. Hell and the devil. What was he doing home in the middle of the afternoon? Then Letty glanced out the window and saw that dusk had fallen. The duchess had stayed longer than she had thought.

"I—I beg your pardon," he spluttered, giving Letty a scathing glare. He swung around and slammed the door behind him so hard that Letty could hear the dishes clinking together in the cupboard.

There would be another argument when he came home later tonight. But Letty found to her surprise that she didn't much care. Not when her arms were filled with an intoxicating woman.

The duchess moved out of her arms and smoothed her skirts, which needed no smoothing at all. Much to Letty's regret. She would have liked to have crumpled a fistful of that beautifully soft wool in her hand, raising it higher on her legs, teasing her with a glimpse of chemise. And maybe more.

Every good intention she had about not flirting with the duchess had gone out the window at the very first hint of temptation. She swallowed. "Your Grace. I do apologize—"

"Do you think we are rather past formalities now, Miss Barrow?" She was...smiling?

"I would like that very much. Please do call me Letitia. Or Letty, if you prefer."

"Letty." She paused. "It suits you. My given name is Anne."

"Anne. How lovely." Letty feared she was grinning like a fool. "Well, Anne, my apologies for my son's poor timing."

"That was Robert?" She seemed delighted. "It is nice to have a face to go with the stories you tell of him."

"You aren't worried about the stories he might tell of us?" Anne pokered up again, and Letty frowned. "Even for your rank, I will not hide who I am. If you would like to go back to being Your Grace and forget that this happened, I would understand."

"I want this," she said, her eyes dark with desire. "If I don't do something different, then I become no different myself, and I am tired of living my life for other people and taking nothing for my own. But I need to be careful. You understand, don't you?"

"I want it too," Letty said. "But I don't keep these things secret."

"You have a lot to lose, too," she pointed out. "Your reputation might not have suffered among rumors of the kind of love you seek. But would it suffer if it became known that you were taking pleasure with the woman who employs you?"

Letty felt the words like a punch. "I would *never* sleep with an employer for a good letter of recommendation."

"Of course you wouldn't. But what would others think?"

"Then maybe you were right, and this was a terrible mistake." Letty felt the unfairness of it deep in her bones, but knew Anne was right. Tongues could wag, and this time it could be disastrous for her.

"If we are discreet, then we can have what we both want, and no one will be the wiser. There is no risk." Anne paused. "I have never felt such desire before."

Letty was surprised. "Surely this isn't the first time?"

"No, no. Not the first. But I've never felt so tempted beyond control."

Letty resisted the urge to puff out her chest with pride. Discretion was a small price to pay for such compliments, and the chance to slake this wild desire that burned between them.

"Shall we see each other again tomorrow?" Anne asked.

"I would love to. And I know exactly where we should go."

Anne frowned. "I thought you would come back to the house?"

"There will be time enough at the house," she promised, enjoying the softness she saw in Anne's eyes. "But there is enjoyment to be had outside, and freedom of its own sort in a crowd. It will still be discreet. Trust me."

There was nothing Letty wanted more than to go back to Hawthorne House and find a bed. But if their liaison was to be secret, then she needed to know that she was wanted for herself— not for convenience. She wasn't foolish enough to believe that there could ever be a proper relationship between a duchess and someone like her, but she wanted more than to trade sexual favors.

It was too much like John otherwise, taking what he wanted because he had access and opportunity. She wasn't a naive girl anymore. She wanted dignity and friendship.

Anne was smiling at her, a wide-open smile that was nothing like her polite duchess demeanor. "I trust you," she said, and the words came with a fierce burst of happiness in Letty's heart.

The wind permeated through Anne's scarf and blew around her ears under her hood, but her fur-lined pelisse was thick enough to ward off the worst of the chill. It was the coldest January that she could remember, with snow banked up everywhere she set eyes.

The sky was blue with enough clouds for snowflakes to continue falling. They sparkled in the sun before melting on Anne's sleeves and gloves, but she wasn't impressed enough with their beauty to be happy about being in the midst of it.

"This is the very worst idea anyone has ever had," she announced around the vicinity of Letty's head, which was bobbing in front of her at knee level.

Letty peeked up, that maddening little smile fixed on her full lips. Her hair was bundled up under her top hat, though a few long tendrils had escaped to dance around her face. "If this is such a poor idea, then pray tell me why we are surrounded by such a crowd? Why are our ears suffering from the happy shrieks and laughs of children?"

Anne scowled. "Maybe this is the right idea for *them*."

"But not for a rarified polished jewel of the nobility, Your Grace?"

Anne tried to think of a retort, but in truth it was hard to think of anything at all through the pleasure that coursed through her at being teased. She was seated on a bench, and Letty was at her feet, lacing blades to the bottom of Anne's boots for an afternoon of ice skating. She had thought Letty an exemplar of efficiency, but she had been in this position for some time now, her hands roving over her ankles in a way that felt most shocking, even through layers of sock and boot and glove.

Especially in public.

Especially beneath her skirts.

Anne's face flamed, and she scanned the crowd. But no one was paying attention to two women preparing themselves for a turn about the frozen pond, and in fact she could see several other couples in their exact same position. They were safe here, protected by the crowd and the nature of the activity which necessitated such intimacies. Letty could have chosen no better public venue which lent itself so well to private flirtation.

"I think that should be secure." Letty's voice broke into Anne's thoughts as she stood, dusting the snow from her skirt. She looked dashing in a dark navy pelisse which set off her pale complexion, and which had been fashioned to look like a man's greatcoat with layers of capes at the shoulders.

Anne gripped her outstretched hand and allowed herself to be pulled up, wobbling on ankles that had never felt a moment's uncertainty before.

"I feel like a kitten learning to walk," she said. She looked into Letty's eyes and felt her stomach dip along with the sway of her ankles.

"Worry not, I won't allow you to fall."

Advancing inch by precarious inch, they made it to the glassy surface of the pond. Anne stared down at it, then at the people who whizzed by, elegant and wonderful. It was that carefree freedom in their faces that encouraged her to make the extra step to the ice.

"Are you ready?" Her voice was quiet, and so close that only Anne could have heard it.

All she could do was nod and they stepped forward together.

The ice was smooth beneath her skates, and she felt her body propel forward a little. Too nervous to let go, she clutched Letty's arm tighter. They began to move together, long gliding strides, one foot and then the other, Letty's encouraging words and instruction all she could focus on as the world started to speed by and her heartbeat picked up in a furious tattoo. Letty was holding her scandalously close, and she reveled in her touch.

It was *wonderful*. Her cheeks burned with cold, but she couldn't stop laughing as they moved farther down the pond, watching as women twirled and men dipped down to one knee to impress their partners, and children played in the snowbanks.

Was this the wild giddy freedom that Hawthorne felt when he first laid eyes on Paris? This was as close as she could imagine to feeling such unbridled joy, the rush of pleasure so heady that she almost couldn't bear it. But if this afternoon was about pleasure, then she would push thoughts of her husband away. She was here, safe in Letty's arms, and she felt a warm glow deep inside her.

"I hate to stop, but we might wish to consider warming up. I think they are selling coffee." Letty pointed to the haphazard wooden stands that looked as if they had been erected the moment the pond had iced over thick enough to skate on.

Anne stepped back onto the snow and sat on a bench to catch her breath as Letty went to the stands. In a trice, she was back with two steaming tin cups and a paper cone of baked chestnuts. She sat and handed a cup to Anne. Perhaps it was selfish, but Anne shifted closer, savoring the press of their legs together. She wasn't usually one to like being touched, but she couldn't get enough of Letty's body against hers.

She slid her gloved hand out of her muff and accepted the coffee, inhaling deeply. "This is heavenly."

"Happily, I brought reinforcement." Letty pulled out a flask from her reticule and tipped brandy into their coffee. "The perfect end to a perfect afternoon."

"I don't want it to end," she said. "I feel like plain Anne whenever we talk, you know. You don't speak to me the way most people address a duchess."

Letty laughed, the sound low and rich. "I suppose I should apologize if I have been rude." Her voice was like a caress.

Anne's heart felt as light as the snowflakes that drifted down around them. "No apologies necessary. It is most refreshing." She hesitated, but any conversation between them was lost among the noise from the crowd. Even their closeness on the bench went unremarked as others also huddled together for warmth. "In fact, I have a question that may be too rude for you to answer."

"You may ask away. I have no secrets," Letty said, popping a chestnut in her mouth.

"I was wondering how you came about Robert."

"By the usual way, I suppose." Her smile was wry. "His father, Mr. John Wilson, was the dashing heir to a barony. Nothing to speak of compared to what you have, obviously, but to a young girl in a small village, it was the moon and stars. My friends swanned after him for years, making cakes of themselves to attract his notice."

"But you didn't?" Anne sipped her coffee, grateful for its warmth and the fortification of the brandy. She was fascinated. She had enjoyed a few short liaisons over the years, but she realized that she had never actually talked about them before. It had always seemed too dangerous to explore in conversation.

"My father had been a captain in the army, and we were well enough off, but I would never have dared dream of ensnaring an heir. Besides, I had never felt a physical attraction for any man. I had no thought of marriage."

"I felt the same way about men," Anne confided, after darting a look around them. "Though my marital dreams were limitless."

"When I turned eighteen, John's mother was doing poorly so he was in the village more often. I suppose he was looking for a distraction. We fell into the habit of talking after church and going for long walks." She was quiet for a moment, and Anne dared to cover her hand with her own. "I started to have ambitions that my mother chided me for. A lord's heir would never stoop to marry outside his class, she would tell me, but still she let us walk together on Sundays. I convinced myself that my life could be a fairy tale in truth. It didn't worry me that I didn't feel any desire for him. I was always told that good girls don't feel anything so base as *lust*."

"Until, of course, they do. But then they're ruined, aren't they?" Anne shook her head. "I was told much the same thing. It took me a long time when I was young to sort through how I felt for one of my friends. I never had the courage to tell her, but it helped me to understand who I was. I have never forgotten her, or how important it was to have the realization that I did not wish for a husband unless it was in name only."

"Isn't it awful? Girls deserve better education. I certainly could have used it. When John convinced me to leave a dance early and pulled me into his arms in his carriage, I thought my lack of passion was proof that I was destined to be his wife. After all, I was such a good girl that I didn't even enjoy my sin. I did it because he was charming and he made me laugh. I was safe when I was with him."

"Until you weren't."

Letty sighed. "Until I wasn't. And then I had the shock of my entire family telling me exactly what a bad girl I was. My father refused to allow me to stay at home, so I left my village in disgrace with nothing but the clothes on my back and a babe in my belly."

"How on earth did you succeed?" Anne's admiration grew.

"John eventually settled a stipend on me. I made some wonderful friends in London, and their love and support sustained me. I found happiness, and purpose, and I have been very happy. And very lucky." She smiled.

"You have been lucky," Anne agreed. "But you also worked hard. You are wonderfully strong to have succeeded so well in raising your son and starting a career for yourself. It's impressive, what you have achieved with no help from family."

Was that a blush on Letty's cheeks? She cleared her throat. "Now I have talked so long that you have taken a chill."

Anne smiled. "Do feel free to make use of my muff, if your hands are suffering also from the cold."

Letty's smile was amused. "Now that would be my pleasure."

Anne's face burned as she remembered, too late, the double meaning of the word. She hadn't engaged in such banter in a long time. Then Letty slid her hand in the muff and clasped her own, and it didn't seem to matter much anymore.

"I don't often have the occasion to feel so free," Anne said. "Out here, with everyone so dedicated to their own pursuit of fun, I feel unnoticed, for once."

"I suppose you often are the center of attention."

"Everyone is always watching. They all seem to want something and are calculating how best to get it. Social prestige. Business favors. A mark of favor from the Hawthorne name can have an impact, and I try to always be sensitive to it." She frowned at her coffee. "But the demands are never ending."

"When you are with me, I promise you don't have to worry about that," Letty said softly.

"I know," she said, smiling. "You see me as more than a duchess."

"I have always seen you as a woman first." Letty's eyes were sincere, and her fingers brushed lightly against Anne's inside the fur muff. "Duchess is a distant second."

The wind picked up and Letty shifted, positioning her body to bear the brunt of it, sliding an arm behind Anne to steady her.

"Here you are, protecting me. Do not consider me unappreciative, but I wish to sit here as equals." Yet her arm felt warm and secure, and she felt cozy.

Letty's smile was slow and sly. "Oh, this isn't because of your rank. It is most definitely because you are a woman who I am trying to impress. And not with my design skills."

Anne smiled. This was the perfect end to the day, indeed.

Chapter Thirteen

A nne shivered in bed late that night. She was staying in one of the guest bedchambers on the second floor down the hall from the suite that Letty was renovating for her. Her usual bedchamber had a wardrobe that was kept stocked with extra blankets in case she had need of them, but it hadn't occurred to her to ask a footman to move them to the guest room. The air tonight was too bitter to be cut with the fire, no matter how high the maid had stoked it before retiring for the night.

There was one alternative that kept teasing her.

The new bathtub.

Blinking into the night, as if she could see anything in the darkness, she marveled at the luxurious notion of turning the faucet and slipping into a warm bath. But when Letty had the hot water pipes installed, it couldn't have been midnight baths she had in mind.

The very idea felt preposterous. Too indulgent even for a duchess.

But the more Anne thought about it, the more she wanted to yield. The true beauty of the new bathroom was that she needn't bother anybody if she wished to make use of it. She wouldn't be rousing a yawning chambermaid to heat pails of water, or arranging a pair of footmen to haul buckets upstairs to fill the bath. She wouldn't have to wake her maid, who always helped wash her hair and toweled her dry after bathing.

She could be alone.

It wouldn't do to hesitate, she told herself. A duchess had no need to deliberate over such a thing in her own home. She had every right to do as she pleased.

She flung off the covers, her skin prickling as she sought her dressing gown in the darkness. Lighting a candle helped her to find her slippers, and she walked down the hall and through her empty bedroom to the brand-new dressing room. She lit a few more tapers and placed them on the dresser and the table to brighten the room.

Letty had been right—the room was well-organized. She found bars of soap perfumed with her own lavender scent in the first drawer of the dresser. She ran her thumb against the letter pressed deep into each bar, feeling absurdly touched to see a fanciful *A* for Anne instead of the customary *H* for Hawthorne which marked so many of her belongings.

One more tiny rebellion. Despite the cold, she felt warmth in her heart.

Everything looked simple enough that she could draw the bath herself, which was a novel thought, but of course Letty would be accustomed to thinking of ways that a single woman could do things alone. Anne rarely did for herself, and she had never in her life bathed alone without anyone in attendance.

The stopper went into the drain easily enough, and she remembered which tap was hot and which was cold. The stream of hot water flowing was a marvel. She sank to her knees onto the thick rug beside the tub and peered over the rim, letting the steam warm her face.

This was bliss, and she wasn't even in the bath yet.

A rush of pleasure settled deep in her belly as she watched the water rise, the candlelight flickering on the surface. She remembered that her maid sprinkled drops of scented oil into her bath, and she went in search of the little vial to add a few drops to the water.

Such a little thing. But she was pleased to do it for herself.

She swept her hair away from her neck and secured it atop her head with a pin. She untied the sash of her dressing gown and folded it on a chair, and her chemise soon followed. There was a mirror in the corner, and she caught sight of herself. Half in shadows, she stood still with her hair mussed, the golden kiss of candlelight dancing on her breasts and thighs.

She looked different. Not physically, though she didn't often see her naked self in this light, and it was remarkably flattering. But the expression on her face was eager, her eyes bright with anticipation. She was poised and ready to submerge into the bath. Ready for pleasure.

It didn't feel decent to stare at herself once she started to think of pleasure. Rather, she wished there were someone else here.

Not a maid.

But a lover.

Swallowing hard, she lifted a leg and dipped a toe into the water. She hissed a little as the heat lapped at her cold skin, then it acclimatized as she stepped fully into the water and sank down. It felt like heaven. She rested her head against the curve of the tub, which felt like it was made to fit her neck.

Letty had chosen wisely. Had she thought of this very moment when she selected this very bathtub?

She swallowed again, but this time it was because she was thinking of Letty. The woman who had put all of this together. The woman who had listened to her, both to what she said and what she didn't, who had studied her on walks and on ice skates and in carriages, who had noticed her aversion to the cold and had given her the priceless gift of heat at her command.

She was a handsome woman. Anne had thought so from the start. Strong. Capable. Her eyes always had a light in them. Her mouth was made for those quick generous smiles that took her face from handsome to captivating. Her hands, whenever she removed her gloves for tea, were broad with neatly trimmed nails.

She wanted those hands on her body.

Anne's eyes drifted closed and she hesitantly pushed through the oil-slicked water to slide over herself, cupping her breasts. Holding them as she thought Letty might hold them, gentle and sweet. She had seen the appreciation in Letty's eyes. She knew she wasn't imagining it.

What she imagined now was Letty's hands gliding down her stomach, smoothing over her hips, tracing little circles over her thighs before gently nudging them apart. She shifted and raised one soapy knee to lean it against the lip of the bathtub. The movement exposed her breasts to the cool air, and her nipples puckered as they rose from the warmth of the water. She slid her hands over her breasts again, thumbing over her nipples, before slipping back down her body.

She ached to be touched by a hand not her own, to be loved by another woman so thoroughly that she could forget her name and rank and exist in the soft bliss of pleasure.

But if all she had was herself tonight, then by God it would have to be enough. Biting her lip, she stroked herself between her legs, the fragrant oils on her fingers easing the friction as she touched her clitoris. If only Letty were here. If only she had stayed to see what wonders her work had wrought on Anne. If only her hands were pressing against her opening, sliding a finger inside, then another, filling her deep with pleasure, again and again.

As she reached her climax, gasping, she caught sight of herself in the mirror. Her eyes were wild, her hair damp and curling in the steam, her lips reddened and fuller than usual. She looked like a woman on the cusp of an affair, she thought, delighted with the idea.

Letty's warm eyes and generous mouth haunted her thoughts long after she had drained the water from the bathtub and put the creams and lotions back in their drawers.

Warmed and sated, Anne slid back into her bed and fell asleep.

The ache in Letty's back told her that it was the end of a very long day, more so than the darkness outside, or the candles that continued to burn though they were but stubs. The wind howled and rattled the windowpanes. Letty wasn't looking forward to going outside to return home in this weather. Pressing a hand to the small of her back to ease the pain, she peered out the window. Snow had begun to fall while she was working, drifting into piles against the house.

She had braved worse weather, but she was surprised at how fast the snow had accumulated. She would ask Mrs. MacInnes for use of the Hawthorne carriage tonight, so she could be in the hands of an expert driver.

A shadow appeared from the doorway, and Letty turned to see Anne. Her mouth fell open. "We had an agreement. You weren't supposed to peek!"

"No one can tell a duchess what to do," she said with a smile. "I couldn't resist."

There was something in her eyes that caused a frisson of awareness to prickle over her body. Her hand dropped from her back. "You couldn't resist?"

"I had to see what you were so busy with," she said. "You have been working long hours with the crew for days, and I was intrigued."

Anne studied the walls, her hands clasped in front of her. She looked like she was in a museum, Letty thought with amusement, studying the wainscoting with the same gravity that she would give to priceless artwork.

"I like it," she said.

"I knew you would," Letty said, walking over to join her. "I drew it up for you."

Anne darted a look at her. "Tell me about it."

She pointed up to the ceiling. "The crown molding that used to be fixed to the top of the wall boasted an elaborate design of strawberry leaves, covered in gilt. I thought you might prefer to leave the ducal symbol behind, so I drew up a geometric oval and square dentil pattern, with nice clean lines, and arranged them to be cast in white plaster."

"It isn't fussy," she said. "I appreciate that. Even though the room is smaller, it already feels less closed in than it had before."

"Exactly. I wanted it to feel neat, linear, and very airy. Less furniture, less ornamentation. I added a new ceiling rose where the light fixture will go. That one I sculpted by hand, which is why I wasn't here much last week. It took forever to slice out the little details from the clay mold. It's geometric, but it's not entirely symmetrical. I wanted something organic, more natural, instead of perfectly arranged."

Anne blinked. "*You* made it?"

Letty shrugged. "I wanted something that bore the mark of my own hand in here, not just things that others put together from my imagination."

It had become important to her to put something of herself in the duchess's bedchamber. She had wanted something permanent, some reminder of herself that Anne could look at long after all the work was done and she had moved on from the house.

After all, her work was the only thing that belonged here. Not her. She felt a little pang at the thought and pushed it aside.

Anne's smiled warmed her heart. "I love it," she said, then paused. "You have been working so late. Have you had dinner?"

She shook her head. "Mrs. MacInnes offered to send me up a plate, but I was busy with the workmen fixing the wainscoting to the walls. I wanted to finish up before leaving tonight."

"Wait here."

Anne reappeared some time later with a small basket, two wineglasses balanced on top.

Letty grinned. "To think that I have a duchess waiting on me. Not many can say the same."

She was touched by her thoughtfulness. Was tonight to be the night, then? A week had passed since their ice skating rendezvous, and they had stolen no more than heated kisses, the air heavy with anticipation between them. She enjoyed their slow flirtation. She liked handling the duchess carefully, delicately, like the finest porcelain. She wanted to unwrap her like a delectable Christmas gift.

Letty took a clean cloth from the stack of supplies that she kept by the cans of paint and spread it over the worktable. She went to snuff the candle wicks, intending to replace them with fresh tapers, but Anne stayed her hand.

"The dim light is beautiful," Anne said. "The servants never allow candles in my presence to burn more than a fourth of the way down before they whisk them away to the lesser used rooms, or to their own quarters."

"Such a hardship," Letty said dryly.

"Oh, hush. I know how good my life is, and I appreciate the servants' thoughtfulness. I'm glad that they get the use of fine candles this way instead of using tallow in their rooms. But it is nice to be plain Anne in an unfinished room, with a makeshift table, and an informal meal."

"Far be it for me to deny a woman her simple pleasures." She brought one of the stools to the table and presented it to Anne with a flourish. "May I invite you to sit with me?"

"I would be delighted."

They unpacked the hamper and spread its wares onto the table. Cold chicken cutlets, soft bread rolls, a selection of firm cheeses, and a bottle of merlot. Anne pulled out two slices of cake to finish the feast. One was a narrow cylinder of cake with a clever chocolate curl on top, and the other was a sponge with custard and fruit.

"If I had my way, I would start every meal with dessert," Anne said, eying the cakes as Letty poured them each a glass of wine.

"There is no one to impress here," she said. "Have you never done something against the grain?"

She considered for a moment. "Before this year? I daresay I haven't."

Letty thrust the plate with the cakes at her. "Then you should."

Anne took the plate with a little laugh. "I can't eat both of them!"

"Try some of each, at least."

Anne took a sip of wine first. She was enjoying herself, perched on a stool that was a fraction too high and seated at a table a fraction too low, Letty's pale face gleaming at her through the shadows, framed by snowflakes falling fast and thick out the window.

It was *romantic*, she realized, in a way she could have never predicted. The room held the strong scent of paint, and there were hammers and nails and discarded wainscoting strips in the corner. This was no place fit for a duchess.

But maybe it was a place fit for a woman who wanted two slices of cake, who wanted to tumble with a lover tonight, who wanted to let her hair down and laugh and tease.

She took a forkful first of chocolate, sighing in pleasure as the cake disappeared on her tongue with its luxurious cream filling. She didn't miss how Letty's eyes seemed fixed on her lips. She darted her tongue out to catch a crumb and watched Letty's throat move as she swallowed.

This was wonderful. She felt a power that had nothing to do with her title. She sipped her wine, then moved her fork to take a bite of the sponge cake. She closed her eyes to savor the sweet vanilla custard and hothouse berries, a true luxury in the middle of winter.

When she opened her eyes, Letty's face was all she saw.

"Are you enjoying yourself?" she asked, her eyes intense.

Anne smiled. "Immensely. However, I do believe that I could be enjoying myself more." The wine had made her bold, she told herself, but in truth it was Letty who intoxicated her.

"Perhaps we could find a way to enjoy ourselves in a more comfortable setting?"

"We haven't even eaten our supper," she said, but her knees were already weak.

Letty grinned. "Tonight, I plan to feast on you."

She bent down and scooped Anne up, and Anne felt herself sinking into untold joy. She wrapped her arms around Letty's neck as they left the unfinished room behind them.

"I want you," Anne said quietly after Letty put her down in the guest bedchamber.

"How do you want me?" she asked.

Anne frowned. It was impossible that her intent was unclear, wasn't it? She tried to speak plainly. "I want you in bed."

Letty laughed, the low rich sound filling the room with light and warmth, like firelight. "Yes, but how do you want it? Fast? Slow? Rough? Do you like staying in control, or do you want it stripped away from you?" She ran a finger down Anne's throat and over her breast, finally resting her hand at her waist.

"Oh. All of those options sound good," she managed to say, her legs trembling. *There were options?* Her heart hammered. Her previous affairs had been tidy, discreet, and delicate.

Ladylike.

She didn't want to be a lady tonight.

Chapter Fourteen

Letty's eyes gleamed. "Perhaps you would like me to discover your secrets for myself? That suits me fine."

What once had seemed so unattainable now felt so easy—they were but two women, sharing space and heat and desire. What could be more natural?

"I would hazard a guess that a duchess desires to be served," Letty murmured, her eyes intense as they locked on Anne's.

How was it possible for words alone to wrench such feelings of need and heat and lust from her?

The crackling of the fireplace roared in her ears along with her heartbeat. Anne licked her lips, unsure of what to do next, and watched as Letty's eyes turned dark.

"Turn around," she said. Her voice was husky now, and Anne could feel the timbre of it pulsing through her.

She turned, and Letty stepped so close that she could feel her unsteady breath on her neck. Good. She wasn't the only one affected by this wave of passion that threatened to undo her with no more than a touch.

Letty unhooked the buttons on her dress, her fingers moving down her back as she worked. Then she spent an inordinate amount of time loosening her stays, lace by lace. Anne ached for the full press of those bare hands on her, freed of all the layers that distanced them. Finally, she took a fistful of chemise and pulled it up over Anne's head and nudged her until she was facing her again.

Naked.

She had no time to feel shy because Letty cupped her neck in one hand and claimed her lips again, pulling her tight against her body. Her other hand was firm on her hip, almost possessive, and Anne thrilled at the touch that told her without words how much she was wanted.

Letty was still clothed, which didn't seem fair. Anne writhed, the twill dress rough against her sensitive nipples. She was startled to find that she enjoyed it, and she was ready for more. This was the part where usually she would urge her lover to rush off her clothes and be done with it already, stealing kisses and touches during an illicit visit, speeding toward the quick press of fingers against her center where she needed it the most.

But Letty didn't seem inclined to speed.

Instead, she drew Anne away from her and studied every inch of her body from her hair, still swept atop her head and secured by jeweled pins, to the tips of her toes, curling into the rug. The intensity of her gaze left trails of heat everywhere she looked. She had never been so bold with a lover, standing for the pleasure of being looked at. Anne shifted and noticed Letty's eyes moving with her. A shiver of delight raced up her spine.

"I told you once if I had the opportunity to do what I want with you, I would look my fill."

"You were speaking of my bedchamber at the time," Anne managed to say.

Letty quirked a brow. "Oh, was I?"

"Yes."

"I think we both know that I was speaking of you. Glorious, splendid you." She looked her up and down again, this time lingering on her breasts, and on the curls between her legs. Her stare was as good as a touch. Almost. "If you hadn't been born into riches, I daresay you could have made a marvelous living as an artist's model."

The notion pleased her.

"But sadly for you, you were born to be a duchess, so I must ask you to stand over there."

Anne blinked. "I beg your pardon?"

"Oh, I do apologize. Stand over there, against that wall—*Your Grace.*"

On unsteady legs, Anne walked to the wall and gasped as Letty gently pushed her flat against it.

It was cold against her back, and she had a sudden memory of reviewing swatches in Letty's workroom. If only she could have imagined at the time that such a moment could have an impact now, because tonight she felt alive solely to experience the texture of the rug thick and silky beneath her feet, and the smooth matte wallpaper beneath her palms.

Letty knelt before her, a mischievous smile on her full lips. "Some of us are born to rule, and others of us"—she brushed a kiss against Anne's thigh, as hot as a flame—"well, we were meant to serve."

She licked the spot where she had kissed. "And I am very good at serving."

Letty leaned in and inhaled her, and Anne didn't think she had experienced anything so intimate in her life. She exhaled as Letty's mouth found her center. At first, she was gentle, her lips caressing her quim and her tongue darting out for a taste. Then she moved her tongue faster and harder in forceful strokes, and Anne's legs trembled so hard that she felt in danger of falling. Letty held one hand firmly on her thigh to steady her. She moved her other hand up until she touched her heat, sliding a finger inside as her mouth worked on her. The pressure of a second finger undid her, Letty's tongue sliding over her nub until Anne cried out, grasping Letty's head, working her fingers through her braids and angling her hips to press herself hard against her mouth until the last wave of pleasure rocketed through her like a falling star.

She slipped an inch down the wall as her legs buckled. Letty rose in one quick movement and wound her arm around her waist to support her and guided her over to the bed where she drew her down and pressed a kiss to her lips.

Anne propped herself up on an elbow. "I fear you are not dressed for the occasion."

Letty laughed. "Am I in danger of being shown out the door by the butler? I am grateful that it's an easily remedied problem."

She pulled her cravat away from her neck and began to unfasten her dress. Anne made a move to help her, but Letty stilled her with a hand.

"I am well accustomed to undressing myself and consider myself lucky enough to be doing it in front of such a charming companion."

Where Letty had taken her time disrobing Anne, her fingers flew over her own clothes. She disrobed in no more time than it took to blink. The fire behind her cast dramatic shadows that flickered across her body, both highlighting and hiding the curves of her luxurious body.

"You are beautiful," she said, gazing at her large breasts and full hips and soft belly.

"I've always thought so," Letty agreed cheerfully.

Anne laughed. "I thought one was meant to be modest in the face of a compliment."

"I see rather more than your face right now, so I thought I should respond with my full opinion of myself instead of a dainty untruth."

"For all that we are speaking of rank tonight, you are the one with the confidence of a queen."

She joined Anne on the bed for another kiss.

"Wait," Anne murmured, pulling away. "Your hair. I want to see it down."

"Anything my duchess desires," she said and sat up to unpin the braids from the crown of her head. She worked her fingers through the braids to loosen them, until her thick brown hair with its streaks of silver was cascading over her shoulders down to her waist.

"You have lovely hair," she said.

"I am partial to it," she said and grinned. "There, was that modest enough for you?"

Anne took her face in her hands and kissed her, then kissed her cheek and scattered a dozen down her throat and across her shoulder. For a moment, she pressed her face between her lush breasts then kissed them each thoroughly, examining them with lips and tongue and the barest scrape of her teeth. She cupped one breast and stroked her thumb across her nipple, and moved her mouth to lick and tease her other nipple.

Letty made a sound that Anne quite liked, somewhere between a groan and a gasp, and it encouraged her to move her hand down between her legs to find a most welcome warmth, her center slick with desire. She found a rhythm that had Letty sucking in a breath and bucking beneath her, then slid her finger inside and found the angle that made her moan her name. She pressed her thumb against her most sensitive spot as her fingers moved inside, and Letty cried out and went limp beneath her.

"Now I know all your secrets," Anne said.

Letty kissed her and gathered her tight against her. "Not even close. We have plenty more discovering to do yet." She drew away and got out of the bed. "But not tonight, I'm afraid. I think I have stayed late enough for tongues to wag, so I should call the carriage to take me home."

Anne sat up. "Wait. I thought perhaps you might stay the night?"

She was already re-braiding her hair. "I don't know if that's wise. The servants might talk."

"You could sleep in another bedchamber, if that's your concern. It would be no great shock to the servants to discover that it was too unsafe for you to return home in the snow."

"It's best if I leave." She had turned away to pull on her dress and her face was in shadows, but Anne thought she saw a scowl on her face.

"Take the carriage at least, Letty. Please. It's late, and dark, and there's so much snow."

"I shall call a hackney. I can take care of myself. Don't worry about me."

Letty strode out the bedchamber without a second glance behind her, leaving Anne to fret in bed alone.

❖

Anne was so distracted the next morning that she wrote the same letter twice to the estate manager at Hawthorne Towers. It was difficult to concentrate with the memory of Letty's lips roving across her body. Last night had been a revelation.

The butler cleared his throat at the door. "Your Grace, I have been asked to tell you that you are wanted in the grand hallway."

Anne wondered if Letty had arrived. She hadn't shown up at her usual time this morning, but perhaps she had been arranging a surprise. That would be entirely in keeping with her nature. She tried to hide her smile. "Who is calling?"

"Why, the duke, Your Grace."

Anne dropped her pen, ink spilling in a black wave over her letters.

Her secretary blinked.

It wouldn't do for a duchess to run, Anne told herself before she picked up her skirts and sprinted to the hall.

Hawthorne stood at the base of the staircase, one hand on the newel post, directing the servants to distribute the mountain of luggage beside him. Sir Phineas came in through the main doors with an armful of—she stared—was that a *dog*? In the *ducal estate*? Her mind reeled. Hawthorne's father would never have allowed such a thing.

The dog barked.

"What are you doing here?" Anne asked.

"I told you I would be moving home in the new year." He bowed. "Welcome to 1814, Your Grace."

"Did you not get my letter? This house is under renovations. Your suite, I am sorry to say, is in shambles."

Hawthorne gazed at her. "You're not sorry at all. I admit it was a good gambit, but it won't do, unfortunately."

"You can't mean to stay anywhere but your own rooms. Nothing else is fit for a duke."

Her heartbeat picked up speed. This wasn't supposed to be happening. Most of the bedchambers had been pressed into use to house furniture or paint or wood or the miscellaneous odds and ends that Letty liked to explain to her. She had been positive that the mess and chaos would deter him, as well as the lack of proper ducal accommodations.

Why was he so adamant to be a guest in his own home?

"I was the duke from across town, so I can well enough manage to be the duke in my own home." He leaned forward, locking eyes with her. "Even if it is from a cot in a basement room beside the second footman."

Sir Phineas bowed. "I am pleased to see you again, Your Grace."

Anne appreciated that he was trying to ease the tension, but she couldn't help but feel a wave of rage toward him, this interloper into her life.

Hawthorne nodded at the butler. "Find me a place to rest my head, be it the meanest accommodation or the best we have."

The butler cleared his throat. "The best we have would be the duchess's own rooms, Your Grace. There is not much to choose from at the moment."

Anne gasped. It had taken all of five minutes for the staff to turn against her. But of course they would. As the duke, and as a man, Hawthorne held more power. More prestige. Years of devoted service to her paled in comparison to centuries of wealth and tradition.

"I would not dream to disrupt the duchess," Hawthorne said. "She may keep her bedchamber. I shan't be needing it...for any reason." He smiled pleasantly at the butler. "Do close your mouth, lest you let in flies."

He exchanged a smile with Sir Phineas, and Anne's hands clenched.

He had everything.

And now he was coming for everything of *hers*.

She would have the unwelcome task of trying to shield the staff from their affair, though the servants must have heard all about their master's exploits over the years. All of London seemed well versed in the scandal. But she also couldn't bear to have the staff thinking that she didn't support the duke's return. Her thoughts and feelings on the dukedom were private.

"This isn't fair," Anne said. He had promised to be *discreet*.

"None of this has ever been fair," he said. He strode away with his hand on Sir Phineas's back.

The dog barked once, then ran after them.

He had left her again to pick up the pieces of the life he insisted on tattering. No more, she thought with a burst of anger. For the second time that day, she took her skirts in hand and ran, the clack of her shoes pounding in the same rhythm of her heart. It felt good to run, to feel the blood coursing through her.

She found them in the library, standing together. Too close, of course.

The dog whined and wagged its tail.

Anne snapped the door shut behind her. "You cannot stay here."

Hawthorne shook a pinch of snuff onto Sir Phineas's wrist, lifted it to his nose, and inhaled. He pressed a kiss to his skin. "And yet I feel remarkably comfortable."

Sir Phineas shot a look at Hawthorne. "I thought this was settled between you both? Perhaps I am *de trop*."

"You most certainly are," Anne snapped.

Hawthorne put a hand on his shoulder. "Stay," he said, his voice soft and warm and inviting. Anne remembered the hypnotic appeal of his persuasion and wasn't surprised when Sir Phineas sighed and dropped himself into the armchair by the fire.

"There isn't much you can do," Hawthorne said, and there was a note of apology in his voice.

"Such is the lot of women. I suppose I have no choice but to bow my head when the lord and master appears." The anger drained from her and a headache pulsed in its wake. She spared one last look at her husband and his lover and flung the library door open to leave.

"Shall we see you at dinner?" Hawthorne called after her.

If she had known any obscene gestures, she would have flung one at him, but instead she stalked off to lick her wounds alone in the single untouched bedroom of the second floor.

Chapter Fifteen

The pounding on the front door was so loud that Letty could hear it clear into her workroom. She looked up from her sketches, smearing a dab of paint in the process. Was Fraser not in his showroom to handle his clients? It was early evening, so she supposed he had already locked up for the night.

She pushed her book aside and took off her painting smock. Fraser's workroom was dark, and so was the furniture showroom at the front of the building. She knew the layout so well that she didn't need a candle to find her way to the front door.

Letty unlatched the door and poked her head outside. Shock raced through her as she saw Anne standing at the other door beside the showroom, the one that led to her own apartment upstairs. Her hood was down and her hair was mussed, blond strands dancing in the wind and catching against her eyelashes and lips. Her ears were red. More concerningly, so were her eyes.

"Anne! What's wrong?" When Letty raised her head to look for the ducal carriage and the habitual footmen that accompanied it, she was surprised that they were nowhere to be seen.

Anne threw herself at her. Her arms snaked around Letty's waist, and she wedged her head under her chin. Letty's hands were ungloved and icy, but she didn't care. She clasped Anne tightly to her.

Anne couldn't possibly be so upset at the way Letty had left her last night, could she? Guilt panged through her. She hadn't been able to bear another minute in the magic of that bedchamber, the world that she and Anne had created for the two of them, filled with cake and firelight and laughter.

The problem was that it was a night encased in a bubble, an illusion of what Letty yearned for. They were of two different worlds, and once the lust had been slaked, the stark reality of it had torn at her heart. She couldn't imagine staying the night in a duchess's bedchamber, in a mansion where she didn't belong.

She also hadn't been able to convince herself to go to Hawthorne House today, deciding to stay home and work on plans from her workroom. Perhaps it was cowardice, but last night's lovemaking had surprised her. Not the fiery passion that burned between them, but the deep well of emotion that she had felt afterward when she fled into the night.

That emotion pressed up against her heart again as soon as she saw Anne.

"I'm here," she murmured, rubbing a hand up and down Anne's back. She glanced around again. It was a quiet street, and no one was around. But she knew there were plenty of people who liked to peer from windows and gossip about the goings-on of their neighbors. "Come, let's go inside. I shall make you a cup of tea and you'll be right as rain in no time."

Anne allowed herself to be led upstairs. "Where is Robert?"

Letty shoved coal into the fireplace. "He is working. Or perhaps socializing with dreadful Mr. Selkirk."

Deciding tea was in order, she hung a kettle in the fire and measured out leaves for the pot. She nabbed a shawl from the hook by the door and drew it over Anne's shoulders, earning a listless smile in return.

She couldn't help herself. She wanted to be the one to take care of Anne, whether she had caused harm or not. It was dangerous, these feelings that she felt so helpless against, and which she didn't dare name. She pushed them aside and busied herself with a tray of biscuits.

Before long, Letty slid two steaming teacups onto the side table.

"Thank you," Anne said, but didn't reach for the cup.

"What's wrong?" Letty asked. She reached over the arm of her chair to take Anne's hand in hers and rubbed a thumb over her knuckles.

"We lost, Letty." Anne closed her eyes and leaned her head back, her hand limp. "The duke has returned."

Letty sat upright. "Hawthorne moved back home?"

"With his lover, no less. Sir Phineas and the Duke of Hawthorne—and their dog—are currently quite cozily ensconced in the Blue Suite on the third floor."

It was one of the few suites that Letty hadn't crammed full of furniture and artwork, but it was a small room with poor lighting next to the busy servant's staircase. Neither of them had thought the duke would ever condescend to stay there.

"I am so sorry, Anne."

"I thought I was being so clever, and it didn't matter at all." She opened her eyes, and they were full of misery. "Nothing we did mattered."

"I wouldn't say that. You made your point to him."

"If I did, then he ignored it. The proof is that he's the one at home, as comfortable as can be."

"It's worthwhile that you stood against him. The changes we've made to the house show that it's a different space than the one he left. It represents different things. You've become a different *wife* from the one he left. Maybe you need to talk to him about your ideas for the dukedom, Anne."

"I would rather never speak to him again," she said, her voice flat. "Perhaps I shall leave him the London estate and go back to Hawthorne Towers in the country."

Letty froze, her teacup halfway to her lips. "Leave? No. You can't go." Things weren't *finished*.

"I have been the recipient of both snide and pitying looks from the staff. I imagine half of them think Hawthorne to be the devil incarnate. The other half think I'm a poor example of a wife, unable to keep her husband in her bed." Anne laughed, but there was no humor in it. "Maybe he truly is the devil, and this is hell."

"Hell is what you make of it," Letty mused. "I could redecorate it for you. Fewer flames. Maybe add some flowers."

Her lip trembled. "I could think of nowhere else to go, except to you."

"I am here for you," Letty said, touched. "Always."

Anne sprang from the chair, taut with energy, and paced in front of the fire. "I could not bear to stay another minute. How can I look at Hawthorne, or his *lover*, across the table at dinner? And yet what will the servants think of me if I do not appear, and hide away in my bedchamber?" She laughed again. "But I am forgetting. We already tore my bedchamber apart. No one is where they are supposed to be in that house."

"Maybe you're finding your way back together," Letty said. Her heart ached to see Anne so pent up with anger. "Maybe it's time to speak to him."

Anne whirled around to face her, her shawl slipping down one shoulder. "I was thinking we should accelerate our plan and proceed to strip down the public rooms. Leave nothing untouched. How long will he stay if the very *house* becomes unlivable?"

Was that why Anne had come all the way from Mayfair to see her? To talk more about the plans for the house? Unease prickled Letty's skin. When she had accepted the job, she would have loved the chance to work on the public rooms. Yet the circumstances felt different now.

The public rooms of the house mattered for her career. The bedchambers were specific to the people who inhabited them, seen by no one except maids and lovers. But the main rooms of a grand estate were meant to dazzle. And Hawthorne House's rooms attracted the likes of princes with deep pockets.

"I could have a work crew at Hawthorne House in a few weeks to start moving everything out of the first floor."

"Excellent. Let's tear it all down."

Anne's dark blue eyes were wild and angry, but they were also covered by a sheen of tears. Letty leaned forward and caught one on her thumb as it escaped down her cheek. "Don't worry about it tonight. I have modest accommodations, compared to your own. But you would be more than welcome to share them."

"It is just as well that my thoughts are immodest enough to convince me to stay." Anne tossed aside the shawl.

Her bedchamber didn't have a fireplace, but it had a potbellied stove in the corner. Letty fetched a shovel full of coals from the sitting room, careful not to spill any ash as she tipped them into the stove. "It will warm up in no time at all." She grinned. "In the meantime, I shall warm you wherever you have need of it."

"Have you no servants to help you?" Anne asked, sitting on the edge of the bed.

"We have two. But our housekeeper is sixty if she is a day, and she and the maid-of-all-work are bundled up already in their attic rooms for the night. I don't wish to disturb anyone if I can do for myself." She smiled. "Do you not like the privacy, and the sight of a woman working on your behalf to comfort you?"

Anne crooked her finger in reply, and Letty fell into bed beside her. She covered Anne's body with her own and moved her lips down her throat as she cupped her breast through the thick winter dress.

"I believe I have demonstrated a few talents that I can offer as a prospective lady's maid." Letty tugged Anne to her feet and made good on her words, moving faster than she had last night, letting wool and linen pool at their feet. She kissed her way across the skin she exposed before toppling her back onto the bed.

Anne's legs wrapped around her waist, and she arched up underneath her, urging her on. Letty caught Anne's wrists in one hand and pressed them into the mattress above her head as she reached her other hand between them, moving against her slick center and pushing deep inside. "I've got you," she murmured, her breathing ragged against Anne's cheek as she quickened her pace. "I'm here for you." She wanted to release her from any more decisions tonight, to accept what was being offered and to allow herself the pleasure and comfort of being taken care of. "You can let go. You can trust me."

She worried she wanted this too much, this wild desire to have Anne any way she could have her, to bring her to release under her hands and to make her squirm and writhe and beg for her touch. But that was a worry for another day. Right now she wanted all of her attention on Anne.

Anne cried out as her body tensed beneath Letty, before she went limp. Letty eased off and pulled up the blankets. Her body was aflame, but she felt as satisfied by pleasuring Anne as if she had achieved her own release as well. She kissed her forehead and gathered her close, listening to her breathing grow slow and steady.

After a few minutes, Anne shivered. "All I brought was the clothes on my back. I have no nightwear."

Letty drew out a pair of thick flannel nightgowns from the dresser and tossed one to Anne. "This will swallow you whole, but it will do the trick for tonight."

Anne stood and pulled it on over her head, then gazed down at her bare feet. "I shall freeze with my extremities so ill taken care of."

"And so you remain a duchess to the core, even outside of your natural habitat. Worry not." Letty went to the fireplace and came back with a bulky towel in her arms. "Earlier, I put bricks in the fire to warm them up for this very moment." She lifted the edge of the blanket and tucked the towel at the foot of the bed.

"You assumed we would end up in bed?"

"I had my hopes," Letty admitted. She liked the thought of Anne in her bed. It felt different from last night at Hawthorne House. Easier. Safer. Here in Holborn, she didn't have to pretend to be something she wasn't.

"Well, your bed seems rather nice. I never thought to be so well-pleasured on only one thin mattress."

Letty laughed. "How many do you deem to be satisfactory?"

"I think my bed has at least three. It's quite high."

"High in the instep, high off the ground, I suppose. Though you may not be royalty, I should be calling you Your Highness instead of Your Grace."

Anne laughed. "Around you, I am decidedly *not* high in the instep."

Letty rummaged in her drawer. "Speaking of your instep, I can think of no finer duty for my lumpy woollen socks to perform," she said, drawing a thick sock up Anne's leg. She pressed a firm kiss in the hollow of her knee.

"You are indeed a most gracious host."

"I try my best."

With Anne tucked up snug beside her, Letty felt her eyelids grow heavy. A sense of peace stole over her. Everything in the room was the same as usual, except for the presence of Anne, her hair spilling over the pillow, her hand tucked up beneath her cheek as she relaxed into sleep. But the room somehow felt fuller than usual. More settled than it ever had with just her in it every night.

If only it could last.

CHAPTER SIXTEEN

L etty's apartment had been cold the previous night, but in the morning with the fires banked, it was nigh unbearable. Anne curled her toes in her socks and tried to warm herself by thoughts of last night's unbridled passion, but it was difficult to lose herself in fantasy.

To start with, there was a moody young man staring at her across the tea tray.

Robert was well-dressed and censorious, with a big chin and a chiseled nose and hazel eyes, none of which resembled his mother in the least. It wasn't often that Anne was at the receiving end of a judgmental look. But here in humble Holborn, things seemed to be a little different.

Robert looked like he hardly knew where to rest his eyes. It took all of Anne's years of acting like the perfect unflappable duchess to remain seated across from him without fidgeting.

Letty flipped a shilling to her son. "Why don't you run down the street and fetch some buns for breakfast?"

Robert caught the coin with ease and hurried out the door without even taking the time to pull on his coat.

Anne gazed at Letty. "I don't suppose I could stay here for a while?" Maybe if she pleaded, she wouldn't have to go back to Hawthorne House. Or her husband. Or his lover. Not yet.

The look in Letty's eye could have cut glass. "You cannot allow your husband to push you from your home. It's your house as much as it is his. Don't let the servants bow to him and disregard you. You should go back and live your life."

"What else *is* my life than my work as Hawthorne's mouth-piece? I work hard for the dukedom, but solely on his behalf. If that's all I am, then maybe I should give it up." Her stomach twisted at the thought of failure, and she pulled her shawl closer around her for comfort.

"No one knows what goes on inside another's marriage," Letty said. "And no one will know what goes on inside your house."

"Come with me," Anne said suddenly. "*Live* with me. For a few weeks, at least, while I grow accustomed to having my husband and his lover in residence." She stared into Letty's eyes. "Please."

Excitement coursed through her. If she had her own lover in residence, then she could show Hawthorne that she didn't care about what he did. Besides, Letty had such a calm presence. She could steady her through the indignity of living with her husband again. She wanted comfort, like the warm brick at nighttime.

Letty's face was serious. "I am a captain's daughter, the mother of an illegitimate son, and a working woman. I'm not the usual type to be a duchess's guest."

"You are so much more than that," Anne said, swallowing hard. "You are changing my house, but I think you're also starting to change my life. I have never had a…a friend like you. You are kind, and generous, and thoughtful. As well as an endlessly talented designer."

"Oh, I am talented at many things," Letty said, and the little quirk of her lips was back.

Anne laughed. "I know you are."

"But I value my independence too much."

Anne swallowed her embarrassment. She hadn't expected rejection, and it hurt all the more for being delivered kindly. "Well then. I have a meeting this morning with the orphan's committee," she said, the lie springing to her lips. She tugged off Letty's woolen socks and folded them before rummaging in the bedroom for her own bedraggled silk pair. "Could your servant please flag down a hackney so I could return to Hawthorne House?"

Letty rose. "I will do it."

Anne flushed. "You are no servant."

"I am your employee, am I not? Ready to serve, if not a servant in truth." There was an unfamiliar bitterness in her tone, and her movements were jerky as she shoved her hat on her head and grabbed her walking stick. "Come then."

Robert almost collided with her as he flung the door open, his arms full of a basket that smelled like heaven. Anne's mouth watered. The scent of sugar and almonds and warm fruit jam was irresistible, and she cast a longing look at the basket.

Letty grabbed two pastries and wrapped them in a cloth. "Robert, I am going out."

His eyes narrowed. "You weren't scheduled to work today." He cast an accusing glare at Anne.

"I am now," she snapped. "Enjoy your buns."

The door almost slammed in Anne's face, and she struggled a moment with it before following Letty's quick step down the stairs and into the street.

Letty, efficient as always, found a cab in a trice and hustled Anne into it. To her surprise, she leapt in after her. After sitting across from her, she thrust a bun at Anne. "Breakfast?"

Anne took the gruffly offered confection. She was confused by Letty's presence in the cab with her, but grateful that she was there. She sighed in pleasure as she took a bite. Crisp flaky pastry, layers of sweet marzipan and raspberry filling, a dusting of sugar on top as fine as the snow on the ground. "This is perfect."

Letty's eyes were hungry as she watched her, even as she bit into her own breakfast. Anne felt a pleasant tingling low in her belly, which came as a surprise. She had never had so much sex in such a short period of time. With her previous liaisons, she had mapped out almost to the minute the appropriate length of time between intimacies, so as not to arise suspicion with neighbors or staff. A week would pass, or more, and the union itself was always fast and furtive.

But Letty without so much as a by-your-leave swooped in and gave her what she so badly needed, for as long as she needed it, almost before she could express to herself what she wanted. She had no idea that intimacies could be so liberating.

She watched Letty lick sugar from the corner of her mouth.

Oh, she wanted more. Much more.

"I didn't think you would come with me," she said at last, as they sped through the streets to Mayfair.

Letty shrugged. "I won't move in with you. But I can be there for you if you want, for the day."

Faint hope stirred within her. She knew she could rely on Letty. "Stay through dinner with me tonight?" Anne asked hesitantly.

Letty blinked. "I only have what I'm wearing."

"It's fine."

"Not fine enough for dinner with a duke and duchess."

Anne sniffed. "As said duchess, you may let me be the judge of that."

Letty grinned and took another bite of her bun. "I would love to stay for dinner."

Anne wondered if maybe she could convince her to stay forever.

Letty tried not to fidget on the stool in front of the vanity mirror. It felt odd to have maids fussing with her hair, slicking cream on her face, and spritzing her with unfamiliar perfume. She was accustomed to doing for herself, and she itched to shoo them away. But out of respect for Anne and Mrs. MacInnes, who both would frown at her for straying from convention, she stayed her hand and allowed herself to be dressed in borrowed finery.

It had been determined that Letty and the dowager duchess were much the same size, and there was still a trunk of her clothes in the attic. A handful of pins and a few stitches later, Letty was wearing a white satin dress that was cut far lower than her usual standard.

It had been a decade or more since she had worn white. It was a color she associated with her youth and the foolhardy notions of purity that had misguided her, but also it required such dedicated cleaning. Even in the townhouse, she hadn't been able to afford to wear white often.

Anne had lent the gown to Letty out of kindness, after she had protested again that her sturdy day dress wasn't suitable for dinner. But the dowager's castoffs reminded her that she didn't belong here in this guest bedchamber where she was getting ready for the evening. For all her time spent at Hawthorne House, this was the first time she was experiencing it as a guest and not as a worker.

If only the Wilsons could see her now. They hadn't considered her deserving of even entering the front door of their country manor.

Maybe it had all been a mistake. Was she here because Anne truly wished to dine with her? Or was this one more way to needle her husband? She wanted to be here for Anne's sake—the memory of last night's tears still pulled at her heart—but what right did she have to be seated at a table with a duke and duchess?

Anne was so much more than a duchess. Over the months that she had known her, Letty had watched the layer peel away from the cold surface to reveal a passionate, warm woman full of integrity and kindness. Letty felt helpless against her attraction, and last night proved it. She would have done anything to stop those tears. Her feelings for Anne were different from every other woman she had loved and lusted after.

On the way to dinner, Letty passed the drawing room and heard her name called out.

"Miss Barrow, our estate's honored guest tonight. Do come join us for a drink before dinner. Let us play at civility, shall we?"

The Duke of Hawthorne was lounging in a chair, with Sir Phineas standing at his side. She hesitated. But despite her feelings toward the man who had caused Anne such hurt, he was a duke and she was in his house. She could not ignore him outright, though it felt like she was entering murky waters.

"A duke needs to *play* at civility?" she asked. "What an awful world we live in if our betters must lower themselves to playacting."

Hawthorne barked out a laugh and handed her a crystal glass of brandy. "I thought I might be met with rancor, Miss Barrow. It is to you whom I owe the pleasures of being placed in the draughty corner bedroom instead of my own master suite, is it not?"

She curtsied. "Guilty as charged. You have a poor reputation, Your Grace."

"Every scrap of it is well deserved," he said. "Some might say you have an interesting reputation yourself. I always say that it's in the eye of the beholder, is it not?"

She wondered what reputation he was referring to. The fact that she had an eye for a pretty face, including his wife's? Or that she had an illegitimate son? All of it was true, and she felt no shame over it. "I think you are very wise."

"Shall we enjoy a hand of whist after dinner? We could get to know each other better. I am intrigued to know more about the woman who has caught my wife's notoriously discerning attention. Already I think I quite like you."

There was something engaging about the duke. She wondered how many secrets he kept behind those fathomless eyes. His deep voice was like a caress, his dark eyes were watchful and mesmerising. His features were more interesting than classically handsome, sharp lines and hollowed cheeks and eyes. "I have heard you to be quite free in your affiliations, Your Grace," she said, taking a sip of brandy and settling into a chair.

"Perhaps you could use it to your advantage. You could have your hands full with designing additions to Hawthorne House to fit all of those whom I have...*affiliated* with." His mouth quirked up.

"Pay him no heed, Miss Barrow," Sir Phineas broke in. "It can be difficult to know when he is serious and when he is not."

Sir Phineas was an elegant man, tall and lean. Letty was surprised to see a small black patch below his eye in the shape of a heart, an affectation from a previous century. It suited him with his elaborate lace cuffs and cravat. He had an air of fashion that would be intimidating if the look in his eye was not so kindly. "I apologize for any discomfort."

"I apologize for nothing," Hawthorne said, sipping his brandy.

"And you also don't speak for me, may I remind you," Sir Phineas said. "Again, I apologize, Miss Barrow, for any tension or stress. I would never wish to cause you harm." He kissed her hand.

Anne entered the room. Letty's breath was gone as she took in the full sight of her draped in silk and dripping with sparkling stones, her face transformed by cosmetics that heightened the arch of her brow and the sweep of her lash, her blond hair piled high on her head beneath a tiara that flashed so much in the candlelight that Letty feared a moment for her vision.

Anne, the Duchess of Hawthorne, was magnificent.

How was this the same lover who had worn her darned socks last night? How had she dared reach so high to bring a duchess to her bed?

Letty knew Anne's stride well enough to catch the infinitesimal hitch in her step as she saw them. "Hawthorne. Sir Phineas. What a pleasure to encounter you both." Anne's voice was even, but her fingers twitched as if she wanted to clench them into fists.

Hawthorne raised his glass. "Well met, fair Annie. I see you wasted no time in adding your own guest to our party. It makes things quite fair on both sides, do you not agree?"

"Miss Barrow is a brilliant designer and an honored guest for dinner. Not that I need to explain anything to you. And I am not your *Annie.*"

He sipped his brandy. "I'm aware of Miss Barrow's expertise. I recommended her to your secretary."

Anne's eyes widened, and Letty fought the urge to rush to her side and steady her. But she should have known Anne needed no such coddling as she watched her lift her chin and clasp her hands in front of her.

"Is this true, Miss Barrow?" she asked, her voice cool.

"Yes." Letty hadn't thought twice about it since she had started working for the duchess. "I heard about the opportunity from a friend of the duke's, and he said he would ask if Hawthorne would be able to put my name forth."

"I see."

Hawthorne smiled gently. "And everything worked out splendidly, did it not?"

A footman announced the imminence of dinner. Letty thought at first that Anne would eschew the offer of Hawthorne's arm, but protocol had been too deeply ingrained. She laid two fingers on his forearm and stood as far as she could from him as they walked to the dining room. Letty trailed behind with Sir Phineas, and they sat at an enormous table that felt intended for twenty. She lost count of the courses that were set in front of her and whisked away amidst the arch exchanges between the duke and duchess. She contented herself with sending looks of commiseration across the vast table at Sir Phineas, who mouthed the words *God help us all* more than once, which made her bite her cheek to prevent herself from laughing.

It was a far cry from the boisterous dinners that she enjoyed with Fraser and Marcus and their friends at Swann's. Anne glittered, her face full of defiance and grandeur, commanding the table while Hawthorne leaned back in his chair, emanating warmth and silken innuendo.

Two more mismatched people she could not think of. However had they come to marry?

"Miss Barrow, may I interest you in tea in the drawing room, and we shall leave the gentlemen to their brandy?" Anne's eyes were bright.

"I would like nothing better, Your Grace." It would be a relief to leave the tension behind.

Anne nodded down the table. "Please do not rush yourselves. Hawthorne, the brandy arrived yesterday from France—I believe it will be quite to your taste."

Tea was brought to the drawing room, and Anne thrust a cup at Letty. "Why didn't you *tell* me?"

"Tell you what?"

"That my husband is the reason you are here." Her face was cold as marble.

CHAPTER SEVENTEEN

Letty held up a hand. "I heard about a once-in-a-lifetime chance to renovate one of the grandest houses in all of London, and of course I took it. In my business, one uses the connections one has in order to get ahead."

"When I hired you, I thought I was taking control of my situation. Of my *life*. I thought I was being independent. And once more, I find I have Hawthorne and his machinations to thank for the opportunity."

"All Hawthorne did was put my name forth to your secretary," Letty said, her eyes narrowed. "You hired me of your free will. Hawthorne didn't add any of the pages to my portfolio when I showed it to you. He wasn't whispering into my ear during the interview, instructing me how to best curry your favor." She didn't remind Anne that she hadn't even hired her on merit. No, she had been hired because Anne had considered her the *least* likely candidate to succeed at the task. It still stung, even though Anne had long ago realized how talented she truly was. But this wasn't about her. Anne was hurting, and she craved to comfort her. "Hawthorne had nothing to do with your decision. He had nothing to do with why I'm here." She took Anne's hand. "Or why I stay."

She wanted to sit in this drawing room for more than an evening, wiggling her way into Anne's real life where she entertained guests at dinners like this and served the Queen. She wanted more than the fringe of her life and her affections in the bedchamber.

But that was a fool's desire.

Anne sighed and squeezed her hand. "I know. I *do*. But everything Hawthorne does rubs me the wrong way. I cannot be easy around him, even though he has the easiest manners in the world. He has the ability to make the world fall in love with him. I don't know how he does it."

"It doesn't matter," Letty said. "It needn't affect you."

"He hurt me," Anne said, her voice low and fierce. "I cannot forgive it."

Before Letty could answer, the men entered the drawing room. At dinner, the duke looked like he had been poured into his coat, with nary a wrinkle to be seen, and Sir Phineas's cravat had been tied in a lovely mathematical. Now, his cravat was a limp knot, and the duke's waistcoat was missing a button.

They must have enjoyed themselves well, and not with brandy. Letty knew the signs of men in love, and these men had caught it hard. It would never do to draw attention to their pastimes. She respected Anne's wish for discretion too much to say anything in front of her.

"What on earth do you think you're about, Hawthorne?" Anne snapped. "Do you wish the whole household to guess at your endeavors?"

Letty smothered a grin into her teacup.

Hawthorne scowled. "We can do as we wish in the privacy of our own house."

"It isn't just our house. It never was, and it never can be. Not when dozens of others live here, and gossip about us to the neighbours. There is privacy enough in the bedchamber."

His eyes could have sparked a fire. "The bedchamber that you dismantled prior to my arrival? I rather thought you were encouraging me to seek respite outside the traditional arena."

"You *cannot* be so careless. Not when we have a reputation to uphold."

"Perhaps I care more about my reputation than you may think."

"You don't act like it, giving anyone leave to think what they will about your pastimes."

"Ah, but you have never understood, Your Grace. Maybe that's exactly the reputation worth fighting for." Hawthorne stalked out of the room, with Sir Phineas following close behind.

Letty took in Anne's pale face and pressed lips and decided to try to lessen the tension. "Perhaps we should retire to your chambers. For dessert."

Anne let out a shaky breath and leaned her head on her shoulder. Letty shifted and wrapped her arm around her waist. The long ruby-studded loops of Anne's necklace dug into Letty's arm, and her own dress constricted her from moving as much as she would like, but it didn't matter. All that she cared about was having this woman in her arms, so close that she could smell her lavender perfume.

"We did miss dessert in my haste to leave the table, didn't we? I believe Cook had prepared a strawberry torte, which is one of my favorites. I could ring for it now—"

"No, Anne," she said gently. "*You* are the dessert." She grinned as she saw the startled realization bloom in Anne's eyes.

"I am the dessert." She sat with it for a moment, then her eyes sparkled. "Yes. I do believe I am."

The wonderful thing about one's lover working in one's house, Anne discovered, was that the opportunities were limitless. Letty arrived early most mornings and spent most of her days on the second floor with a congregation of her work crew and a smattering of footmen who seemed happy to shuck off their livery and powdered wigs to haul furniture around, instead of standing at the doors. Her work lasted well into the evenings, with Anne insisting on the carriage to be called to bring her back to Holborn if the hour grew too late.

For all that Letty was busy double-checking deliveries and arranging schedules and pitching in with plastering the walls, there was plenty of time for secret kisses and private rendezvous. The presence of the estate's duchess typically cleared any room Anne entered, and when it didn't, it was easy to have a maid bring Letty to her sitting room or her parlor. Soon, Anne had more memories than she could count of being pressed up against a bookshelf in the library, and bent over her desk panting Letty's name while she slipped a hand up her skirts, and of straddling Letty's lap while being pleasured in the morning room.

She flushed as she remembered how censorious she had been of Hawthorne and Sir Phineas doing the exact same thing in the dining room, when she was so easily persuaded by Letty's clever fingers and talented mouth to be loved wherever she could find the space or time.

Anne curled up against Letty, seeking her warmth beneath the covers after having pulled her away for an afternoon meeting that had ended in the guest bedchamber. She drew one leg over Letty's hip and pillowed her head on her shoulder. There was nothing quite so comforting as a warm woman on a cold day.

She still couldn't convince Letty to stay the night with her at Hawthorne House, but sometimes she thought these afternoon pleasures were just as nice.

Anne sighed.

Letty kissed her forehead. "What is on your mind?"

"Lovemaking has been the most marvelous way to use up all this excess energy I have these days," she said. "It feels like every moment that I am not with you, I am so angry. I am growing tired of it."

With Letty, there was always a sense of peace. Anne craved that comfort, that steady security. Whether they were talking or working together or in bed, Letty had proved over and over that she was reliable.

Letty twirled a lock of Anne's hair around her finger. "Are you still angry about Hawthorne?" she asked.

"Yes," Anne admitted. It was no secret, after all. "He can be so provoking. He knows how best to rile me."

It was one thing to see Hawthorne from across a crowded ballroom, and another to know he was somewhere in her own house. Dining with him every night was rustling up bittersweet memories of the way things had once been.

"He told me when he wanted to move in that he was extending an olive branch. I flung it in his face." Anne hesitated. "I wonder if perhaps it's time that I should extend it back to him."

"Well, if you want to understand your husband better, your lover may not be the best one to ask for advice."

Anne snuggled closer. "You have so many male friends, and they seem to be—well, similar in nature to Hawthorne."

"You can say it, Anne. They're sodomites. Mollies."

"When I say those words, I cannot unhear all the prejudice and shame that society attaches to them."

"But the more we say it, and the more we are comfortable with it, maybe the less harm the words can do to us."

"I can understand that," Anne said. "I don't understand *him*."

"You could talk to him."

"Every time I try, I get so angry." She was quiet for a moment. "Hawthorne was once the most important person in the world to me."

"Do you remember when we had our first walk together, and I asked you what your favorite memory was? You told me it was your wedding night."

"It's the truth. It was the best night of my life."

Letty blinked. "But—"

"We didn't consummate it, of course. Neither of us was interested in *that*. But it was magical. The day had been so long and so..."

"Exhausting?"

"Perfect," Anne said instead. "The Prince of Wales was there, and the Queen, and hundreds of others. I had been so well-rehearsed by my mother and the dowager duchess that I could have rivalled an actress. Finally, Hawthorne grabbed a bottle of pink champagne with one hand and took my hand with the other and pulled me up the grand staircase to the hollers of the cheering crowd."

"In all apparent haste?"

"Exactly." Anne could remember his face, thinner and less lined than it was now, his eyes brimming with excitement. "We stole upstairs to the balcony outside his bedchamber. He tore the foil from the bottle and opened the champagne with a cracking good pop, wine spilling all over us both, and we laughed and laughed. He hadn't thought to bring glasses, so we took turns sipping from the bottle and toasting our good luck."

"So you were happy together in the beginning," Letty said.

"Ecstatic. We had managed to fool them all. My parents. His parents. Royalty. Despite growing up on neighboring estates, I hadn't been the previous duke's first choice for marriage to his precious son. It took years of persuasion, but our plans came to fruition." She remembered orchestrating endless social calls to the duchess, which her mother thought was her own idea.

"But why were you so set on marrying Hawthorne? Was it the title? I suppose I might have set my cap for a duke if one had been in my neighborhood when I was young." Letty's tone was wry. "Such a union has a way of setting one up for life, after all."

Letty wrapped an arm around her waist. It wasn't just her physical warmth emanating from her body that Anne so loved. It was also her open personality, warming up her soul.

"When I was sixteen, I saw Hawthorne kissing a friend of his when they were on holiday from Oxford." She laughed. "Of course, he tried to convince me that I had seen nothing. Then he tried to bribe me to keep my silence. But I told him that I understood—I felt the same way for one of *my* friends. It was a tremendous relief to discover that other people had thoughts like mine. It felt like my whole world had broadened, and so our plan was born. We would have as long an engagement as we could possibly manage, marry when the pressure became too much to bear, and all the while enjoy the freedom and secrecy to pursue our own attractions."

"What on earth happened to turn Hawthorne from husband to rakehell?"

"It wasn't one month after the wedding before he hated the hypocrisy of it all." She frowned, remembering nights of tears and fights. "He fled to Paris. Childhood friendship and chaste vows don't compare to raging passions, after all."

"And he left you to handle everything alone." Letty tightened her arm around her. "That wasn't well done of him."

"He wrote me a letter, explaining that it was best if he took all the blame. That way I could have the secrecy that I desired, and no one would ever guess at my passions. He was generous, in his own way."

"Or in his own opinion."

"Well. At least we had the wedding night. For one glorious night, I felt the weight of the future like a feather in my palm, light enough to blow forward with ease. I will never forget that moment, for as long as I live. The moment in which I truly felt like a duchess. Powerful. Unstoppable."

"You no longer do?"

"It's different now. I have shouldered so much on my own. Hawthorne's father lived for five more years after that, and he and his duchess had things well in hand. In the absence of Hawthorne himself, though, I had a lot of responsibility as I learned how to manage the estates and the households."

"I suppose everything is different again, now that he's back."

"Different doesn't begin to cover the half of it." Anne sighed. "I miss my friend."

"I have learned one thing to be true over the years. You can't ever change the past, but you can always make new friends." Letty's eyes were warm and shining, and Anne felt a weight lift off her shoulders as she gazed into them.

"New friendships can be so very interesting," she managed to say, her heart thumping in her chest.

But friendship was what she had once had with Hawthorne, and it hadn't stopped him from leaving her as soon as it was convenient to him. She was afraid that she was starting to want something different with Letty. Something more…permanent.

Letty held her tight for a moment, then drew back. "This has been a lovely interlude, but I have a meeting with the furniture maker soon. I have to get back to work."

She pulled on her chemise and stays and started to button her gown.

Anne cleared her throat and shifted in the bed. "I don't think Mrs. MacInnes mentioned it to you yet, but now that you have been spending so much time here, I arranged a workroom for you. It's not grand, but it's for your use as long as you like."

Letty's smile was unexpectedly shy. "You did that for me? That's so thoughtful. I would love to have my own space for my materials. Thank you."

"It's the little sitting room near the front of the house, so I thought it would be convenient for your meetings with the vendors and suppliers. I noticed you storing some of your supplies in the servants' quarters and thought it easier and more practical if you had your own space. I had the footmen move a desk and some shelving there already."

Letty strode back to the bed and cupped her face in her hands. "You are wonderful for doing this. Thank you." She kissed her, tender and sweet, and Anne felt like swooning beneath its spell, but all too soon Letty pulled away and left the room for her meeting.

Anne lay in the bed alone, lost in thought, after Letty left. She wished she could be sure that she meant more to Letty than the house did. That this was more than an easy opportunity to satisfy sexual desire.

If Letty felt friendship for her and nothing more, then maybe all she wanted was to complete the job as fast as she could so she could make her name for herself. And then move on.

Anne didn't want her to move on.

These new intimacies were all very terrifying.

Oh, but they were also *thrilling*.

Her heartbeat felt almost painful, full of impossible emotion.

How could she want a relationship with someone who couldn't begin to understand the pressures and demands of the duchy? How could she yearn for permanence with someone who, outside of the walls of the estate, was as casual as Hawthorne about her romantic inclinations? Letty hid nothing of herself and had a blithe disregard for public opinion, and Anne admired that about her. But it wasn't something she could afford to have for herself.

She couldn't bear to watch the same thing play out as the last time she had felt so close to someone.

Last time, it had been hard enough to lose a friend.

This time, she couldn't bear to lose her heart.

❖

Letty laid the plans for the estate flat on the table and moved her reference books to the shelf in the little parlor that Anne had set aside for her. It was starting to look like *hers*, with a box of fabric swatches and trims beside the desk and color swatches fanned out on top of it.

She tried to ignore the sting of disappointment that she felt when she looked around the parlor. It was luxury indeed to have her own space. It was twice as large as her workshop beside Fraser's at home, and it was thoughtful of Anne to think about what she needed.

Letty had been working in the same rooms as the workers as they removed sideboards and installed new chandeliers and painted the walls. It was how she was accustomed to working for the businessmen of Holborn. She felt it was important to keep an eye on the crew, to direct where it was needed, and to pitch in when someone needed a hand. She had always liked the camaraderie of it.

The quiet was nice, and it looked more professional to greet the vendors in her own parlor. It lent more prestige to her name. Not quite as if she had her own showroom and office, like Fraser had. But it helped associate her name with a little more polish. A little grandeur.

But although she was grateful, she couldn't help but feel that Anne was pushing her into a corner of her life. Could she have made it any clearer that this was where Letty belonged? Not as a friend. Not as a lover. She wasn't to be given any personal space. Only a space to work.

To be fair, she knew Anne had invited her to stay at the estate for a few weeks. But that offer had been *worse*. She couldn't bear to feel like a kept woman, set up in a little room for Her Grace's pleasure. How was that any different from the townhouse that John had paid for?

She had been forced out of too many homes to be casual about where she laid her head these days.

A footman rapped on the door and told her that she had a visitor.

"It must be the carpet merchant again," she said, brushing dust from her hands. "Could you please show him up here?"

He cleared his throat. "It isn't a merchant, Miss Barrow. It's a rather young person claiming to be a relative of yours. He is waiting in the blue parlor."

Robert, she thought, and her heart contracted with fear as she left the room. Was he unwell?

Chapter Eighteen

Robert was facing the window, his hat tucked under his arm. Seeing his broad frame silhouetted, Letty had a shock of realization that he truly was a man full grown now. She had known it, of course, but it struck her all of a sudden how far removed he was from the gawky boy that she had scolded and hugged.

"Robert, it is good to see you."

He turned, and her joy shriveled as she noticed the set expression on his face, the coldness in his hazel eyes.

"Mother, I hope you are doing well."

Even his voice sounded different. Cool, distant, and with a little clip to the words. No doubt an affectation picked up in the presence of Mr. Selkirk.

"I am very well indeed. I am surprised to see you paying a call to me here."

"You spend all your time here, so I can't see why it would be surprising."

"Hardly. You exaggerate."

"When was the last time you saw me?" he shot back.

His eyes were sunken, and his cheeks hollowed, and with a start she realized she hadn't seen much of him lately. "It seems we have both been busy with work."

She sat and gestured at him to do likewise, but he gave a stiff nod and clutched his hat tighter, refusing to sit.

"I shan't be here for long," he announced. "I come on a matter of some sensitivity."

Letty took a breath. "Well, you can come to me for anything. You know that."

"I am in need of funds."

She wished he had come out of a desire to see her, but she dug a few shillings from the pocket tied at her waist. "This is all I have."

He glanced at the antiques in the room. "All of this around you, and *this* is all you have? I'm not here for shillings, Mother."

Letty stared. "This isn't my estate. These aren't my things. What on earth do you think I have?"

"Here I am, literally with my cap in hand, my palm outstretched for the barest crumbs of your largesse! You have everything you dreamed of. Including the duchess," he sneered. "And you deny me a decent living? I thought our fortunes had turned after I saw her stay the night at our apartment in January. The last time you did such a thing with my father, you negotiated far better terms than what you seem to have done here."

His words tore into her as sharp as if they had claws. "I don't know what undignified thoughts are going through your mind, but for God's sake, Robert, this attitude is beneath you." Too upset to remain sitting, she got to her feet. "I am *working* here. You are earning your living, too. Where is the shame in earning a decent wage?"

Robert snorted. "Why should I have to work, when there are other means for a gentleman to get money?"

"What does that even mean?"

He shook his head. "I thought we could come to an agreement. I thought you would provide for me, with your new riches, but you're no better than my father, leaving me with *nothing*."

Rage threatened to throttle her. How dared he speak to her like that? After all she had done his whole life for him? After all her careful plans to earn enough from this job to give to him?

"If you can't keep a civil tongue in your mouth, then it would be best if you left."

He gave her a cold bow and Letty sank back onto the sofa. What on earth had happened? Robert had his share of wild moods these days, but nothing could have prepared her for this callous rudeness. Her heart was thumping, and when she raised her hand to tuck her hair behind her ears, she saw that it was shaking.

It was only two in the afternoon, but Letty decided a stiff drink was in order. She didn't want to spend another minute here with Robert's words echoing through her mind, and she also didn't want anyone to see her and gossip about the state she was in, so she decided against ringing the bell for refreshment. It may have taken her months, but she understood now Anne's reticence to draw attention from the servants.

There would be decanters in the library, so she set off at a brisk pace to try to set herself to rights. Though she was no guest here, she didn't think anyone would begrudge her the use of a restorative after a shock.

She wasn't two steps into the library before she noticed that it already held someone slumped in a chair with a glass in hand and a dog on his lap. "Sir Phineas, I didn't expect to see anyone in here."

He tipped the dog off and bowed. "Miss Barrow, you are welcome to join me, as long as you don't mind the companionship of an overfed pug. You don't seem like you would have a fit of the vapors from an over-early glass of brandy."

She managed a smile. "If we are to be drinking companions, I would far rather you called me Letty." She nodded at the pug, who was staring at her with big eyes. He was tan with a black muzzle and rather a lot of wrinkles, and somehow he was rather adorable.

He poured a glass, passing it to her and then nudging it with his own. "To your health, Letty. Please do call me Phin. To what do I owe the pleasure of your accompanying me today in seeking a little Dutch courage?"

"I seek not courage, but rather something somewhat closer to oblivion." The brandy was smooth and strong. It was perfect.

"I too have such days," Phin said. "Today, for example."

"What happened?" She took another sip and settled into a deep leather chair. They were both outsiders here so she decided that social niceties could go hang, and she toed off her shoes and tucked her legs under her. The pug put his paw on the chair and wagged his tail, and when that didn't garner him the attention he wanted, he gave a little whine and pushed his nose against her knee. Charmed, she scooped him onto her lap.

"I suppose I'm dwelling on my purpose these days. Since I moved in here, I feel as if I am not much more than an appendage instead of an autonomous man of my own accord. I love Hawthorne, but I wonder if it was wise to move in. Especially as it has upset the duchess so much." He threw his drink back and poured another. "What about you?"

She hesitated, then took a deep drink to fortify herself. "My son paid me a visit. Frankly, he behaved so poorly that I am ashamed to admit that I taught him his manners. He had the gall to try to extort money from mentioning my supposedly lucrative affair with the duchess."

Phin laughed, then shook his head. "It isn't funny, but your son sounds priggish and rather foolish. Doesn't he know you would have heard much the same or worse, from people far less sympathetic to you? Haven't you had washer women spit at you and men spill things on you in the taverns? God knows I have."

She raised her glass to him. "I certainly have. I would give most anything to have things be easier and to never experience such things again."

"We are in perfect accord, my dear Letty. I used to throw the occasional party at my townhouse and invite people like us for some comfortable socializing. We can't have any parties here with Her Grace in residence, of course, but I sorely miss them. Is this getting older, do you suppose? Growing more responsible and respectable by the year?" He stared down his glass, one eye screwed shut as he contemplated it, then drank.

"I'm forty-two and sometimes I still wish to fling all my cares to the wind and run away from my responsibilities."

It was horrible to remember the hard times, yet it felt good to talk with someone who had experienced some of the same things as herself. Letty felt some of the tension ease from her body as she scratched behind the dog's ears, which seemed to meet with approval as he gave a little huff and settled his head down on her thigh.

"I can't begin to imagine having the responsibility of a dukedom," Phin said. "I worry enough about managing my own household, which is far and away much smaller than this mansion. Of course, I've made things complicated in that regard, but I can't help myself," he said.

"How are your household affairs complicated?" she asked.

He leaned in. "Sadly, I seem to be the softest touch of any man I know, and thus I've employed more chambermaids with a history of theft than any one man ought. My heart bleeds for them when I hear of them being fired from other households for being generous with their favors or being with child, so I keep hiring them, knowing that most will turn their hand to thieve me the same way they've done others."

She stared. "If you know they'll do it, why do you keep them in your employ?"

"One shudders to think where they will end up next with no employment. I console myself with the knowledge that I have the opportunity to indulge in new cutlery and candlesticks at least once a season, so I am always in fashion." He wiggled his brows.

She was touched. "You're a generous man, Phin."

He gave her a sidelong glance. "Speaking of fashion, you *are* going to finish the designs for Hawthorne's rooms at some point, right? I have a vested interest in that ducal bed, you know."

"You aren't terribly inventive if you need to wait for the bed."

"Oh, I haven't waited." He smiled wickedly. "It's just that one's knees also are getting older, and his bed is sure to be wondrously soft."

"I will take care to select the very softest mattress out of consideration for your poor knees," she said, patting the one nearer to her and taking another drink.

"It's the duke I was speaking of," Phin confided.

She laughed. "I promise I will finish his room next. Anne's chambers will be done tomorrow, and I admit I am looking forward to her seeing it."

"*Anne*, is it? What are your intentions toward the lovely duchess?"

Letty paused. Her feelings for Anne were complicated, and she didn't know how to categorize them. She loved spending time with her and learning more about her. She had a deep-seated need to give her every comfort and pleasure she could imagine, so she could see the smile on her face in return.

But *intentions*? That implied something rather more serious. That was the kind of question an overbearing father asked of a suitor.

She decided for the moment she didn't have to worry about it. After witnessing Robert's awful behavior today, something felt different inside. She had spent her life focused on raising her son, but he was a man now, free to make choices and mistakes without her hovering over him. For the first time, she felt free to focus on herself.

She wanted to see where this relationship with Anne could lead.

"My intentions are my own, good sir," Letty said. "A lady never kisses and tells."

He bellowed with laughter. "Perhaps a lady doesn't, but I thought a miss would be more than happy to reveal her all."

"The miss may have revealed, but her lips are firmly sealed." She mimed locking her lips and dropping the key in her brandy glass.

"You may keep your secrets from me, Letty, but I hope you don't keep them from the duchess. You both deserve happiness."

They did, didn't they? Even if that happiness was fleeting, one was alive to embrace every moment of it that they could grasp to their bosoms.

"You have not only a soft heart, but a wise one." She set her glass down and rose. "Thank you for the indulgence. Now I am restored and ready to seek my happiness. I bid you good day, sir."

She strode out of the library, feeling more confident. The sooner she finished Anne's bedchamber, the better. She wanted to show Anne that she cared about her, and she wanted to do it by making her most private space the most comfortable and sumptuous that she could manage.

It was time to forget about her problems and take what she could for herself.

CHAPTER NINETEEN

Letty sat on a stone bench in what was once the statuary but was now empty of all adornment save for the immovable pedestals and benches that were placed at even intervals through the long room. She wasn't finished with the second-floor bedchambers yet, but she had stolen down here with a cup of tea to check that the workers had done the job well of moving everything out.

It was nice to have a moment to herself. Robert's visit yesterday had taken a toll on her. He hadn't been at the apartment when she had returned last night, and she hadn't seen him this morning either. She also hadn't seen Anne since then, though she wasn't confident if she wanted to talk to her about Robert and his wild accusations.

She took another sip of tea, trying to focus on the job at hand. Letty was pleased to see that the first floor was now a maze of empty hallways and alcoves, with barren walls and floors. But it still hadn't dissuaded Hawthorne from staying, and Anne had flatly refused to hear any of her ideas for potential themes for the new rooms.

It was a shame, because Letty was brimming with ideas.

When she started the job, she had thought it would be a simple matter of filling the rooms with riches. Maybe it was because she had spent months drawing up plans for bedchambers and dressing rooms and private sitting rooms, but now she wanted to personalize the public rooms of Hawthorne House—which was the exact opposite décor approach of the other great houses in Mayfair.

She wanted to evoke an emotional response from visitors to the estate with designs that suited the dukedom in its grandeur, but also celebrated the specific inhabitants of the house. She had never thought to do such a thing before, but the people in this house were becoming dear to her. Letty wanted to give them something special.

One room would signify the rebirth that she was seeing in Anne. The walls would be painted as a beautiful dawn morning, in gradient colors from softest peach at the ceiling to radiant magenta at the baseboard. The room would be filled with modern furniture and sculpture, its modernity signifying the new life that Anne was carving out for herself.

Another room would be designed around the idea of fire, for the passions that flared between them, and another for ice to remember the winter that they met. She couldn't help but insert memories of their time together into the designs. This winter was changing her, and she wanted to mark it down. She wanted hints of their relationship to last in architecture if it couldn't last forever in the real world. She had laid out dozens of sketches in her sketchbook and filled it with notes for fabrics and materials.

A shadow fell over her page, and she gasped out a swear.

Hawthorne chuckled. "Apologies, Miss Barrow. I came to see what wonders you have wrought thus far in our humble abode, but you seem to have removed far more than you have replaced."

She didn't care for the interruption but couldn't deny that the duke had the right to enter any of these rooms and to investigate as he chose.

"This isn't what I would call 'humble,'" Letty said.

"This isn't the most marvelous of our estates. Hawthorne Towers is the real masterpiece. Though the chateau that I own in Paris is grander than any of our British imaginations could dream up, I'm afraid."

Letty wished she could see it, but she bit her tongue.

"You know, I have a great many treasures in storage. You should come with me and bring some of them back here. These rooms are looking sadly empty, I think."

Letty stilled. It would be wonderful to see what art he had collected. Before she had emptied them, the galleries had favored landscapes and hunting scenes, which she didn't think suited the current duke or duchess. The statuary had housed nothing but marble busts of Hawthorne ancestors.

She was tempted. "The duchess has charged me with the bedchambers first, Your Grace," she said, swallowing her ambition. "Perhaps at a later time we could discuss the galleries."

He glanced outside. "I am on my way now to the docks, actually, as I'm expecting a shipment from France. I'm in the process of bringing over my collection. Would you care to join me?"

Her heart pounded. This was a rare opportunity.

Even though she was at the estate far more than her own apartment these days, it wouldn't do for Letty to forget her true purpose. She didn't belong here as part of the nobility, sipping lemonade and gossiping over biscuits. She didn't want to be like Phin, fretting over his usefulness or lack thereof. She was here to *work*, and she was proud of it. If viewing art with Hawthorne helped with the house renovation, should she not take the opportunity?

Anne had been delighted when Letty had surprised her with the hot water in the dressing room. Wouldn't she be pleased for Letty to take the initiative for the public rooms, if she revealed them to be as thoughtfully designed as the dressing room? Anne's bedchamber would be finished soon enough. She could easily divide her time between the first and second floors in the meantime.

She said yes.

It was a long carriage drive to the warehouse by the docks, and Letty let herself be entertained by the duke's observations and witticisms. He had the talent of flattering without being effusive and his manner was engaging without being too familiar. She knew Anne would be furious if she ever told her, but she couldn't help but feel charmed by the duke.

Letty stopped short once she entered the storage facility at the docks. It was an enormous warehouse, and the duke had been right— everywhere she looked was *treasure*. Marble statuary. Filigreed furniture. Antique chairs, priceless silverwork, painstakingly embroidered tapestries. Onyx and emerald and opals, ebony and maple and rosewood. Clocks and candlesticks cluttered the tables, and everything from the smallest of snuffboxes to the largest of ornamental jars were stuffed on the shelves.

This is what she wanted for her own, one day. She had dreamt of collecting beautiful things, waiting for the right moment to part with them and place them in the homes she yearned to arrange for other people.

Hawthorne led her through several large rooms, each more astonishing than the last, and then they set to work marking what they wanted to cart back to the estate for display.

"These are beautiful," Letty said, looking closer at a shelf full of Greek vases. Vase collecting had become quite popular over the past fifty years, and she had seen many examples in the museums.

But the vases in the museums were nothing quite like this.

"Ah yes. This is what I love most to collect but have never found the right place for them." He picked one up, a large black vase with stark red outlines of two naked men embracing. "If I am not mistaken, Miss Barrow, this is part of our shared heritage, is it not? Does it not deserve to be displayed? Love should never be something to be ashamed of."

She couldn't find it in herself to disagree. Not when it was so important to her to live as openly as she could. She gazed at the dozens of vases and plates before her, all of them depicting illustrations of men in various stages of undress, all in the company of other men.

"I have been collecting for years," Hawthorne told her. "I had many wonders in my Parisian estate. Perhaps you would have enjoyed a visit. I have marbles from Claude Ramey, bronzes by Donatello, paintings by Caravaggio. I have been shipping items here during the past decade and am still deciding what to bring from my Paris home as I have no plans to return there anytime soon. Looking at all that I have amassed now in one space, it seems...well, rather a waste."

Letty nodded. "I understand what you mean. There is too much here for any man to display in his lifetime, even if he had dozens of homes instead of the six estates that your duchess tells me you own."

"Exactly so. They deserve to have eyes on them, instead of languishing here in the dark." He brushed a finger over a small bone carving of an owl with jade eyes. "They would fetch a pretty penny at auction. Perhaps I should contact Christie's."

She wanted to snatch it to her chest and forbid him to sell. But perhaps it was the right choice. He couldn't display everything.

"Would it be unforgivably rude of me to wonder how an army captain's daughter came to be so knowledgeable about fine art?"

"Rude to wonder? Perhaps. The answer is quite rude as well, or rather indelicate might be the better word. However, I shall answer."

"Do go on," he said with a raised brow.

"I left my village pregnant and alone save for the promise of my ruiner to provide for me. While I dreamt of wedding bells, he quietly set me up in a house with a stipend and paid me quarterly visits when he came to London. I was so green, I wasn't even aware that I was his mistress."

"That is the action of no gentleman."

"I was desperate to fit in with his family, and because I wasn't of the same station, I found myself in need of education. I began to take an interest in the newspapers and joined a lending library. The British Museum wasn't a far walk, so I frequented it every day. I made friends first with the guides, then the curators, and then friends of the curators. Before I knew it, I had surrounded myself with art collectors and furniture makers and silversmiths and painters, and I never stopped learning."

"I presume you ended things with the cad?"

"Yes. I realized that John was never going to marry me, and by that time, I loved my life in London. I promised myself I wouldn't let myself live in shame as his secret mistress, so I stopped agreeing to see him. He was a faithless liar, yet generous in his way. The townhouse was lovely, and I had a nursemaid to help with Robert, as well as tutors as he grew. I began to organize and design rooms for my friends as they married and moved into larger houses, and I helped the local eating houses when they chose new chairs for their diners or art for their walls, and that's how I began to grow my reputation for design."

"How very enterprising."

By the end of the afternoon, Letty had compiled several pages of notes detailing what they would bring back. Her mind was whirring with ideas, which she was eager to sketch up into plans for each room. She couldn't wait to arrange for her crew to visit the warehouse and start retrieving the goods and placing them where they belonged.

She returned to the estate with hope in her heart and energy in her step.

And then she saw Anne, arms crossed, a scowl on her face.

When Anne saw Letty laughing with Hawthorne as they walked up the grand staircase together, she felt for a moment like the air had been removed from the estate as well as most of the furniture. What was Letty thinking, to be seen with him? Her hand was on his arm, and they made a pretty picture together, Letty's mischievous smile paired with Hawthorne's sardonic smirk.

She hadn't even realized that they had left the estate together. Anne had been on her way to the room that Letty was working on to entice her away for a moment or two, and now she stood in the hallway at the top of the stairs with no thought of where to turn.

"Anne!" Letty cried. "Hawthorne was kind enough to bring me to the warehouse where your art is kept."

"*His* art," she corrected her, hating the short clip to her words. What good was all her practice before the Queen if she could not keep her composure now when it mattered?

"Ah, but what is mine is yours," Hawthorne said.

Like the dukedom was? It was hers within reason. Within boundaries. He had yet to take their business affairs into his own name, but every day the threat hung over her like a thundercloud. She clasped her hands tight in front of her.

Hawthorne bowed to them both. "We must do this again sometime, ladies." He swirled up the next flight of stairs, no doubt to meet his lover.

Letty smiled at her. "He has the most wonderful collection."

"Why did you go with him? Alone in the carriage?" It wasn't right to start flinging accusations, but she was so hurt. "Do you love him too, like everyone else?"

"Of course I don't love him. I don't even know him. But I support his choice to live openly. That is what I myself do." She smiled. "As to being alone together, I hardly think a chaperone would have been necessary."

Anne flushed. "Your reputation is not enhanced by spending time with him."

Letty's eyes narrowed. "All he did was show me the warehouse and allow me to choose a selection of art and furnishings that will display your house to your advantage. He is helping me to *work*."

"I thought we had planned to leave the public rooms alone, and then Hawthorne might choose to leave again."

"That was your plan," she said. "Not mine."

"We were meant to be conspirators together." Here they were, bickering in the hallway like a pair of chambermaids where anyone could chance upon them. Couldn't they retreat to her rooms and forget everything in a frenzy of lovemaking?

"It didn't work," Letty said. "Your husband is going nowhere. And I must start work on the public rooms."

"Why?" she asked, her heart hammering. Starting the first floor was one step closer to Letty finishing the house, and she didn't want her to leave.

"Private rooms don't have their etchings displayed in architectural magazines."

"Is that all that matters?"

Anne had thought that Letty was thinking of *her* when she chose the furnishings and selected new paint and carpets. She had thought her home was being designed for her pleasure. But the rooms that Letty touched were more than just pretty. They were imbued with meaning, with emotion. She refused to believe otherwise.

"How is this any different from Hawthorne preventing you from executing your ideas for the dukedom?" Letty said, exasperation on her face. "You hired me. I want to work. But you let me do nothing that will advance my career."

"It's different because you can stop your work while we think things through, and there are no consequences. If I stop work for the dukedom, people in the villages might starve, or endure life in cottages with rotted roofs if they cannot afford the upkeep and we don't intervene. Any manner of things may happen. My rank carries the burden of enormous responsibility."

"No consequences?" Her face turned rosy. "I have workers who depend on the labor I can give them. If the work is halted because you have changed your mind yet again, but it's too late for them to pick up work with a crew somewhere else, what do you think happens to them?"

Anne was silenced. She hadn't thought about the ramifications to the web of people connected to the renovation. "You're right."

"I can see the fire in your eyes when you talk about your charities, and when you tell me about your own ideas to improve things for the tenants. You are as passionate about work as I am. We simply do different things. My work is creating something that one can touch, and your work is to make decisions that put a whole slew of actions into movement, but what we both do is important. You can't take that away from me when you yourself know how important it is." Letty's face softened. "Let's sit together. We can call for tea."

"And cake," she sniffed.

"Of course."

They went to the sitting room attached to Anne's temporary bedchamber and were brought an arrangement of frosted squares and chocolate delicacies on a silver tray with their tea. Anne was soothed by the routine of pouring and sipping and tasting.

"I was upset when I saw you with my husband," she confessed, taking a nibble of cake.

"I suppose not for the usual reasons that a wife might be jealous," Letty said, her eyes dancing.

She laughed. "No. But everyone loves him better than I, and I cannot bear it if you do too."

"You don't trust me?"

"Of course I trust you." She poked at her cake, but her mouth was too dry to take another bite. "But you didn't take my feelings into consideration about Hawthorne. You didn't speak to me about it. You knew I would be shocked and upset, but you did it anyway."

"Because it's good for my career," Letty argued, setting her teacup down.

"Exactly—your career comes first. Not me." Anne's heart was hammering in her chest. These were thoughts she hardly dared to voice to herself. What if Letty decided that it was not worth the headache of being embroiled in the midst of her strange marriage?

"I didn't realize you wanted to be ranked." Letty's voice was quiet.

"Of course I do. I spend all my waking time trying to devise ways to spend time with you. I—well. I care for you. Deeply." *I might love you*, she wanted to say, but couldn't bear it. Not when Letty's face was so unreadable. What if she didn't feel the same way?

"Ever since Hawthorne moved in months ago, we have only spent time together in the corners of this house." Letty's voice was flat.

"What is so wrong with taking pleasure where we find it?"

"Remember how glorious it was when we went ice skating?"

"Yes." Anne remembered it vividly. The freedom of flying, the ice forming on her eyelashes from the cold, the hot chestnuts that Letty had bought for her.

"That's what I want for us, Anne. Not just moments between meetings and work. I want to spend time with you, doing things together out in the world. I understand I can't accompany you to Society balls or the opera or wherever else a duchess might socialize, but there are other places where we could spend time."

"It's dangerous out there."

"You trusted me to take you skating. Trust me to take you somewhere safe." She leaned forward and took her hand. "Since Hawthorne has returned, you have been so angry. You have spent your time retreating and hiding yourself away."

Anne took a breath. It was time for her to face the facts, to stop burying her head beneath her pillows like a child. "I suppose I thought if I never left the house, Hawthorne couldn't take control of it." She shook her head. "But I already lost that battle, didn't I?"

"Why don't you come to an eatery with me and have dinner to meet my friends?" Letty asked. "I would love for you to get to know them."

She stared. "You wish for me to go to a *public eatery*?"

"I live my life in public. If you want to be part of my life, then you would have to accept that." She paused. "I care for you too, Anne. More than I've cared for any woman. But there are things about my life that you would have to accept, if you want to accept me."

"It's much more comfortable in here."

"Comfortable, but invariable. What is it you want? To stay here and have nothing ever change, or to go out and seek happiness?"

Anne hesitated.

"Take a risk. Meet my friends. See the lifestyle that we live that your husband has risked everything to embrace. Understand me, and you might start to understand him. If you don't like the outing, we can always talk about it afterward—but haven't you always wondered what it would be like?"

"I've always been afraid," Anne said quietly. "It hasn't been righteous judgment that earned me the title of the Discerning Duchess. It's been fear."

"You're thirty-four years old, and one of the most powerful women in England. Isn't it time in your life to stop being afraid?"

"Yes." She felt a thousand times lighter. "Yes. It's time."

Chapter Twenty

It felt odd going somewhere with Anne without the security of the Hawthorne carriage. The choice was met with obvious disapproval from the butler when Anne also refused the protection of a footman, but as she had told Letty earlier when they had made their plans, they couldn't very well take the servants with them to an oyster tavern run by sodomites without expecting some degree of gossip.

Letty rarely felt afraid in the streets of London. Many of the walking sticks in her collection had a thin sword tucked in the shaft, hand-crafted and gifted to her by Fraser over the years. She gave the ground a quick tap with her stick. She wasn't nervous for herself, but tonight she was traveling with something precious. Tonight it would fall to Letty to protect the duchess if anything should happen. The notion made her stand a little taller and puff out her chest a bit.

She could take care of Anne.

The problem was that she was starting to want to take care of her forever. Not just for a night on the town, or a night of pleasure. She wanted to draw up a future for them together, after the work on the house was finished. But how could it ever work? Anne was a duchess with duties to society, and Letty wasn't willing to live in the shadows forever, stealing time where she could while Anne lived her life.

Tonight wasn't wholly about showing Anne what it was like to be in spaces designed for people like them, or to help her understand her husband.

Introducing her lover to her friends was the first step toward seeing if they could fit their lives together.

Letty flagged down a hackney and tucked Anne inside before giving direction to the driver and stepping in herself.

"My friends should already be there by the time we arrive," she told Anne. "You'll have plenty of people to look out for you."

"I feel safe with you," Anne said.

Her chest warmed. Making Anne feel safe and comfortable gave her a feeling more potent than wine.

Light from the lantern that hung outside the carriage fell on Anne's face, and Letty saw that her lips were set tight together.

"We can turn around, Anne," she said softly. "We don't have to do this if you don't want to."

"I want to," she said, lifting her chin and meeting Letty's eyes. "I want to understand."

Donovan's Oyster Tavern wasn't far from Mayfair. The wind was strong enough to make the big wooden sign swing from the iron bar above the door, and Anne tugged her hood closer over her face as they made their way from the carriage to the red brick building. Letty slid an arm behind her to steady her. "Here we are."

Opening the door to the eating house was like coming home. Letty relaxed the moment she was inside as warmth slid over her body like an embrace, the noise and chatter of familiar voices filling her ears and her heart.

This is what she had been missing at Hawthorne House. Community. Camaraderie. The press of bodies on all sides, waiters darting around them and through the throng. It was a stark contrast to the aridity of the ducal dining room.

Letty heard her name being called. She grabbed Anne's hand. "Come, meet my friends."

They wove around tables filled with laughing men, past lanterns that glinted off oyster shells and glassware, and finally found themselves in front of a table in the corner that was already littered with empty glasses of blue ruin.

"Gentlemen, this is Anne," she said, dispensing with the title to protect her identity, though of course her friends knew who she was with all she had said to them about her.

Letty held Anne's chair as she sat, pushing it in before taking a seat beside her. "Anne, may I present to you some of the dearest men in my life? Fraser is a woodworker with his own business, and also my neighbor. Marcus owns a stationary shop on Chancery Lane."

"I am pleased to make your acquaintance, good sirs." Anne gave them the fraction-of-an-inch nod that Letty remembered well from when they first met.

Letty narrowed her eyes. Fraser and Marcus were sitting close enough together that they might as well be on each other's laps, and they were grinning like fools. "What's happening here, fellows? Why are you in such a good mood?"

"You haven't been around much these days, Letty lass." Fraser tried to look reproving but his smile ruined the effect. "If you weren't too busy to check in on your friends, maybe you would know."

That stung. "I've been working."

"But when is the last time you let work get in the way of your life to this degree?" Fraser nodded at Anne. "Begging your pardon, but we saw rather more of Letty before she started your renovations."

"I have told her she keeps long hours," Anne said, nodding seriously. "I quite agree with you."

"Some of those hours are because I am in your bed!" she protested, but she saw the little upturn on Anne's lips that meant she was teasing.

"Nothing like a romp in the hay to resettle one's priorities." Marcus smirked. "I finally convinced Fraser back to my bed and we have made our amends, happier than ever."

Fraser shoved him. "We had much more than a romp, you dolt." He beamed at Letty. "We had a talk, and we've decided to try our hand at being exclusively with one another. It's been weeks, you know, since you've seen us. You've missed rather a lot."

Letty shook her head. "These accusations are rather unfair when all I am trying to do is earn my bread." She hesitated and thought of Robert claiming much the same thing. "Though I get your point. I shall make more of an effort to see you both. You deserve better."

"Duly noted, and we love you too. By the way, I like this woman of yours, Letty," Fraser said with a grin.

"I do too," said Marcus. "But why aren't you playing the gallant and ordering her a drink? She will think you a poor host indeed."

"Very true, I am remiss in my duties." Letty flagged down a waiter and ordered wine for the table.

The air was warm, and redolent with cigar smoke. Anne had worn her hair down tonight for the first time that Letty had known her. At least, outside the bedchamber. Her hair fell in thick golden ringlets that helped to obscure her face, and the tendrils at her temples were damp with sweat from the heat of the room. She caught Letty's eye and grinned, exuding a joy that Letty also hadn't seen much of outside the bedchamber.

In the carriage, Anne had seemed hesitant, and Letty had expected her to be shy once inside the tavern. Instead, her eyes were bright with curiosity, scanning the crowd and the staff and décor and catching the occasional sight of a man slipping up the stairs in pursuit of another man. Anne slid her hand onto Letty's thigh, and she gripped it tight.

This was a woman to keep.

Platters of oysters and glasses of ale and wine were brought round in a ceaseless dance, clattering down on the table and disappearing down gullets, then the empty vessels removed and replaced with efficiency.

"Try the oysters," Marcus told Anne. "They're famous here."

Anne eyed the platter. "I'm accustomed to a different method of serving."

Letty nabbed an oyster off its thin bed of ice, gleaming and quivering in its iridescent shell. She sucked it out, tasting its sweetness with a tang of salt and a squeeze of lemon. "Is it so different from how you are served at the best of dinner parties that London has to offer?"

"I use rather more cutlery," she said with a hint of a smile.

"I see. My fine lady doesn't wish to put forth any effort." Letty selected an oyster and brought it to Anne's lips. "Here you are. Just bring your lips together, and suck."

The look that Anne gave her was sharp enough to cut, but Letty was having too much fun. She pressed the shell gently against her bottom lip. "Go on," she urged her.

Anne lowered her lashes and sucked the oyster into her mouth, then swallowed. Her tongue swept across her bottom lip to catch a drip of lemon and brine, and Letty ached to be underneath that mouth.

"I could grow accustomed to this," Anne said, fluttering her lashes at Letty, and allowed herself to be fed another oyster.

"We're still here, darlings," Marcus said, refilling Letty's wineglass. "My word, Letty. After all your ribbing about our flirtations, you're no better. I am blushing to see it."

"I never claimed to be better," she said. "Though my lover certainly is in a category all of her own, leagues above me."

It gave her pleasure to say the word, to claim Anne as her own in front of her friends. To pretend that all of this meant more than it did. To indulge in the illusion that it could last, and that Anne would be part of more dinners like this, or that she would sit with them buying oranges in the cheapest seats of the theater, or that they would someday walk hand in hand as they laughed their way home together after a night out with too much wine.

But that wasn't Anne's life. Her life involved tea with the Queen, and fine dinners with princes.

Letty knew it was greedy, but she wanted it all. No matter what it was. As long as Anne was involved, she wanted in.

Anne laughed. "I am cut from the same cloth as you all," she said, a little smile on her lips, and Letty wanted to believe it.

"We want to know that our lass Letty has someone who values her," Fraser said, tapping his gin glass on the table for emphasis. "She's been burned by the fires of love before."

Letty snorted. "That's poetic of you." She turned to Anne. "And categorically untrue, I might add."

"What's more poetic than watching you mourn and sigh after love lost? You're like a sad puppy every time." Fraser wagged a finger at Anne, who likely had never been scolded in such a manner before, though she bore it with equanimity. "We don't want that for her."

"We certainly don't." Marcus snagged an oyster and gulped it down.

Anne leaned forward, settled her elbows on the table, and propped her chin on her hand. "Do tell me more about these contentious lovers Letty has had."

Letty groaned. "Please don't."

Fraser stroked his goatee. "I think the worst was the artist who did those dreadful oil paintings and thought she was above us all."

Marcus roared. "Oh yes. Miss Priss, is what we called her."

"You did not!" Letty gasped.

"We certainly did. She was terrible. Prim and proper. Can't imagine what she was like in the bedroom."

Letty swatted his shoulder. "That is *not* for you to imagine."

"Are you not looking for bedroom sport?" he asked. "Miss Anne here is dressed up like one of us. There are rooms upstairs if you want to both pretend to be other than what you are, for a quick jaunt. It can add spice to the occasion."

Anne might be pretending not to be one of the Quality tonight, but Letty knew with every fiber that she was quality. Real quality. Genuine, passionate, determined.

"We shall pass on that charming offer," Anne said with a little sniff.

Amid the laughter, and the drinking, and the stories from her friends, Letty and Anne continued to flirt with each other with their tongues and lips devouring piles of glistening oysters.

Letty brushed her lips near to Anne's ear. "Among all these oysters here tonight, you're the only pearl," she breathed.

Anne laughed. "Do I owe these pretty words to too many tankards?"

"The drink loosened my lips. It didn't plant the idea inside."

Anne's hand moved to Letty's thigh again, and she sucked in a sound of pleasure along with her next oyster. "I want *you* inside," she said, her hand firm on her leg.

"That can be arranged," Letty said with a wink, delighted that Anne felt relaxed enough to tease and flirt in public.

A sudden ruckus had Letty on her feet and in front of Anne in an instant, reaching for her walking stick at the same time.

Hell and the devil.

The watchmen were here.

Chapter Twenty-one

Anne gripped the edge of her seat, every sense on high alert as a pair of jeering men clattered down the stairs of the oyster tavern, hauling a young man between them and being none too careful about his person as his head smacked against the doorway to the stairwell.

Her shift was damp with sweat low on her back and her mind whirled. In all of her fretting about the evening before it had started, she had never anticipated the presence of the night watchmen.

"Let this be a lesson to you," one of the watchmen bellowed. "If you're looking for a night of pleasure, go visit the lightskirts up the road. Falling in bed with your fellow man will get you naught but endless nights in prison."

"We run an honest establishment here," a tall, bearded man called out, shoving people aside as he made his way to the stairs. "You've made some mistake, sirs. Let me make it right and you can be on your way."

The silence that had fallen meant that they could all hear the jangle of silver crossing palms. Anne held her breath. The watchman pocketed the coins but didn't let go of the pale man that he held in a twist of his arm.

"Alas, I think I know what I saw," he said, chortling.

Anne felt the punch of fear deep in her belly. She was well aware that sodomy was proven in a court of law by witnessing a man in the middle of committing the act, with proof of the man's release. If this man was claiming to have witnessed such things in the upstairs chambers, it meant a death sentence.

She couldn't let it happen.

Before she could fully comprehend what she was doing, Anne jerked out of her chair and marched to the fray. Her legs felt like rubber, but she was confident that no one would be able to tell as she put every ounce of energy into an effortless glide.

Letty hurried after her. "Anne, don't do anything rash," she hissed.

Anne tossed a look behind her. "I cannot stand by and do nothing."

She stopped in front of the men. "I am the Duchess of Hawthorne," she said coldly. "Unhand this man."

He looked surprised for a moment, then looked at his companion over the head of their prisoner. "Duchess?" he repeated. "These actresses get more nervy all the time, I swear. Go on then, sweetheart, you can duchess me all you like in the carriage while we take this miscreant away."

She dug out a ruby ring from her reticule and thrust it at him. "Unhand him and you may have this."

"Paste jewels look more real by the day, too." He dropped the ring back into her hand. "We've got business to do, miss."

"I am a duchess, and you will rue this day." Fury built in her. How dared this man behave with such insolence?

"Maybe you are, and maybe you aren't, but I don't much care either way. In a place like this, whose word has more authority?" He glanced around at the silent crowd. "I think it's the one with the bully stick. Begging your pardon, Yer Bloomin' Grace." He laughed and shoved past them into the night.

The owner clapped a hand on her shoulder. "Thank you for your help, miss. I appreciate it." He moved away into conversation with other patrons, their voices sober with concern.

"I cannot believe that it accomplished nothing," Anne said to Letty. It was warm in the tavern, but her blood felt ice cold as it ran through her veins. "The title *means* something. I have always been able to get what I need on the power of my name alone."

"Not in places like this," Letty said gently. "Not always."

"What purpose is rank if it can do nothing when it's important?"

"Come, let's get you home."

Anne watched through the carriage window as the tavern disappeared from view. "I can see why you might wish to spend time there. There's an electric kind of energy that I don't see at the private suppers or eating establishments that I am more accustomed to."

"These people feel free," Letty said. "We all agree to it when we enter, no matter how tacitly, and we leave behind any gossip when we leave. It's usually safe, but there's always risk. Sometimes a deadly one. You can be yourself—not the self you want others to think that you are. But your true self. That's what Hawthorne's doing by not hiding his inclinations."

"Did you recognize that man?" Anne asked quietly.

"Personally? No. But it could have been anyone. It could have been Fraser, or Marcus. Tomorrow, we will go back and each contribute some money and try to set this man's affairs to right. If he has a wife, or a business, or a child, we will come together to ease their hardships."

"That should be the role of society." Anne frowned.

"Not when society shuns us. This is what *community* does." Letty cupped her cheek, her eyes shining in the darkness of the carriage. "You were so brave. My beautiful, proud, defiant duchess."

Anne flushed. "I am ashamed that I have done nothing in the past," she said, the words burning her throat.

"But you did something tonight. You didn't hesitate to use your name and your title to help."

"Instead of hiding behind it to protect other rich people who don't need it. What punishment is social censure compared to the reality of people's lives?" She had never thought about it that way before.

They were silent the rest of the way home.

❖

The next afternoon, Anne found Hawthorne slouched down on a chair in the library, one of the few rooms that had been spared from the chaos that reigned in the rest of the estate. One Hessian-booted leg stuck straight out in front of him, the other bent at the knee. He was scowling down at a book open on his lap.

For the past decade, she had tackled the dukedom's problems without hesitation. But now, faced with her biggest problem—the duke himself—Anne realized that Letty had been right. She had done nothing more than hide since Hawthorne returned.

It was time to confront him.

He unfolded himself from the chair and bowed, looking at her thoughtfully with those heavy-lidded eyes that she knew so well.

"We need to talk," Anne said.

"I am at your leisure, Your Grace."

She resisted the urge to twist her hands in her skirts. Good lord, that was a habit she had left behind in the schoolroom. Instead, she sank into the armchair nearest the fire, watching the flames twist and spiral and collapse upon themselves before flickering anew.

Much like their marriage.

Anne meant to ask him how long he was planning to stay in London. She wanted to know why it had been so urgent that he move into Hawthorne House. She thought about him and Sir Phineas and had a thousand questions.

But what came out was something else entirely. "Why did you leave me?"

The instant the words were out, she wanted to retract them. She couldn't tell if the fire flamed hotter in the grate, or on her cheeks.

Hawthorne gazed at her, and her stomach churned with the sweets that Cook had served earlier. Then he drew near and sat on the arm of her chair, and his scent was so familiar even after all these years that her eyes stung with unshed tears. The crisp starch on his collar mingled with the smoky amber cologne that he must still favor.

"It was never about you," he said, his deep voice filled with regret. "You were my best friend, Annie. The only one I ever trusted.

I am sorrier than I can ever express because I know I hurt you." He looked away. "But I couldn't bear it any longer, hiding my true self at balls or the opera, then sneaking into the shadows to risk a kiss or more."

"Do you think it wasn't difficult for me?" she asked. "I was in the same position."

"I know. And I ruined it. You were the strong one, while I failed us both. If it means anything to you, please know that I have regretted it every single day of my life."

"We were meant to handle things *together*." Pain lanced through her as she remembered the morning that she had woken up to the news that her husband had left.

His mouth tightened and he looked away. "I left the duchy in the best possible hands. I would trust in your integrity with my very life, so why would I not trust you with my family and our livelihood? I know you must have done a better job than I would have."

"You didn't have to stay away for a decade."

"I never meant to make things harder for you. I thought what I was doing would make it easier. I swear to you, I always meant to come home."

She shook her head. "If you were gone for a year or twenty, it wouldn't have mattered. When you leave, you change. And when you come back—you don't quite fit."

When they had first devised their plan so long ago, she had thought them two halves of the same piece. Now their edges bumped up against each other, raw and ragged. Her heart twisted, thinking of how young they had been. How naive.

"None of us stay young forever," Hawthorne said. "You have grown and changed as much as I have."

She stiffened in her chair. "How can you say that? I have fought to stay the same. I dedicated my life this past decade to safekeeping everything this dukedom stands for."

"Then you don't remember who you *were*. The memories I have of that bold, passionate woman are as strong as ever. You are cold now. Severe." He smiled. "You used to be wild."

Anne was shocked to the core. "My mother would have sooner hidden me away in an attic than married me into a dukedom if she had ever thought me wild."

"Would a demure young miss plot with me to hoodwink everyone we know into thinking that this was a love match? I never would have chosen *her*. There was a reason I chose *you*. We chose each other." His eyes burned into her own. "Do you ever feel like we are on a trajectory, bigger than ourselves?"

"Of course. We have a responsibility to those who work for us."

"But plenty more depend on us to help. People like us, Annie. I cannot stand by any longer and watch the violence, the hatred. I must do something."

"Doing something may invite more violence," she said, fear causing the pulse at the base of her throat to throb. It was the same fear that woke within her when she stared too long at a pretty face in public. She was long accustomed to its presence. Her evening with Letty last night made her realize how much she hated it.

"I went with Miss Barrow to an oyster tavern last night," she said. "She told me it was one frequented by…well, mollies." It was the first time she had ever said the word aloud and it felt foreign on her lips. And yet, maybe Letty had been right. Maybe talking about these things was the only way to make them feel familiar. Normal. "The night watchmen were there, and they hauled away a man." She struggled to find words to express herself. "It was abhorrent."

Hawthorne's eyes sharpened. "Which establishment?"

"Donovan's. I believe it was on Piccadilly."

He scribbled something on a piece of paper and rang the bell for a footman, then gave the note to him with a terse word.

"What are you doing?"

"What do you think I've been doing since coming back to London? I've greased the palm of plenty of watchmen and jailers. I've sent along the promise of a significant payment to release this man with no questions asked."

"Even our fortune isn't enough to rescue everyone," she said softly. How many other men were out there that they didn't even know of, languishing in a cell? She hated to think of it.

"Nothing will change unless we start to create change. It might take years, decades, or hell—maybe even centuries. But we have to stand with our own. We have to show them that the love we have for our own is decent. Honorable. Meaningful. We can't hide in the shadows forever."

"But what if something happens?"

"You and I have the privilege of power. We can hide behind our name, our wealth, our rank, if need be. No one else can afford this risk. No one else can do what we alone can do. Maybe kinghood really is bestowed by divine right. If that's true, then doesn't it stand to reason that so does dukedom? Why else could our union be so blessed, if not for us to stand up for who we are?"

"We were not blessed with children," she said quietly. "That is what is said of us, anyway."

"That's not the only blessing, and you know it. We never planned on children. There's plenty enough in the world already, and my sister's family is more than willing to take up the mantle of the dukedom. You've handled Edward's education, haven't you?" His eyes burned into her own once more.

"Of course I did." How could he even ask? It had always been a matter of utmost importance to them both. "I stuck to the plan. I chose the most liberal of tutors for Edward, and the most free-thinking of governesses for his sisters. I provided the best education that I could think of in order to favor people like us."

"Good. Those are the people I plan to represent."

"What do you mean?"

"Isn't it clear yet why I returned to London?" He cleared his throat and shifted, his posture straightening. Gone was the languid pleasure-seeking man that she had married, and in his place was a hard-eyed determined duke. "I am taking my rightful place in politics and claiming my seat in the House of Lords. I stayed away from England for long enough. Maybe even too long. But I was caught up in my duties there."

"Duties." She gave a hollow laugh. "Parties, you mean."

"Yes, there were parties," he snapped. "And through them, I created a network across all of Europe and even beyond. People who learned that they can trust the name Hawthorne. People who came to believe the symbol of this duchy meant protection." He paced in front of the window, clasping his hands behind his back. "The rules are far less strict in France, but men still risked their necks seeking out companionship if they were in a place that was unfriendly to them," he said flatly. "If I had not been so flagrantly public myself, creating a place in my estate where other like-minded men knew they could go, I could not have sheltered them under my name and under my roof. Sometimes, secrecy begets greater risk than publicity."

"You couldn't turn your back on them," Anne murmured. Understanding washed over her. It had never been just about his personal desires, his wish to live outside of society's rules. He had been as committed to his duty as she had been, albeit in a different way. It felt as if the world was tipped on its axis and everything had been shaken upside down.

"It became too much this past year. I knew I could trust you to run things, but I also knew it wasn't fair to burden you alone with it. I had to come home. To make it right. To rule this dukedom together."

The flame of anger that Anne had tended to for ten years was finally extinguished. She felt exhausted when she thought of all the energy that she had spent as the Discerning Duchess—years of being tense, worried, hypercritical, and overextended on behalf of the dukedom. She leaned her head back against the chair. Who had she *been* before she had become the duchess? She hadn't remembered, so focused on her present anger and on preserving the shine on her name.

Memories rushed back. Arguing with her father as a girl about outdated methods of working the land. Snapping at ladies who dripped bigotry along with their gossip into the ears of debutantes. When had she changed? When had she started to fear the threat of people's opinions, even when she had never encountered anyone disagreeing with a duchess? When had she dedicated her life to being as invisible as possible, and trying to convince others to hide away too?

It had done no one any service. She had thought it wise to retreat, and to warn young ladies against overt public displays of affection to protect everyone's reputations. Ladies who stood and flirted too close to each other could beget rumors that could spread to implicate other ladies, and then other behaviors could be called into question. She had feared the gossip. But without any corresponding actions to combat the root of the issue—Society's strict rules and expectations of behavior—how had she really helped?

A representative from the House of Hawthorne had not been present in politics in decades. His father had preferred not to dabble much in politics, so it was no surprise when Hawthorne had followed suit.

"Why now?" she asked.

"Now that I'm back in London, I am part of the community here. I used to gather people to my chateau to meet in safety, but now that I walk among them in their own haunts, I see the intolerance firsthand. I've seen the raids. I know people who have been persecuted." His face spasmed. "I can bear it no more."

"I misjudged you all these years," she said. "I'm so sorry. I thought you cavalier with your reputation. When the truth is far from what I believed." She paused. "I apologize for the state of your bedchamber, but I have been so angry. I wanted to take up the axe myself and strike down the furnishings and break the windows. I wanted to erase the reminder of our union, and to be quite frank— the values of the dukedom that I can no longer stand. Propriety. Severity. Virtue. Judgment."

"It is I who must apologize to you, and you know it. You had every right to your anger, and I'm sorry to have caused it." Then Hawthorne grinned, and she saw a flash of the youth he had been. "If there was an axe to be had, I would take it up beside you and swing at these old beams myself. Tear it all down, Annie. We'll build it back stronger than ever."

"For us," she said. "For *our* values."

"Exactly. Honesty. Openness. Acceptance. Protection."

She paused. "Taking your place in politics means you will be more exposed to the public than ever."

"I know it's a lot to ask. If we remained separated, I could spare you the worst of the scandal. But your good name and unblemished reputation and endless work with charity would help me and give legitimacy to my cause. Our cause." He looked at her steadily. "I told you, we were born to rule. We can do this. *Together*. It's not much different from how we originally imagined our lives—helping each other by hiding in full view."

"After all, who would challenge the duchy?"

"Words to live by," he said, raising a brow at her.

They had never been in romantic love. But oh, there certainly had been love between them. Maybe there could be again.

Maybe she had her friend back.

Chapter Twenty-two

The next day, after Anne recounted her conversation with Hawthorne to Letty over a slice of cake and tea in her sitting room, Letty grinned at her and set her fork down.

"I have a surprise for you today. Your bedchamber is ready," she said, standing up and extending a hand to Anne.

Anne didn't think she had ever raced up the stairs so fast, but she had waited a long time to see the finished room. A thrill went through her as Letty opened the door. The bedchamber was magnificent. Gone was all the gold that had dominated everything from ceiling to floor, and gone were the heavy curtains that had blocked the light from the windows. The windows themselves had been replaced by larger ones, and the upper panes now featured gorgeous stained-glass rosettes.

Everything was different.

The room now was lush but elegant. The walls were papered with thin pink and white stripes, and filmy white curtains hung over the windows from ceiling to floor. There were no more hard edges or elaborate metalwork to clutter the room. Instead of ornate brass candelabras, there were crystal candlestick holders that sparkled in the light. The chaise lounge had been recovered in black velvet and the wood trim painted a clean white, with a thick pale pink blanket folded on it.

"I added ceramic braziers underneath most of the chairs to fill with coals when you need more warmth," Letty said, pointing to one painted with blue and white flowers.

"I shall never again be cold," she said, squeezing Letty's hand, and was startled to hear her voice sound thick and rough. She put a hand to her cheek and found it wet with tears, which made sense because her heart felt about twice its usual size. Filled with love.

Best of all was the elaborately embroidered *A* that dominated the face of each plump pillow on the bed.

"I told the embroiderer to include parts of your family's crest, as well as Hawthorne's," Letty said, picking up a pillow and pointing at the bright silk threads. "See, there's a thistle, and there's an oak leaf, from your family. There's a lion for the Hawthornes. You are still Lady Anne of Clydon, as well as Anne, Duchess of Hawthorne." She picked up another pillow and her face softened as she looked down at it. "And this one is for plain Anne, my lover. I sketched it up and gave it to the embroiderer after our night at the oyster tavern." There were delicate pearls sewn to the white satin pillow, embroidered with pink shells.

"You thought of everything," Anne said, reaching for her hand. "You brought pieces of me together here. You know me better than anyone ever has." She was touched to see the work that Letty had put into every detail, all the personal and private preferences in this room that once was designed to dominate and impress, and now was designed for her comfort.

This room was proof of Letty's affection. It had to be. All the evidence she needed was right here in front of her. She couldn't stop smiling.

"You haven't seen the pièce de résistance." Letty flipped back the corner of the dark pink bedcover and eased the sheet away from the bed. "There are now seven mattresses instead of the three you had before," she said cheerfully. "All thick enough for a princess. Together, maybe they're enough for a queen." She curtsied, then winked at her. "All for you. Your Highness."

Each mattress was covered in a different brocade fabric, wildly contrasting colors and designs. Paisley marched across one, forest animals on another, florals were scattered across a third. They were different thicknesses, and when she touched them, she found to her delight that they must all have different fillings. Goose feathers, she guessed as she squeezed one, and another felt like lambswool.

Anne laughed and wiped away another tear. "I may not be a princess, but this is indeed a bed fit for fantasy."

"Everything else is restrained and elegant, but I thought the bed was a suitable place for surprises."

Anne sized her up and thought she might have enough momentum. She tackled Letty to the bed, catching her off guard. For a moment, they tussled, laughing, and Anne felt blissfully aware of the freedom of falling and rolling and gripping and tugging. There was no center of balance, and everything was a blur.

She had never so enjoyed feeling off kilter.

"You told me once that designers are not magicians," she said, pinning Letty down beneath her, "but today I beg to differ. This room is magic. You are *magic*."

Anne pressed her lips against Letty's, tasting heat and chocolate and feeling all her inhibitions falling away. With Letty's hands pressing against her waist, she felt safe. Protected. This was a woman who had planned every last little detail of this space for her, with her pleasure in mind.

Anne slid off the bed, as unsteady now as she had been when they were ice skating on the pond. "You saw all of me," she said, "and you created all of this."

Letty propped herself up on her elbows. "Yes." Her eyes, often full of mischief and light, were serious.

"I want you to see *all* of me, like you did that first time. But I want to be the one to show you."

The weak winter sun slanted in through the stained-glass windows, showing a pattern of beautiful color on the rug. She didn't need a mirror to show her that her lips were plump and rosy with need, or that her eyes were luminous with desire. The reverent look on Letty's face was the only reflection of her desire that she cared about.

Anne slid the diamond-tipped pins from her hair one by one, dropping each to the carpet.

"I worked so hard on this room, only to have it in disarray almost at once," Letty said, shaking her head.

"How shall I ever make it up to you?" Anne teased her. Her fingers hovered over the buttons of her frock.

But her dresses weren't meant to be undone without the presence of at least one maid, and the buttons proved decorative in nature. Letty started to rise, but Anne stilled her motion with a gesture.

She wanted to be in control this time.

Biting her lip, she considered her options. She spared a look of longing for her frock, which was a favorite, then decided there were more important things than fashion. She fetched a pair of heavy shears from the dressing room.

Letty was frowning now and sitting upright on the bed. "Anne, let me help you."

Anne stepped away and snapped the shears open and shut. "I have this well under control."

She slipped the cold blade between her chemise and the dress, and before she could change her mind, she slid the scissors shut and heard yarns rip and stitches pop. Done was done, she thought, moving the scissors again, snipping down the bodice to the waist, feeling the cool air on her skin and feeling gloriously alive. She had cut enough now to wiggle free of the dress, leaving her in a sleeveless chemise, stays, a petticoat, and stockings.

"You are beautiful," Letty said, standing up, a hungry look in her eyes.

Anne took a deep breath and eyed the shears once more. She felt so light with the remnants of her frock at her feet, like she had shed a layer of herself in the process.

She craved *more*.

Thankfully, clothing was not the only thing that a pair of scissors could cut.

"Anne!" Letty gasped, her hand flying to her mouth as a hunk of golden hair floated to the floor.

"I am returning to myself, at long last," Anne announced. She considered for a moment. "Or I am something new entirely. Either way, I feel different. I want to look different too."

With a few unconcerned snips, she hacked her hair above her shoulders. "I shall have a hairdresser come in the morning to put it to rights, but this is a good start." She ran her hands through her hair, shaking any loose strands free.

Free.

At last.

Anne sashayed to the chaise lounge, putting as much wiggle into her walk as she could. She sat and drew her legs up beside her, giddy with pleasure and heady with desire. "Maybe I wish to be admired as much as the room is," she said and slid her petticoat up her legs to bare her thighs to the winter light and Letty's gaze.

She felt scandalous. It was *wonderful*.

Letty was at her side in an instant, her hands warm and firm on her legs. "I definitely admire you." She knelt in front of her, looking up at Anne. "It's a good thing I ordered the rugs in this room to be extra thick. It was intended to keep the warmth better, but I must admit it has multiple benefits."

Anne sucked in a breath as Letty thrust her petticoat and chemise to her hips, then gasped as she was readjusted so that her legs were over Letty's shoulders and her head was buried between her thighs.

It turned out, as always, that the magic was in Letty's mouth.

Letty flicked her tongue across her quim then sucked gently on her nub. She slid her tongue against her opening, then slipped her tongue inside, thrusting until Anne was begging for release. Panting, she threaded her fingers into Letty's hair.

Letty raised her head. "I chose each mattress, but I admit that I didn't test them out in the way that they were meant to be used. We should check that they are up to the job of servicing a duchess." She picked Anne up and tossed her onto the bed, then made quick work of disrobing.

Anne flung off her stays and chemise, wild to continue, but stopped when Letty held up a finger.

"Keep the stockings on."

Anne obeyed, delighted at the adoration in Letty's eyes as she stood there naked except for her sheer silk stockings held up at mid-thigh with pink satin beribboned garters.

"Pretty as those sweets you like." She grinned lasciviously. "And twice as delicious."

Letty covered her when she joined her on the bed, and Anne loved the weight of her as she pressed her into the mattress. But she wanted something different today. She nudged Letty off, then straddled her hips so she was sitting on top.

"This is a good angle for you," she said, looking up at her. "*Very* good."

Letty cupped her hand under Anne and stroked her with her thumb. Her other hand was on Anne's gartered thigh, and her fingers slid beneath the ribbon against the delicate flesh of her inner leg.

Anne arched her back and cupped her own breasts, and ground herself against Letty's hips and her hand, feeling the pressure build from the friction. She worked slowly, teasing them both, watching as Letty's eyes grew dark and luminous and her full lips parted. She had never felt so uninhibited, and she wanted to enjoy every moment of it.

She tipped forward until she could capture one of Letty's breasts with her mouth, teasing her nipple. Still straddling Letty and holding her in place with her thighs, she slid a hand between their bodies and touched her, stroking her until she could hear her moan.

Anne slid off and settled herself between Letty's thighs, then moved her head down so that she could taste her quim. She had never done this before, for Letty or for any other woman. She had always been shy of it, unsure. But today she felt bold.

The feeling of losing control under Letty's touch always worked her into a fervor, but she discovered there was deep pleasure to be had in loving Letty with her mouth, and in hearing Letty cry out her name as she found her release.

Anne curled up beside her. "You made something perfect for me with this room. I wanted to give you something perfect in return," she said. She hesitated, then clasped her hand in her own. "Stay with me tonight, Letty. Please."

After all this time, could she finally convince Letty to stay? She feared her heart was in her eyes if Letty looked too closely, but the feeling overwhelmed her. She yearned to spend the night in this ludicrous seven-mattressed bed with her, their hair tangled together on the pillows, their limbs tangled together beneath the covers.

Letty's smile was hesitant and warm, and when she gave her reply, Anne's heart felt near to bursting.

She said yes.

Chapter Twenty-three

Six months ago, Letty could never have dreamt that she would one day walk in Hyde Park in the presence of a duke and a duchess, but today she strolled beside them with Phin. As it was the beginning of April, the air was still chilly, but the promenade was well populated with people wearing the fanciest clothes that Letty had ever seen. She didn't fit in among them, with her sturdy twill dress and her ebony walking stick and her top hat, but she was beside Anne, wasn't she? Did it matter that she was on her husband's arm, and Letty was on Phin's?

She wanted to say that it didn't, but it was difficult to shake the notion that she had no right to be by their side, looking quite as comfortable as if she were their equal. She tried to shake such thoughts away.

She could see Anne's hair beneath the elegant bonnet perched on the crown of her head. The hairdresser had done a wonderful job after Anne had cut it, trimming it into a sleek little cap that feathered around her ears and nape.

Letty loved seeing Anne out of doors. It had taken some persuasion to convince her to walk to the park instead of taking the carriage, but the fresh air seemed to fill her with joy, and it put rosy blossoms on her cheeks that were most charming.

The purpose of the walk was to continue to reshape Hawthorne's reputation by association with Anne's pristine reputation, so they stopped frequently to talk to anyone willing to obtain the good fortune of a ducal greeting.

"How do you think you shall fare in politics?" Letty asked Hawthorne after he had tipped his hat to a baron and his wife.

"I am a most persuasive speaker when I have a mind to be."

"I suppose that's what politics is about, is it not? Smooth talking and charming manners," Anne said.

"I rather think there is meant to be some importance attached to the ideas behind the facade. Or so I'm told," he drawled. Then he sobered. "I plan to stand for our rights, when they are threatened. To stand against bills that may threaten us."

"I wonder what the others in the House of Lords will think," Anne said.

"I cannot imagine it will come as a surprise to most of them. But this is why I wanted your help." He patted Anne's hand, tucked into the crook of his elbow. "With the guise of a traditional life and a traditional wife, I am less of a threat to them. I think I could further my agenda if they think they are working with a middle-aged married man instead of remembering the Paris rumors."

"But you don't want them to completely forget," Phin said, an easy grin on his face.

"Is that your purpose in our house, Sir Phineas?" Anne asked. "To remind any in danger of forgetting Hawthorne's true nature?"

Hawthorne barked out a laugh. "I wish I had thought of that. But no. Phin is here because I have a deep and stubborn love for him and his affectations, and I fear wasting away in Mayfair without his entertainments."

Phin sketched a bow. "I aim to please."

They paused to congratulate a viscount on his engagement and Hawthorne gallantly kissed the prospective bride's hand before they moved on.

"This is positive," Anne said. "People are accepting you."

"It behooves them to be polite here," Hawthorne said, scanning the crowd. "I need to see them in different circumstances."

"How is it with the gentlemen at White's?"

He shrugged. "I wager. I read the papers. I talk with some of the young bucks, who seem rather admiring of my gall. The older set, the ones I need to face in parliament—they nod at me when they enter but take care to sip their cognac in another room. I don't care about their acceptance, really. Or their offers to buy a matched set of bays." His eyes glittered. "I need them to know that they must listen to me when I have something to say in parliament."

Anne pursed her lips. "We should host a dinner to invite some of these more influential politicians to Hawthorne House. You could talk to them in more detail than at a ball, or even at the clubs. There, you would have the picturesque setting of your devoted wife."

"That will confound some of them and encourage others." Hawthorne looked thoughtful. "I think dinner is an excellent conceit. I will draw up a list of names that we can review together."

"Together?"

"I wouldn't dream of doing this without you by my side. All of you, in fact." He looked vulnerable for a moment, tension around his eyes. "If I don't present a strong front now, I worry that I will be ridiculed, my ideas dismissed. They cannot remove me from the House of Lords, but they can disregard what I say. I need to show that I have strong allies. That the Duke of Hawthorne is a force to be reckoned with."

Letty felt a burst of pride. "Hawthorne House will be ready when you need it to be," she vowed. The work on the first floor had progressed quickly after she and Anne had agreed on the themes for the public rooms. An idea struck her. "You have said this house is part of the locus of power."

"Yes. Generations of Hawthornes have ruled from there."

"Then why not showcase it?"

"What do you mean?" Hawthorne looked confused. "We have dinners. Annie hosts a ball every season. Royalty has taken tea in those parlors."

Excitement pulsed through her. "Royalty is one thing, but do you want to only show the nobility what you stand for? Why not show everyone? Some other houses have public days, where the house is opened once a week to anyone who wishes to purchase a voucher. Why not open yours? You could gain the support of the people."

Anne stopped short. "Letty, that's brilliant. That's what is important, isn't it? People will know us, and they will know they are not alone. The House of Lords is not the only venue that matters."

"How will they know us?" Phin asked.

Hawthorne grinned. "It's because of my art, isn't it?" he asked Letty.

"Exactly. Your Greek vases and some of the more risqué marbles would give anyone the hint that you share the same inclination."

"What if they think he likes to collect antiques, regardless of what is on them?" Phin frowned.

"If people choose not to see what's in front of them, then it can provide total privacy in plain sight," Letty said. "But for those who choose to look and to understand, it sends its own message. This house can be powerful in ways other than as the address of the Duke and Duchess of Hawthorne."

"This is a wonderful idea," Hawthorne said.

Anne looked thoughtful. "Instead of hosting a dinner with parliamentary men, should we instead plan a grand opening of the house? Guests could walk through the new statuary, the vase room, the gallery, and the other public rooms."

"You could have a little light luncheon available in one of the parlors, and champagne offered at the door."

"Through your art, they shall know you," Letty said. "I can arrange the rooms to draw attention to what you wish to highlight. It shall astonish and delight."

Hawthorne nodded. "Those who wish to open their eyes and notice the themes in my art and remember the rumors about me will know that our house is a bastion of safety for them. That someone among the highest of the land is one of them and will fight to protect them."

"You can invite members from both the House of Lords, and the House of Commons," Phin said. "And the Prime Minister. They shall all see what you stand for."

Hawthorne took a pinch of snuff. "And the Prince Regent. Anne, if your sterling reputation can convince him to come, and if everyone can see that I have the favor of the prince—then I shall have it all." He bowed. "It's as I told you. Together, we rule, my dear duchess. It's simply an unconventional coronet that we wear on our heads."

Anne and Hawthorne spent the next few weeks planning the details of the grand opening and debating over guest lists and menus. Letty focused on the finishing touches for the first floor. Most of it was complete, and it gave her a strange feeling to think of the house being finished.

Endings were always difficult.

When she had started, it had been difficult to conceive of an end point, but Anne had eased off on the initial instruction of redoing absolutely everything. All of the bedchambers had now been refreshed, and all of the important public rooms had been redone, but there were several parlors, the library, and the ballroom that they decided didn't need to be touched.

The public rooms were exactly as Letty had envisioned them. She had completed the rooms inspired by fire and ice, and the one that, to her, symbolized Anne with the morning dawn. Instead of massive displays of wealth, she thought the rooms conveyed something meaningful, of love and perseverance and growth and change. She was proud to think of people viewing her work.

Letty was now arranging things in the statuary, which she called the Ocean Room. It represented the tide change, the ebb and flow of relationships, bringing people back together. It was a room meant for Anne and Hawthorne. Filmy turquoise and blue curtains hung from ceiling to floor, which would move in the breeze like waves when the large French doors were open in the summer. She had designed a set of wind chimes that would tinkle in the air like rocks washing together at the seashore, hoping that the illusion of the ocean could be brought together by both visual and aural cues.

The walls were lightest seafoam green, and the trims were white. She had hand-carved the molds for the plaster baseboard and crown molding, with bold swirls and curls for the froth of the ocean's waves. Seashells were arranged along a narrow ledge that ran the length of the room, and Letty hadn't been able to resist adding clam shells with handfuls of pearls shining all around the room.

Anne studied the statues that had taken all the footmen she could find in order to move them into the room. Some of them were nudes, classical Greek statues of Adonis and Zeus, and some were animals, including Letty's favorite from Hawthorne's collection—a hawk with outstretched wings, so realistic that she felt it could take off in flight at any moment.

"It's marvelous," Anne said. "I had never thought to see what Hawthorne had collected over the years. Perhaps I was too afraid to open the warehouse stores, scared of what I might find."

Letty stood on her toes to hang a painting on the wall, a furious oil painting of crashing waves and shipwreck. "He has a wonderful collection. I would welcome any chance to go back if you would like a guide through the warehouse."

The butler entered the room. "Your Grace, Miss Barrow. I apologize for interrupting, but there is a party to see you in the blue parlor."

Chapter Twenty-four

Twenty years had passed since Letty had seen most of them, but the Wilson family looked much the same as ever. Lady Wilson had rather more wrinkles now compared to when she had scolded Letty all through their town for trying to abscond with her son, but she still had the same nervous habit of tapping her fan. Currently, it was bouncing against her knee. Beth, John's eldest sister, had the same snide look on her face that Letty remembered from when she used to chaperone them. Susan, the younger sister, was preening at herself in the mirror above the mantel. The Wilsons had always been boisterous and snobby, and they remained true to form even in a duchess's parlor.

The butler, of course, had announced them by their married names. Beth was now Mrs. Anderson, and Susan had become Mrs. Talbot, but Letty had such vivid recollections of John's sisters as how they *were*. She couldn't break the habit of thinking of them by their Christian names.

Letty tried not to take their manners to heart, but it was difficult. She had furnished this parlor, from the royal blue carpet to the stately Windsor chairs to the elegant brass chandelier. Watching the Wilsons looking down their noses at them set her teeth on edge. The room wasn't meant for the likes of them. It had been designed for Anne, and for the people who fit into her life.

Which the Wilson family decidedly didn't.

They were the ragged edges of Letty's past. She had tried to leave them there where they belonged, but they managed to crawl their way to the forefront of her life when they so pleased.

Her mouth felt unaccountably dry, and she wished Anne would call for tea. Then a shudder ran through her at the thought of prolonging this visit by even one extra minute. She despised that their presence still made her heart race, but she had been thrown out of her father's home because of them. They had thrust her into destitution after John's death. Only her own wits and skills had saved her.

What was Robert doing here with them?

"Not enough embellishment for my tastes," Beth murmured in sotto voice. "Rather plain, isn't it, Susan?"

"Indeed it is," Susan agreed, then blanched as she caught Anne's eye. "Not to say that Your Grace doesn't have impeccable taste!"

"Miss Barrow was of infinite help in decorating the room," Anne said. "It is marvellously well done."

Beth tittered. "Miss Barrow is an industrious woman indeed. How good of you to work, poor dear, to support yourself."

She managed to smile without baring her teeth. "Needs must. Especially after you cut off my stipend."

Lady Wilson gasped and rapped the table with her fan. "How very rude, Miss Barrow! Discussing financial matters in front of the Duchess of Hawthorne!"

"However did you think the duchy came to have such a house without stooping to discuss a financial matter or two?" Anne asked, her voice cold with displeasure. Her eyes glinted with fury that the Wilson family didn't seem to pick up on.

Robert had edged to the far side of the room, looking more than a trifle indisposed. Letty couldn't blame him. The Wilsons were enough to give anyone indigestion, and she had shielded him from the worst of their qualities for so long. This must be one of their very first encounters.

She frowned. "What brings you to Hawthorne House, Lady Wilson?"

"We are here to pay our respects to Her Grace, of course." A bevy of simpering curtseys followed, each more ridiculous than the last.

"This is a social call?" Anne queried.

"When Robert told us that dear, dear Miss Barrow was working for you, we told him we simply must pay a visit and catch up!"

Alarm bells were ringing in Letty's belly. "How did you have Robert's direction? We were forced to move after John's death. I never updated any of you to our whereabouts."

There was no doubt about it. Robert had a greenish tinge to his face.

"Why, Letitia Barrow!" Beth cried. "Do such old friends need a reason to visit? Remember when you thought we would be *sisters*? Now look at you." Her smile was pitying.

Letty raised a brow. "How long have you held onto that grudge? Have you come all this way to rub it in my face? I daresay I am far better off now than I ever would have been if we had called each other kin."

"It isn't a grudge." She sniffed. "I wouldn't have thought twice about you except that your son wrote to me."

It felt like ice was running through Letty's veins. She turned to stare at Robert. "Robert wrote to you?"

"Yes. He mentioned he needed help. I suppose you couldn't provide." Beth eyed her. "What could I expect, knowing of your poor circumstances and straightened means?"

A situation that she had helped to manufacture, of course.

"Miss Barrow is well on her way to becoming illustrious." Anne's voice was sharp.

"I'm sure," she said in placating tones. "Your Grace does have excellent taste."

"If the chit has wormed her way in here through some illicit means, Your Grace, do not hesitate at once to turn her over to the authorities," Lady Wilson bellowed, striking her fan against the table with enough force that Letty wondered if the sticks would break. "I cannot expect that age would have changed her mercenary ways. She tried to embroil my son in her schemes."

Letty sucked in a breath. She wanted to retort that she had gained this job through her talent and skill, neither of which any of the Wilsons would be capable of recognizing, but the words died on her tongue.

Because she hadn't.

She had gained it through George's help, and Hawthorne's word, and Anne's judgment of her talents to be so poor as to be unable to finish the job.

Every confidence that she had in her ability and in the hard work she had put into the estate felt like ashes where her heart should be. Her palms felt sweaty in her cotton gloves, and she wanted to tear her cravat away from her throat.

"You have quite some nerve to show up to my home uninvited, insult the décor and my esteemed guest, and then to expect niceties in return," Anne said.

"Robert said this would all be quite all right!" Susan exclaimed.

All eyes turned to Robert, who smiled weakly.

"I do not presume to know what Mr. Barrow may have promised you in exchange for the currency of my favor, but I would wager it to be a pack of lies," Anne announced. "I do not look kindly on people who treat their family in such manner."

"Family?" Lady Wilson laughed. "Miss Barrow is nothing more than a cast-off courtesan, and her son is a bastard who can't even get the lowliest solicitor to sponsor him. They are nothing to us. Why, my dear John always did used to call them his little burden, didn't he? What was the phrase he would use? Off to London to take out the rubbish?"

Robert looked stricken.

Letty glared at her. "You dare to discredit your own son in front of your grandson? Robert has grown up to be a worthy, fine young man. You did yourselves a disservice by never owning up to the connection. You may condescend to look down your nose at him, but he's thrice the man his father was." Her heart might be breaking over Robert's involvement with them, but she would protect her son to her dying breath.

"He is no grandson of mine." Lady Wilson eyed him like he was a three-day-old cut of beef in her pantry.

Anne rose. "You have severely overstayed your welcome, Lady Wilson. My butler will show you out."

Lady Wilson sniffed. "I thought to pay you a visit and give you a warning about Miss Barrow out of kindness, Your Grace. Your faultless reputation would indicate that you would welcome such news of poor behavior."

"Perhaps my values have changed," she snapped, "and I no longer look down on people as I once did."

"Indeed I suppose you don't. I've heard the news of resuming your decidedly *odd* marriage." Lady Wilson rose. "Come, girls, let us be away from here." She dropped her voice but it was still audible as she hurried her daughters to their feet. "I regret to admit that she isn't anything like what they say of her, and this is sadly a far cry from the type of environment that could elevate you."

They sailed out in a cloud of white skirts and trailing ribbons and waving fans.

Robert's face was white, his eyes wild. "Mother, I am ruined."

"You think only of yourself, after you invited those horrid people here? In front of Her Grace?" Letty ripped the cravat away from her throat and tossed it onto the sofa beside her.

"I didn't know they would act in such a manner," he muttered. "I thought I must have come from some common sense."

"I am sorry, Robert. I never told you how vicious they are, and how shallow."

"If you had been more forthcoming, I may not have made such a mistake!" Robert's voice was shrill.

"Calm yourself," Anne said crisply. "There is no real harm done. Every family has its difficulties, and at least yours played out in private."

Robert flushed. "That is more than kind of you to say, Your Grace, as *you* were the audience to this miserable play."

Letty struggled to get a hold of her temper. "Anne is right. You have lost nothing—"

"I have lost *everything!*" he cried. "You are so familiar—you call her *Anne* without thinking! You are no better than what the Wilsons said of you, are you? You traded favors with my father for his money, and you trade them now with the duchess for fame and reputation. You told me that hard work would bring its own reward, but I see now what you consider to be 'hard work'—on your back. Your ambition ruined you once and will again. Meanwhile, *my* ambition was to make an honest living, and I have not even that opportunity left to me!"

"Do not speak to your mother that way," Anne warned him, standing up. Letty had never seen her so angry. Her eyes were wide and fierce, and every line in her body indicated she was ready to pounce if necessary. Letty would have felt touched if she didn't feel so humiliated. "Apologize at once."

"She ought to apologize to *me*. Mr. Selkirk let me go from my clerking duties months ago because of her." The color was high on his cheeks, and his eyes were bright. "I wrote to Lady Wilson as a last resort, and she agreed to speak to Mr. Selkirk in exchange for an introduction to the Duchess of Hawthorne, whom she said she greatly admires. But it's all ruined. She won't speak to Mr. Selkirk now."

"You have been unemployed for *months?*" Letty reeled at the news.

He scowled. "He heard rumors that you had taken a job with the Degenerate Duke of Hawthorne, and he dismissed me immediately. I told you for months that we had to be beyond reproach, but you refused to help me. I tried every last resource that I had at my disposal—I worked hard, and when that didn't work, I tried to use what little connection I had and the privilege of my father's family, and that held no water either."

He crammed his hat on his head and strode off.

Letty rubbed at her temple where a headache was brewing. "I need to go after him and check that he's all right."

Anne frowned. "Robert is a man grown, as you've told me many times. He needs to figure out his life for himself, and he certainly needs to work on his manners because he is on his way to being an insufferable boor. He's well clear of his dreadful family at this point, at least, so you have nothing immediate to worry about. Stay."

"Why should I stay? So you can use me as a temporary distraction, something to entertain you while you work through your emotions about your marriage?" Letty knew the words were hateful, but they flew out of her mouth before she could think.

How imperious Anne seemed. Never had Letty so clearly felt the difference between their ranks. Anne might have relaxed her judgment over the months, but she seemed to have kept some of it in reserve. It was warranted against the Wilsons. But how dare she say a word against Robert?

While Anne sat there on the chair that she had designed for her, her hand resting on wood imported from Spain and fabric woven in India, Letty sat across from her and felt as far away as if an ocean had opened up between them.

She didn't belong here.

Anne's mouth dropped open. "How could you think that?"

"Because I work for you, and when I'm not working for you, I'm on top of you. This isn't enough for me, Anne. I don't want to be a noblewoman's dirty little secret." Her voice was bitter. "Robert's father was no different."

"You aren't a secret."

"This whole affair is built around secrecy."

"That's different! It's to protect us. You agreed as much as I did."

"It's no different at all. I am here all the time, in your house, at your beck and call whenever you have need of me." The night she had spent in Anne's bed had been nothing more than her trying to grasp on to a dream. She had wanted so badly to believe in it. To believe in *them*. "I don't belong here in your big fancy house with your big fancy life, Anne. You don't have room for me here. You never made any."

The Wilsons had reminded her of where she came from—nothing. Letty had fought for what she had, and she was proud of it. No duchess could take away the dignity she felt in who she was.

Not even a duchess that she was in love with.

The air whooshed out of her lungs. Was this love? Was that the source of the pain that roared in her chest like an animal?

Confusion was plain on Anne's face. "This house is enormous. There's plenty of space for you. I gave you your own parlor."

"For *work*!" she cried. "That's where you see me. Not as an equal, but as someone who *does* things for you."

"That's not true," Anne said, hurt in her voice.

"I can't stay," Letty said, rising from the sofa. "Robert has never seen the Wilsons before, and there is much that he doesn't understand."

"The problem is easily solved, Letty. I could give him money. You could have asked me for funds, you know. Your son doesn't have to suffer."

Anger coursed through her. "Do you think I can't provide for him? Do you consider working an honest job to be *suffering*?"

"Of course you can provide," Anne said, her tone gentle, "but you said Robert wants to be a gentleman."

"Money won't make him any more legitimate," she snapped. "Working is a better pursuit in life compared to earning no coin and whiling time away on frivolities, like the scores of so-called gentlemen that contribute nothing to society. That's no life for me, and no life for my son. I earn my keep, Anne."

"I know how much you enjoy working on this house."

"I did. But the house is finished."

"No," Anne whispered. "There's still plenty to do. Maybe we should reconsider the ballroom, or the library."

Letty smiled sadly. "They don't need any work. There is plenty more to do at Hawthorne House, but I don't think it's what you would consider to be important. The servants' quarters. The attics. The mews. You aren't considering the places where people work, are you?"

"Hawthorne and I work hard in the estate," Anne said, anger now in her voice. "You know the work we put into the dukedom."

"What about the work that the lowest chambermaid puts into this house? All of us are together in this, working dusk until dawn, supporting the duchy." Letty waved a hand. "They scrub for their living. I dream up space for people to live. You sign off on projects and petitions. We all have different types of work."

Anne didn't say anything, her face white and pinched.

"We should agree the house is done, and then I can find a new job."

Anne frowned. "A new job?"

"This wasn't going to be my last one I ever took. I wanted to make a name for myself."

"And you will. This house will be a showcase. Your name will be remembered."

Letty blinked. "I don't care about being *remembered*. I care about making use of my time *now*, to work to bring joy to other households. Other families."

"The name is always more important than the individual job. The name is eternal, representative of the body of work."

"Maybe when your name is Hawthorne, you can afford the luxury of thinking that way."

"I am trying to help," Anne said.

"I know. I appreciate it, really I do." Letty looked around the room in all its splendor. She appreciated everything that Anne had given to her, and that she had allowed her to put her ideas into action. But was appreciation enough? "I need to see my son." She hesitated. "I don't know when I'll be back."

"How can you go to him after the way he spoke to you?" The shock was plain on Anne's face.

Letty paused, one hand on the back of her chair. "He is my son, Anne. He's hurt and misguided. And he's all I've got."

"You have me," she said, her eyes large and shiny with tears.

"I *thought* we had each other. Now I wonder if we ever understood each other."

She could see the alarm on Anne's face. "You are coming back, aren't you?"

"I think we have a lot to talk about. Right now, I need space."

❖

Letty had gone in a whirl of plaid skirts, leaving Anne alone with only the ticktock of the grandfather clock for company.

Letty hadn't said good-bye, she told herself.

But she had *left*.

Like Hawthorne had.

She had shared everything with Letty and had been her most intimate self with her. Letty had shown her how to laugh again, how to be the woman that she had locked up so long ago. Finally, she was free, but at what cost if she no longer had Letty in her life?

What had she meant when she said that Anne hadn't made room for her? Hawthorne House was enormous—and Letty hadn't even seen the other estates. She had thought of bringing Letty to see them in the summer. She paused. Had she ever said as much? Had she actually told Letty that she saw a future with her?

Or had she made assumptions that of course everything would go the way a duchess planned it?

In truth, she hadn't thought of Letty working past this job. She wouldn't need it. Anne had heaps of money to spend as she pleased, and if she pleased to keep Letty with her, she knew no one would say a word against it.

She frowned. Maybe they did have more to talk about than she realized.

She could only hope that it wouldn't be enough to tear them apart.

CHAPTER TWENTY-FIVE

After the grand magnificence of Hawthorne House, the apartment in Holborn felt small. Once, Letty had found it comfortable enough, but now she saw how cramped their quarters were. It had never bothered her before, and she was cross at the idea that she could have grown accustomed to splendor so quickly. Had she become snobbish by spending so much time at the ducal estate?

Upon her arrival, Robert mumbled something about going out to meet with his friends and made haste out the door. Letty was relieved. She knew they needed to talk, but the opportunity to rest sounded wonderful. She hadn't realized how tired she was from stretching herself thin with work. Marcus and Fraser had been right—the hours at Hawthorne House had started to eat up her life, threatening to swallow it whole. Tonight was the first time she had been at home before nightfall in a long time.

More fool she for trying to grasp on to the illusion of forever.

The blankets on her bed were pulled up to the pillow, waiting for her to crawl in. Alone. It was only four o'clock in the afternoon, but Letty was exhausted. She rubbed her chest, which started aching after her argument with Anne. She rummaged in her chest of drawers and pulled out a thick flannel nightgown. With it came memories of Anne and the night they had spent here together months ago, but she bundled herself in its warmth anyway, with a pair of wool socks that needed darning. It wasn't quite cool enough to merit the outfit, but it was well-worn and snug and she needed the comfort, so she slid the window open an inch to cool the room and then tucked herself into bed.

It was nice to be still enough to allow her thoughts to gather and disperse like smoke, and she fell asleep.

Letty only knew disorientation for a second when she awoke, hours later. The bruising feeling in her chest reawakened with her, but her headache had lessened. It was dark in her room, and cold, and there was a sliver of light beneath the door that told her that Robert was home.

She closed the window and drew on a shawl before she went to face him.

He was fumbling with a teacup on the table, which he dropped when he saw her. "Fancy a cup of tea, Mum? I had the water on for you."

Sure enough, the kettle was in the fire and she could hear the water boiling away. Blinking away a sudden tear, she could only nod. He had never done anything like that before for her.

"Go sit and I'll bring it to you."

That earnest face, so sweet and so dear, brought another tear to her eye, and the bruise on her heart grew. She settled into the chair with the throw blanket and tucked it on her lap.

The tea was strong and hot when he brought it to her.

"We haven't any milk," he said, a trifle defensive.

"I didn't complain," she said, scalding her lips on a sip. It felt so nice to be coddled a little. When was the last time they had a moment like this together? Letty's heart warmed with the tea. She had raised a fine young man after all. A troubled young man, and a complicated one—but a fine one, nonetheless.

She decided it would be best to have it out. "Why did you need the money, Robert?"

He flushed. "I had unexpected expenses."

"Drink? Women? Gambling?"

His lips tightened and he looked away. "Work."

"Robert, what are you talking about? They are meant to pay *you*, not the other way around."

"I was expected to take Mr. Selkirk to dinners. The theater. Gifts of bourbon, or cigars."

"Why didn't you tell me?"

"I tried when I came to see you at the estate. But I was so angry, and—well, I know I comported myself badly. I am so sorry, Mum. I know better than to behave like that." He pushed his teacup round his saucer, and she was reminded of him doing the same thing when he had been a boy, ashamed of being caught in a scrape.

"He took advantage of your inexperience and your lack of options." Letty shook her head. "Robert, you should have said something to the other solicitors you work for. He is a despicable man."

"I wanted to do whatever I could to make my own way," he said, but he sounded more tired than angry. "But after all that, Mr. Selkirk changed his mind. When he told me that he couldn't mentor me, I was wild with rage. I had done only five months under his tutelage, and I need five years to be a solicitor in full! Now I must start all over from scratch with another man."

Youth. So impatient. What was five months of a lifetime when one became old enough to stare back at the decades? Then she thought of the six months that she had spent at Hawthorne House, and how it had changed her forever. She remembered the nine months that she had spent nurturing life in her womb.

"Was that when you wrote to Lady Wilson?"

"I thought she could talk to him, but all she wanted was to meet the Duchess of Hawthorne." He let out a hollow laugh. "More fool me. I thought he might respect a title if he didn't respect me, and then he might let me stay."

"The Wilsons aren't like that," she said. Her stomach felt sour and she took a gulp of tea as if she could wash away the memories. "They aren't kind, and they do nothing from the goodness of their hearts."

"I didn't know. I don't know them at all."

Letty didn't like remembering those times, but it hadn't been fair to keep them to herself. Shielding a child was one thing, but Robert had been old enough for years now. "When they cut off the stipend, Lady Wilson made sure to tell me in person. She was here in London to wrap up some business affairs with the estate, and she was proud to tell me that their good name no longer had to be associated in any way with the muck of ours. She laughed in my face, and that was the last I saw of her until today."

"Why didn't you say anything?"

"You have so little family of your own," she said softly. "I hadn't wanted to disillusion you. We have built a family here in London of friends and neighbors, but the Wilsons are all that you have of your father. I didn't want to tarnish the memory."

"You never thought much of heritage before."

"No." Her own family had treated her so poorly when she needed help the most that she didn't put stock in where people came from. She cared more about what people did with their lives than the circumstances of their birth. Then she thought of Anne and Hawthorne, determined to use their name and connections to help those who might flock to the security of a noble name. She thought of Phin, hiring the worst chambermaids in London because he had the coin to spare if they bent their minds to theft. Heritage and tradition just might be what one made of it. "But I understand it a little better now. I thought you would be too proud of the connection, so I tried not to speak of it for fear that you would think working was beneath you. We didn't have the resources for you not to work."

"And yet then I built castles in the air, from hopes and dreams." Robert sank back in the chair.

"Now you can build something better. Stronger. With a good foundation, and a roof that can last a lifetime." Letty smiled at him. "That's the wonder of endings. You get to create beginnings all over again."

"I don't know what I'm going to do."

"You'll find something." She paused. "And if you can't on your own, then I'm always going to be here to help you to find out what comes next. I should have trusted in you and told you about your family, to allow you to draw your own conclusions. You are an adult now, and while you will always be my son, things need to be more equal in our relationship. I made a lot of money from the Hawthorne job, you know, and I had always intended for the bulk of it to go to you to start your adult life. If you don't consider it to be tainted money, that is."

"That's beyond generous, after the muck I've made of everything. I'm so sorry for all the awful things I've said, Mum. I was angry, and I was proud, and most of all—I was a fool. It was unforgivable. I shall regret it all my life that I spoke to you that way."

"I forgive you," she said quietly. "You have made mistakes that hurt me, Robert. But I will never turn my back on you. You are my son, and as long as we can always talk about the problems we face, we can face them together. We are stronger together. I love you."

Family didn't always mean acceptance, and it didn't guarantee forgiveness. Letty had not heard one word from her parents after they learned that she was pregnant. Robert's father's family had cast him aside since his birth. But she had enough broken bonds in her past to know that she wanted to do all she could to shore up the ones she had.

Robert's smile was like the shawl, the flannel, and the tea. Familiar, comfortable. This was *family*. Her heart soared.

Waking up each morning without the anticipation of Letty coming to work at the estate was a disappointment that Anne didn't like to face. She allowed herself to be bathed and dressed by her maid, finding the morning ritual nigh unbearable today. She remembered the thrill of self-discovery when she had first seen these rooms, finding pieces of herself reflected at her in every careful detail.

Although there was an *A* on every bar of soap and every pillow and every handkerchief, it might as well have been an *L*, because she thought of Letty everywhere she looked.

It had been Letty who chose these towels that the servants rubbed all over her body, and Letty who selected the mirror that she stared into while her maid arranged her hair. Letty had mused over every color, texture, and fabric.

Letty had mused over her, too, and had clearly found her wanting.

But that hurt too much to dwell on, so Anne went to her parlor to see the silver coffeepot and two biscuits set out for her, with the neat stack of leather portfolios and the day's business within.

Just like every day.

It felt different knowing that Letty wasn't bustling around the estate. Of all the wonderful things that she had filled the house with, the most valuable of all had been her presence. Without her, it felt empty.

Hawthorne swept in and Anne was reminded that the house was not entirely empty after all.

"To what do I owe this honor?" she asked, setting aside her pen.

"I have been thinking of our situation. You run the dukedom better than any man," Hawthorne said. "Better than I would do myself. Can't you continue to run things there, while I focus my attention on politics?"

Anne stared. "Wouldn't that ruin the illusion of the duke's power? I thought the point of your return to this house was to strengthen your case in parliament, to be known as a shrewd manager of your affairs."

"I have decided that I would prefer to showcase my excellent taste in choosing a wife, and hand over all decision-making to you. This is your strength, Annie. You should have had the power from the beginning, and I was too foolish in Paris to realize what limits you were working under."

"It is the ducal discretion to change one's mind, after all," she said. Warmth blossomed inside her. "But if I remember correctly, I think I chose you as a husband first."

"This dukedom stands for equality, after all." He slipped a hand into his pocket and withdrew a tiny package wrapped in a scrap of velvet. "Here." He presented it to her with a flourish.

She peeled the fabric away and stared down at a heavy gold ring.

"It's yours and yours alone," he said.

She turned it over to look at it more closely and gasped when she grasped its significance.

It was a signet ring.

He twisted his own from his finger and dropped it into her palm. They were almost identical in design, studded with tiny rubies and opals, but the new ring was smaller. She slid it onto her middle finger and held her right hand in front of her, admiring it. Instead of the swirling Hawthorne *H* by itself, this one had a graceful *A* and *H* intertwined.

"You can sign any document as Anne, Duchess of Hawthorne, and this seal will signify that the decisions are made on behalf of us both in this dukedom. You don't need to use the Hawthorne seal anymore and hide behind my name to approve anything. I know it's unusual to have two signet rings in the family." He grinned. "But I think we are rather unusual."

It was rare for a woman to have her own signet. Anne smiled. They *were* family, the two of them. "Thank you for the gift. I appreciate this more than I can say."

Her name would finally mean something besides self-preservation and condemnation of others. She owned her own place now in the dukedom. Decisions that she made would contribute to her personal legacy.

As she stared down at the ring, she felt a wave of excitement for everything that it represented. Power. Opportunity. Progress.

She had stayed in London all through the winter. Now that she had the power, she wanted to tour their holdings and put plans into action to improve and modernize each one.

But most of all, Anne wanted to tell Letty that they had won after all.

Yet what was winning without the love of her life beside her to share it?

She frowned.

"You seem bereft. Is it the absence of the charming Miss Barrow? I never seem to hear her laughter in the halls these days, and the rooms are remarkably quiet without the work crew."

"I'm not bereft," she muttered, then sighed.

"Come here."

She sat beside him on the sofa.

"Take some comfort. Cry if you must."

"I wouldn't want to ruin your coat."

"Its loss will be a tailor's gain, for I shall simply have another one made to measure."

Anne had shed enough tears last night, but it was surprising how nice if felt to have the offer. She could trust him. She inched closer and settled her head on his shoulder and felt the warmth of his hand as he placed it on her back.

"I suppose we must look as predictable as any old married couple, enjoying the peace and quiet of a spring morning together."

"Ah, but we happen to be much more interesting than anyone gave us credit for in our youth. We reached far beyond the mere *predictable* and are enjoying something altogether better indeed."

She smiled. "I'm glad that this is what we chose."

"I'm sorry that it took so long for us to get to this point. I know you had wanted it from the beginning."

"You're giving it to me now," she told him. "It's enough."

"Now tell me about love lost."

It was a struggle to find words to express the emptiness she felt. "I am unmoored," Anne said after a pause. "Adrift in the sea, no lighthouse, no lodestar to guide me to shore. Letty is so much more to me than a lover. I love her, Hawthorne. But I haven't told her because I don't think she'll have me."

"If there's one thing I have learned about love—and you are free to assume that over the years, I have studied it plenty—it is to take what is freely offered and make sure to give it back in spades."

"What kind of advice is that?"

"If you are lucky enough to find love, then love with your whole heart. Don't hide it. Shout it from the bloody rooftop. Let Miss Barrow know how you feel and let her make a decision. But don't make the decision for her because you were too afraid to tell her how you feel."

Sir Phineas entered, the pug trotting in with him. "I don't mean to interrupt."

"This isn't what you might think." Anne rose from the sofa.

He grinned. "Do you truly think for one moment that I would believe the two of you have changed all manner of nature and have fallen into a deep passion?"

"Stranger things might have happened, but not today, Sir Phineas. Hawthorne remains all yours."

He swept into a bow. "I appreciate you keeping him warm for me, Your Grace."

Hawthorne barked with laughter. "I would have come home a long time ago if I had known what domestic bliss we could have created together."

Anne hadn't realized how much she would gain with Hawthorne's presence. Having someone else inhabit the house who knew her secrets, and indeed shared them—this was indeed the comfort she had thought to gain upon their marriage.

How sweet it would be to have Letty here too. It was more than a house when she was in it, bustling around and fixing it up and bringing her magic to everything she touched. Including Anne. It was a home. It could be *their* home.

If that was what Letty wanted, anyway.

Hawthorne was right. She had to tell Letty how she felt. She had to take a risk if she wanted any hope of the reward of their love.

"How are preparations for the grand opening coming along?" Sir Phineas asked.

"Mrs. MacInnes and I ran through the details together this morning and everything is well in hand. Hawthorne, I thought your speech could be delivered before the musicians started to play."

He nodded. "Excellent, thank you. Has Prince George accepted the invitation?"

"Not yet. But a great many others have confirmed their attendance."

"I had wanted him there to lend more weight behind the speech. But we shall make do." There was strain around his eyes, and Sir Phineas squeezed his shoulder.

Anne threw very few social events, and the prince had never refused any that he had been invited to. Not having an answer at all was unusual, and boded ill. Hawthorne wanted him in attendance to lend legitimacy to his place among the highest of High Society after so many years of absence from the court.

But if the prince didn't show up, would it appear as a mark of disfavor on Hawthorne and the choices he had made in his life? Would onlookers count a royal absence as a slight against them both? Anne's place at her husband's side would give him some credibility, and would smooth over any overt grumbling, but it could only take it so far. The prince was key to social rehabilitation.

"Will Miss Barrow be in attendance?" Sir Phineas asked, wagging his brow. He was clearly attempting to lighten the mood.

The grand opening was for Hawthorne's benefit and the guest list was limited to the people with whom he sought to curry favor.

"If you want her here, send an invitation. Send a footman with the carriage and insist on a reply." Hawthorne's eyes bore into hers. "When you want something out of reach, you must stretch beyond your comfort."

"Letty should enjoy the fruits of her labor." An idea struck Anne. Maybe this would be the perfect time to show her how much she belonged here. "We could make her a guest of honor, could we not?"

Hawthorne grinned. "I should like nothing better."

This would be the ideal opportunity to bolster Letty's reputation among the lords and ladies of the *ton*. All of London would know Letitia Barrow's name after this tour.

For once, she was doing work that she wanted—not what her duty demanded.

Chapter Twenty-six

"O h, look who's shown up? You've become a stranger these days, Letty my lass."

Letty rolled her eyes at Fraser's gleeful face, trying to hide her joy when she glimpsed Robert at the back of the room. She had ventured downstairs to Fraser's workroom with a tray of tea and toast in the hopes that Robert was down here with him.

Her habit was to purchase confections from the bakery up the road for breakfast, but sweets now reminded her so much of Anne that she had decided instead on French bread slathered with butter. She tried not to dwell on how much she missed the marzipan buns.

She tried not to dwell on how much she missed *Anne*.

"I am hardly a stranger anymore, Fraser. I saw you last week at Swann's."

"Yes, and you ducked out before the bill was due because your fancy carriage had arrived to whisk you off to Hawthorne House. You owe me for that drink, you know. Just because you are passing time with a duchess doesn't give you the right to scarper and let the rest of us make do."

She stared into her tea. "I don't think we're still passing time together."

Fraser's eyes softened. "Oh, Letty."

"In fact, come up after work tonight and I'll serve you that drink." She bit into her toast. "Keep me company so I don't wither away from heartbreak, please. And do not rub your own newfound happiness in my nose."

"I'll be there."

"How is Robert faring down here?"

"Well, I must admit your son is useless with a piece of a wood in his hands," he said. "Nothing doing, I'm afraid."

Robert swore from the corner and shook his fingers hard, evidently having hammered them. "I'm fine," he called out.

"I see what you mean. Perhaps life as a woodworker isn't in his future."

"I would be game to have him on for as long as he likes, though. You know I've a soft spot for the lad, and I always need extra hands to sand, haul wood, or load furniture into the customer's carriages. It's a fine arrangement for now."

Letty spent the rest of the day organizing her workroom. It had become easier to work from Hawthorne House, and she hadn't been in her own space in weeks. She jammed a box onto the shelf with too much force and had to steady the fabric rolls that threatened to fall. Her identity was tied up in these paintbrushes and wallpaper swatches, in the wood samples and paint chips. This was her passion. Anne had been kind when she arranged the parlor for her as a workroom, but did she really understand the importance of her work? Did she really think that she would give it all up, when she was working so hard to prove that her talents deserved to be recognized?

Maybe she hadn't been on a Grand Tour to see the wonders that the world had to offer, and maybe she didn't have a storeroom of collectibles that she could use to furnish houses. She didn't have the pedigree, or the social standing. Maybe Lady Wilson's appearance at the estate had shaken her confidence to the core.

But she didn't need any of those things, and she certainly didn't need anyone's acceptance or approval, to be proud of what she had accomplished.

Hawthorne House was the pinnacle of her career. It showcased what could be done with design—to go beyond furnishing a room to imbuing it with personality and ideals and inspiration. Each room had come together in a marriage of breathtaking art and comfortable furniture, private moments presented in public spaces. It told the story of Anne and Hawthorne and embraced who they were. She loved that these ideas would be available to the public who would stroll through the estate for a shilling on Mondays.

Letty hoped some of them would have their own homes in need of refurnishing.

After all, she would have to start looking for another job soon, or Robert wouldn't be the only unemployed Barrow in residence.

When night fell, she set out for Swann's and brought back enough food for a feast. It warmed her heart to see Fraser and Robert here at her table, laughing together. This was what was missing for her at Hawthorne House. It wasn't *hers*. She wasn't free to have her son or friends come over for a casual evening like this.

After all, a true home wasn't about the house, no matter how exquisitely she might furnish it. A home was about the people. The moments. The laughter and the tears.

The love.

When she looked around these rooms, scores of memories swarmed her mind's eye.

The scuffs on the floor near the armchairs from scooting them closer to the fire each winter as she and Robert shared a cup of tea and talked in the evenings.

The patches on the quilt that she had mended near the window because the light was best in the kitchen, and how Robert had laughed when he had seen her stitching while sitting on the counter.

The faint stain in the rug where Fraser had spilled gravy one night when they had too much whiskey while laughing over their exploits from when they were twenty and new to London.

Letty's heart was full, but she felt bittersweet as she dished out portions of tansy pudding for dessert. The reality was that there wouldn't be too many more nights with Fraser, who was settling down with Marcus soon enough, or with Robert, who would be looking toward a family of his own.

Trying to keep everything the same was like grasping at moonlight.

She had to accept that things were changing and allow herself to be swept up in the current of her own life, or else risk being left behind and drowning. Alone.

Her home wasn't this suite of rented rooms, and it wasn't Hawthorne House.

The home she wanted was quite simply wherever Anne was, whether it was gliding on ice skates on a wintry pond, or laughing in bed with a towel-wrapped brick at their feet, or dining at a table built for two dozen and smiling over a shared piece of cake.

She wanted a home made of intimate moments where they whispered truths to each other, where touches sizzled between them, and where the gentleness of their embrace eased them into sleep.

They belonged together, no matter *where*.

That was why she had never bothered renovating her rented rooms here. She hadn't needed to. All she had needed was family, and that was exactly what she had with Fraser and Robert.

It was what she wanted to create with Anne.

How could she have expected Anne to make room in her life for her, when she had been too afraid to ask for it? Why had she been so hasty to assume that a duchess couldn't change her ways, that she wouldn't welcome Letty and her family? Hadn't she witnessed Anne change so much over the months?

Why had she let herself be bound by fear, when she had refused to let fear dictate anything in her life?

Robert and Fraser were laughing together.

"Working with you isn't the hardship I thought it would be," Robert said cheerfully.

"Ah well, such is life. Sometimes you're up, and sometimes you're down. You're naught more than a day laborer now instead of working to be a fancy solicitor with an office in Chancery. It's a sad downgrade indeed."

Robert laughed. "I have plenty of time to turn my fortunes around," he said. "Maybe I can marry an heiress. Would you help me find one?"

Fraser rumpled Robert's hair like he had when he'd been a boy. "I would indeed, if one would have you, lad. We will always be family, blood or no."

"I wish you had been my father, Fraser."

"Aye, I felt enough like it when I taught you how to drink whisky."

"And smoke cigars."

Letty raised a brow. "This is the first I'm hearing of it."

Robert's smile turned sheepish, and Letty joined in the laughter.

"I plan on going back to Hawthorne House soon," she said, breaking into the conversation. "I am wondering if perhaps this time...I might stay there."

Robert grabbed at his dish of pudding as he almost tipped it over, his ears reddening. "I am sorry for the things I said to you and the duchess, Mum. It was wretched of me."

Fraser glared down at him. "What did you say, young man?"

He wilted beneath the glare. "Unkind things that I will not repeat, sir. Unkind, and untruthful in nature."

"They weren't all untruths," Letty said mildly. "Anne and I have been having an affair. I am in love with her."

The rest of Robert's face turned beet red, and Fraser broke into a grin.

"I always rose above it when people told me that I couldn't design because I'm a woman. I put my head down and worked twice as hard as any man, and now maybe I have the opportunity to go twice as far. My work stands for itself. I don't have to care what people may say about it." She took a deep breath. "And I don't have to care what they say about my life. I never have, and I can't start now. People might say I'm opportunistic, taking advantage of a personal relationship with a duchess to further my career. They may cast aspersions on my character. But that's my business, not theirs, and my life makes me happy. *Anne* makes me happy."

Fraser pulled her up for a hug, and after a moment Robert wrapped his arms around the two of them.

Letty held on tight to them before letting go.

She was ready for a new start.

Hopefully to something glorious.

Anne fretted over the letters on her desk, or rather the lack thereof. There was still no reply from Prince George, and the grand opening was a week away. She had sent an invitation to Letty this afternoon with her most trusted footman, but he had come back and said there was no reply given when he had delivered it.

She might be facing the loss of the love of her life. If she hadn't lost her already.

But Letty hadn't said good-bye, she reminded herself. Her belongings were still in the parlor that she worked from. Was she supposed to have boxed them up and sent them with the footman and the invitation?

Anne set her letters aside and went to Letty's workroom. It had been redone in light, airy colors that were perfect for spring. And hope. And love. But what didn't remind her of love these days?

Upon her instruction to the staff, nothing had been moved. Floor plans were still rolled up on the table, reference books were on the shelves with a few cartons of odds and ends that hadn't made it into any of the refinished rooms. Everything was laid out as if Letty were about to walk in with her half-smile and a teasing word and start working.

Anne trailed her hand over the pair of sketchbooks on the desk, brimming with loose papers and fabric scraps tucked between the pages. There was a smear of dried paint on the cover of one, and the binding was unraveling a little on the other. Well-used and well-worn.

It meant she was coming back, didn't it? For a craftsperson to leave their supplies, it must be a sign that they would be back. Letty had gone nowhere without her sketchbooks and her pencil case. But when Anne looked closer, she saw that the books were full. Maybe Letty didn't need them anymore.

Maybe she really was finished with Hawthorne House, and her quick departure would be their only good-bye.

Anne picked up one of the books. If she pressed it to her nose, she could almost smell Letty's vanilla spice perfume, as if the pages had soaked in her essence.

She flipped it open to the middle and found a drawing of her bedroom on one page and notes about the bed on the other. Delighted, she stroked the pencil lines that cleverly detailed the patterns, with tiny squares of fabric glued along the right side and neat arrows pointing to which mattress they belonged to.

Page after page detailed each room that Letty had worked on, with meticulous sketches showing the unfurnished rooms, neatly written ideas and plans for each one, and then the final room with everything perfectly arranged.

It was a book filled with beginnings and endings, and Anne marveled over each page. It was almost as good as having Letty here beside her, pointing out the details that she had missed, and stories about why she had chosen certain elements.

That was Letty's skill as a designer. Hawthorne House wasn't a lifeless showpiece, a testament to power and prestige. It wasn't only a signal to the community that the Hawthornes stood with them. It was a *home*, meant to be lived in by real people with real wants and needs and dreams and desires.

Letty had been right. Her talents should be celebrated, and she should have every opportunity to work if she wanted to.

Anne's hand stilled on one of the pages. She recognized the framework of the room as one of the smaller parlors at the back of the house, a sunny room with a door opening onto the gardens. Though it was pretty enough, Anne had never spent much time there.

Letty had drawn a double page spread of the room and had painted in every detail. Curious, Anne stared down at it. Letty hadn't touched the actual parlor during her stay. In fact, Anne couldn't remember ever discussing that area of the house together. But something must have taken Letty's fancy, because she had filled it with furniture and light and color and plants, and in tiny handwriting in the bottom right corner, she had scribbled *Letitia's Parlor*.

Anne smiled down at the sketchbook as she closed it. Letty wanted to return. She was certain of it.

For all of the loving care and work that had been put into it, the renovated Hawthorne House was missing one important fixture—the designer herself.

No, it couldn't have been good-bye.

Letty Barrow belonged in this house, and Anne was going to prove it to her.

Chapter Twenty-seven

The musicians were warming up their instruments, and Anne listened to the scrape of violin strings and scales from the flute with more attention than usual. If she focused on the music, then she didn't have to stare down at the emptiness of the great hall or pay attention to the emptiness that echoed through the chambers of her heart. It also gave her something to do besides fret about her husband. She glanced up at him. His face was set as hard as the marble in the statuary, and a tick was fluttering at his eye. She took his hand in hers, forced his fist apart, and slid her fingers between his.

"It will all go to plan," she said.

"You can't be quite sure of that," he replied. "But I appreciate the sentiment. The show must go on, come what may." He held her hand in a bone-crushing squeeze.

Prince George had not replied to the invitation.

The grandfather clock down the checkered hallway boomed the hour.

"No one makes an early appearance these days," she said.

He jerked his head in a nod, and she listened once more for the music.

The doors swung open, and guests began to trickle in. Hawthorne strode up to them in greeting, and Anne surreptitiously stretched the cramp from her hand from where Hawthorne had gripped it into numbness.

There was a steady stream after that of men from the House of Lords mingling in the hallway with their counterparts from the Commons, many of whom were accompanied by their wives. Hawthorne's nephew, Edward, was there, cheerfully talking to some of the younger lords. Champagne was popped and poured by a team of footmen.

Anne ensured that crisp pamphlets were pressed into each parliamentary palm. She had paid a visit to Letty's friend Marcus, remembering that he was a stationer, and had begged a favor from him to arrange a rush printing with a publisher for the occasion. The pamphlets were sixteen pages apiece, two pages for each of the eight public rooms that would be part of the public tour. One page featured a detailed illustration, and the other was a description and any notes of interest.

Anne had poured over Letty's sketchbooks for hours to select the best parts to include. If there had been more time than a week, she would have liked to have the illustrations colored, but she decided there would be time enough to arrange a bigger printing which would be distributed to the public when they paid their shilling at the door for their tour.

She wanted people to remember Letty's work, to take it home with them. More than memories of the rooms—something concrete and tangible. It was like giving away a little part of the house to each visitor.

Anne nodded to Hawthorne from across the room. Now that a half hour had passed, it was time for Hawthorne's speech and the tour to begin.

A knot had settled in her belly. Neither the prince nor Letty had showed up. But there would be time enough to soak her pillow in tears tonight. Now, there was still an event to get through.

There was a tapping behind her, and a touch on her forearm, and suddenly Anne's world was complete. Letty stood there with Robert.

Anne sighed with relief. "I knew you were coming back," she said and fought the urge to sweep her into her embrace.

Letty's dress was plain compared to the lords' wives, but she had a distinct style all her own that made Anne's heart swell with pleasure. She was magnificent in a striped twill dress and a neat cravat, her gloved hands folded over the head of her walking stick.

"Of course I came back. I never said good-bye, did I?" Her mischievous smile was a balm to Anne's soul.

Anne wanted to say more, but Robert's presence stilled her tongue.

"No one will know I'm here," Letty said, accepting a glass of champagne from a passing footman. "I shall be quite secretive, worry not. Though it will be nice to see the reactions on people's faces as they see the house, this is Hawthorne's moment, as it should be."

Anne smiled. It wasn't just Hawthorne's moment.

Hawthorne leapt up a few stairs of the grand staircase, where the light shone down from the glass in the ceiling four floors above them. Her husband was no golden god. He had no perfect Byronic looks. But he had charm and magnetism beyond compare, and Anne was so proud of him for his willingness to stand apart from the society that she had always yearned to be part of.

"Greetings, ladies and gentlemen, and welcome to Hawthorne House. Some of you may have been here before as guests of my beloved wife. To those of you who are here for the first time, I beg your pardon as I am far from being as perfect a hostess as the duchess."

He nodded to Anne, who dipped her head in response amidst the crowd's appreciative murmurs.

"In the tradition of some of the other great houses in this neighborhood, I will be throwing open the doors to Hawthorne House every Monday to all and sundry. Any who wish to visit may secure a voucher and walk through these eight public rooms, the same as you will today. Why else have we accumulated art if not to share it with the people? How else can a duke share in the democracy of ideas, if he does not embrace his fellow man? The dukedom may have been granted to me by spiritual grace. This is what my father taught me, though I have kept out of churchly matters for so long that I no longer know if this is true." The crowd laughed. "But what is ours in this house is temporal. There are treasures from past cultures, and wonders from current artists and artisans alike. I wish to share our life with the people, so they may come to understand what it is that this dukedom stands for. Freedom to seek one's own path, and equality for my fellow man and woman."

The applause was scattered, but most importantly, the looks on people's faces were thoughtful. Respectful. Even without the prince in attendance.

Hawthorne raised a hand. "I would be remiss if you all left here today thinking that what you are about to see is wrought from my own inspiration. I owe everything to my wife, the Duchess of Hawthorne." She curtsied to warmer applause. "But most important of all, I want you to acknowledge the brilliant taste and talents of our designer. Please join me in a warm hand of applause for Miss Letitia Barrow."

Letty blinked as the crowd murmured and craned their heads to look for her. Hawthorne grinned and gestured to her, and after darting a look at Anne, she shoved her champagne into Robert's hand and strode up to join the duke on the staircase. Standing there in the sun were two of the most important people in Anne's life. Her heart swelled to see them exchange an easy smile.

"Your mother is the most talented woman I have ever met," Anne said sternly to Robert. She had not forgotten his poor treatment of Letty the last time she saw him.

"Yes, Your Grace." His voice was meek.

"Thank you for welcoming me to Hawthorne House, Your Grace," Letty said, her voice loud and clear. "It has been an honor beyond compare to have contributed to the majesty of this estate. I sought to embody your character and your ideals among the details, and I can only hope that I have met with some small success." She winked. "Now, I am free for hire if any other of your grand houses needs refreshing." The crowd laughed as she curtsied to Hawthorne, and he kissed her hand.

People stopped her to say a few words as Letty made her way back to Anne.

Hawthorne moved to the edge of the great hall, motioning for people to follow and to review their pamphlets as they began the tour.

"Hawthorne has it well in hand now," Letty said cheerfully. "I had no idea he was going to say anything about me. I never thought he would."

"I asked him to," Anne said, and her reward was the delighted grin that spread across Letty's face. She pointed to the front page of the pamphlet. "I created this with Marcus's help, detailing who you are and the work that you put into the house. People will know your name."

It was written there in bold serifed font under an illustration of the front of Hawthorne House. *Miss Letitia Barrow, Designer*. Anne underlined it with her finger and jabbed the page. "This is for you."

Letty took the pamphlet and beamed down at it. "Thank you."

"I rather thought you would like to go through the tour and add your voice to Hawthorne's in each room. Please do, if you want to. I wanted you to come as our honored guest."

"I think I am quite familiar enough with the public rooms," Letty said. "Perhaps we could retire for a brief moment to one of the more private ones?"

Anne nodded.

Letty grinned. "Robert, go expand your mind on the tour."

Anne led Letty beyond the public rooms to the back of the house and stopped in front of a closed door. She stood with her back to it, one hand on the doorknob. "Over the past few months, you have revealed so many rooms to me, Letty," she said. "And with each one, I understood more of myself. I am so grateful to know that someone knows me so well. I don't have your talents for color, or arrangement. But I wanted to give you something."

She wanted to show Letty that she understood what a gift her work had been and how much she appreciated it.

She wanted to show her the love they could share.

❖

Anne opened the door and stood back, gesturing for Letty to enter before her. Letty was touched—no one except royalty preceded a duchess. She stopped short after entering the room. It was the little parlor that she had so admired, the one overlooking the terrace. The room itself was largely unchanged, but it was now overflowing with greenery.

Roses, tulips, and orchids were placed on every available surface. Heavy copper tubs sat at the entrance to the terrace, green leafy trees waving gently in the fresh breeze from the open windows where gauzy curtains fluttered. The door was open to the outside, and although the yard was not yet in bloom, Letty could see the potential in her mind's eye.

"I had the gardeners from Hawthorne Towers send me cuttings and plants from the greenhouses there. I couldn't position things in here the way you would do, with your clever arrangements of furniture, but I had new curtains put up, and here"—she gestured to the table—"I had paint chips and fabrics assembled, to match as close as possible to the drawing in your sketchbook." Shades of pale yellow and light gray fanned out on the table, on top of a dark blue velvet swatch.

"It's beautiful," Letty said. She couldn't find the words to express what it meant to her. She didn't have much in her life these days that she hadn't fought for.

"Like you," Anne said. "I know the flowers are temporary bursts of beauty, but the trees will thrive forever. Like the building that surrounds them. Like what you have built for us inside these walls."

A book lay on the table by the paint chips. Letty picked it up and turned it over in her hands. It was bound in buttery soft yellow leather, with her name etched in gold leaf on the cover.

"Open it," Anne urged her.

Letty thumbed through the pages, bright white and unmarked, and inhaled the familiar crisp woodsy scent of a new book. There was a note inside the front cover, written in a hand that she recognized as Anne's own. She read it aloud. "For your next project. Wherever it may take you, may you always come home to me." She looked up. "Oh, Anne."

"You have made a living creating homes for other people wherever you go. Because you were tossed out of your own, you know the value of it—and I want to share mine with you. This room is for your pleasure, to sit and while the time away, or to take tea with Fraser and Marcus. It's not meant for work. But for *you*. Really, you can have the use of any room you like, though I hope you will consider my bedchamber to be first among them." Anne took a deep breath. "I understand what you meant now about making space. I was so focused on my own pleasures and my own needs, and I'm sorry that I didn't listen enough or pay enough attention to your own. Take me to eating houses and taverns and I'll take you to balls if you wish. I want to spend as much of my life with you as I can—in public and in private. No more secrets. No more hiding."

"I love that idea," Letty said and was surprised to find tears obscuring her vision. "I am sorry for doubting you, and for saying such horrid things. I was so afraid that I didn't belong in your life, and I lashed out in anger and fear. I know where I belong now. I belong with *you*."

"I love you, Letty," Anne said softly. "You are so strong, and capable, but I want you to know that I am here to support you just as much as you have supported me. I want you by my side, in this house or any other. You turned my heart upside down when you tore up the estate, and I don't ever want the work you've done on me to stop. I love how you think, how you challenge everything you come up against."

"I love you too, Anne." Letty's heart felt as light as the gossamer curtains on the window. "Watching you discover yourself has been one of the greatest joys of my life. I want to go on discovering our lives together and creating it new again and again with fresh challenges and projects."

Anne's eyes were bright. "*You* gave me the gift of myself. I didn't know what I wanted until you showed it to me. I didn't know how much I could have, if I could have only dreamt it. Now we have our own fairy tale ending."

Letty wrapped her arms around her and pressed her mouth to Anne's, trying to pour all of her emotion into her kiss when words didn't seem to be enough.

"I don't wish to let you go," Anne said, cupping Letty's cheek. "But you are the guest of honor at this grand opening, and the tour must be done by now. You should greet your adoring public."

Letty laughed. What a gift today had been, in so many ways. "I daresay they are hardly adoring. But maybe they found something to please them along the way."

"I certainly have," Anne murmured, her eyes caressing Letty's body, and they both laughed.

They rejoined the party as Hawthorne was leading everyone into the music room. It was a good crowd, and though there was a polite swell of conversation, Letty was disappointed to see that the guests were still reserving judgment on their host. People spoke to Hawthorne, but in a cool clipped way that didn't speak well of their future bouts in parliament together.

Anne took a leisurely look around the room filled with people, doubtlessly most whom she knew from social events. They were standing at the edge of the music room, but being a duchess meant that Anne had plenty of eyes on her no matter where she was.

She smiled up at Letty, a true smile full of love and devotion, then leaned up and kissed her.

Full on the lips.

Fully in public.

It wasn't a passionate kiss or a long one, but it was firm and decisive, and Letty knew what it meant. It was one more gift, to show her that Anne was serious about their life together.

No more secrets.

Murmurs swirled around them.

Anne smiled serenely and tucked her hand in the crook of her arm as they started to stroll around the room. "People may say what they wish. It is we who have it all. They may well think a kiss is the mark of a duchess's favor, like it was in older times. After their tour with Hawthorne, some may suspect it is much more."

"You aren't worried?"

"I didn't realize until the night at the oyster tavern that I have the immense privilege of not needing to fear for my life, regardless of what people think may be true. We might have a dozen witnesses tonight, but there are no watchmen here. I am safe enough that I can make an occasional gesture such as this, and hope that some may see it and feel less alone with their own desires."

"Will you receive fewer invitations?"

"Perhaps, but would I even have time to attend them?" Anne told her about the signet ring, tugging off her glove and showing it to her with obvious pride. "I want to focus on the estates for now. My concerns are for the people on the land, not the gossip-mongers at the balls."

Letty swelled with pride. This could be a life well worth living together.

There was a commotion in the grand hall, and a heavy booted footfall sounded louder and louder until Prince George stood in the hallway. It only took a moment to see that he was in his cups already though it was but late afternoon, his face florid beneath a crown of unruly curls.

"Hawthorne!" he bellowed, striding into the room, bleary-eyed. He clapped the duke on the back and chortled. "Haven't had the chance to welcome you back to Britain's grand shores. I've heard your gatherings are legendary, though perhaps not quite to my tastes." He cast his eye over the crowd and lowered his voice to add, "This deadly dull affair doesn't seem up to your usual snuff, I must say. We sinners ought to stick together, eh? Thick as thieves, we could be. I can take you round, you know."

Hawthorne took a step back, his lips thinning. "There is no sin here, Your Majesty. There never has been."

Letty understood his meaning, even if the prince didn't. What they did and how they loved was far from sinful. It was joyful.

"Yes," he chortled, "that's quite the spirit. I understand. Plenty going on but nothing to see here, eh?"

Hawthorne took another step back, and Prince George frowned at him. He bowed. "I am gratified by your presence to our humble house, Your Majesty. But please do excuse me as I entertain my guests."

The parliamentary men looked a good deal happier with Hawthorne after he snubbed the prince, who was a disruptive force in politics. A few men even clapped him on the back, and one poured him a drink with a wide grin. Letty smiled. Things may not have gone according to the original plan, but it seemed to work out better in Hawthorne's favor this way.

Prince George fixed his eye on Anne and kissed her hand with a bit more lavish force than Letty liked. "My dear duchess, it has been too long since I have been to one of your elegant little gatherings. May I be so bold as to say that I have noticed a change in the décor since I was last here? Charming. Very charming."

"May I introduce Miss Letitia Barrow to you, Your Majesty? She is the one responsible for all the changes here at Hawthorne House. I am gratified to admit that her excellent taste has elevated our home."

Letty curtsied deeper than she had thought possible.

"Delighted, Miss Barrow. Truly delighted. I like things a bit more fanciful, you know, but it's very fine work you've done here." He nodded as he looked around the room. "Very credible indeed. You know, I am doing great things in Brighton these days. Perhaps you could take a crack at a room or two in my palace there."

He wandered off, plucking a glass of champagne from a tray.

"High favor indeed," Anne said to Letty. "I daresay your name is well established now."

Letty was awed. "This is higher than I ever thought to aspire."

Anne kissed her again. "The very highest is no more than what you deserve."

Hawthorne sauntered up to them. "I see you are making free with your affections, Annie. By the way, your son over there seems like a good lad," he said to Letty. "During the tour, he had a few very thoughtful observations about sculpture. I think he may have absorbed more from your career over the years than you may have thought. He's gone off with Edward now, talking about modern approaches to art."

"I would have loved to be in business with him, but he never showed any interest," she said, blinking in surprise. "He has always spoken of being a solicitor, though he has moved beyond that in recent weeks."

Hawthorne looked thoughtful. "The estate manager at Hawthorne Towers has been talking about retiring in a few years. He could use a shrewd young man with legal training as his assistant for the time being, with the opportunity to become the next steward if he proves capable of it. Your boy seems of an age with my nephew. If they get along, it may be a good idea for them to grow into their positions together. Gives them someone to trust besides us old folk." His tone was wry. "What do you think, Annie? Do you think young Robert might be a good fit? It would be your decision, of course."

Letty saw Robert and Edward talking in the corner, laughing so hard over champagne that Robert was nigh doubled over.

Anne smiled. "It sounds perfect."

Letty couldn't have designed a better ending for her work at Hawthorne House if she had tried. She had ended up with everything she could have dreamed of.

She gazed at Anne.

And so much more.

EPILOGUE

One Year Later

Hawthorne Towers was Anne's favorite estate, and summer was her favorite season. She inhaled the fresh country air, redolent with the scent of the lawn trimmings and rosebushes, and topped Letty's glass up with more wine.

It was dusk, and they were sitting in the gazebo by the lake. Hawthorne had arranged to build it for her as a wedding gift, a fanciful structure of wood and gilt, but he had left England before it had been finished, and she had never much liked spending time there.

Now she had plenty of memories of Letty's warm lips and strong arms from countless rendezvous in the gazebo on lazy afternoons, which meant that Anne added it to her list of favorite things about the estate. She could hear birdsong and the lake lapping at the shore, but as always, most of all she wanted to hear Letty's low voice.

"How is the work coming along?" Anne asked.

Letty took a sip of wine. "I've almost completed the work on the butler's bedchamber, and then I'll move on to the second footman's rooms tomorrow."

Letty had spent the year traveling between London and the six other Hawthorne estates scattered across England, where Anne was slowly implementing her ideas for improvements. When she was with Anne in the estates, she had focused her time on renovating the servants' quarters which had endeared her to the staff immediately and had earned her their loyalty. If any of them thought her relationship with Anne was strange, being her constant companion despite the fact that Anne had a husband, they never said it, and in fact seemed to be staunchly supportive.

Letty's design skills were much in demand after the success of Hawthorne House and the interest from the Prince Regent, so she had as much work as she could wish for. She had started to train an assistant to help her, especially for the times when she was out of London.

Letty and Hawthorne had struck a deal where Letty could furnish the houses she worked on by using his vast collections in the warehouse, and they split the profits on whatever sales she made.

Hawthorne's half of the money went to maintaining a charity in London to help men who were persecuted because of their romantic or sexual behaviors. Phin ran the charity on his behalf and seemed overjoyed to spend his days in London with a fixed purpose while Hawthorne was busy with parliament, where he had become a respected member.

"I am so glad you're here with me, Letty. Life is infinitely more wonderful with you in it." Anne clinked her glass against Letty's and they shared a warm smile.

Letty had given up her apartment next to Fraser when she moved to Hawthorne House with Anne, much to the delight of Marcus, who had moved into her old apartment the very next day. Keeping rooms beside Fraser seemed the perfect cover for their relationship and kept the neighbors' gossip to a minimum.

Robert had moved too, spending his days hard at work at Hawthorne Towers under the tutelage of the estate manager. Letty told her that she had never seen him so happy.

"How is it that I ended up with a duchess in my bed and in my heart?" Letty said, her gold-flecked eyes gleaming.

"I am lucky beyond measure that you did," she said, leaning over to kiss her. "Now I have everything my heart desires."

About the Author

Jane Walsh is a queer historical romance novelist who loves everything Regency. She is delighted to have the opportunity to put her studies in history and costume design to good use by writing love stories. She owes a great debt of gratitude to the local coffee shop for fueling her novel writing endeavors. Jane's happily ever after is centered on her wife and their cat and their cozy home together in Canada.

Website: www.janewalshwrites.com

Books Available from Bold Strokes Books

Business of the Heart by Claire Forsythe. When a hopeless romantic meets a tough-as-nails cynic, they'll need to overcome the wounds of the past to discover that their hearts are the most important business of all. (978-1-63679-167-8)

Dying for You by Jenny Frame. Can Victorija Dred keep an age-old vow and fight the need to take blood from Daisy Macdougall? (978-1-63679-073-2)

Exclusive by Melissa Brayden. Skylar Ruiz lands the TV reporting job of a lifetime, but is she willing to sacrifice it all for the love of her longtime crush, anchorwoman Carolyn McNamara? (978-1-63679-112-8)

Her Duchess to Desire by Jane Walsh. An up-and-coming interior designer seeks to create a happily ever after with an intriguing duchess, proving that love never goes out of fashion. (978-1-63679-065-7)

Murder on Monte Vista by David S. Pederson. Private Detective Mason Adler's angst at turning fifty is forgotten when his "birthday present," the handsome, young Henry Bowtrickle, turns up dead, and it's up to Mason to figure out who did it, and why. (978-1-63679-124-1)

Take Her Down by Lauren Emily Whalen. Stakes are cutthroat, scheming is creative, and loyalty is ever-changing in this queer, female-driven YA retelling of Shakespeare's Julius Caesar. (978-1-63679-089-3)

The Game by Jan Gayle. Ryan Gibbs is a talented golfer, but her guilt means she may never leave her small town, even if Katherine Reese tempts her with competition and passion. (978-1-63679-126-5)

Whereabouts Unknown by Meredith Doench. While homicide detective Theodora Madsen recovers from a potentially career-ending injury, she scrambles to solve the cases of two missing sixteen-year-old girls from Ohio. (978-1-63555-647-6)

Boy at the Window by Lauren Melissa Ellzey. Daniel Kim struggles to hold onto reality while haunted by both his very-present past and his never-present parents. Jiwon Yoon may be the only one who can break Daniel free. (978-1-63679-092-3)

Deadly Secrets by VK Powell. Corporate criminals want whistleblower Jana Elliott permanently silenced, but Rafe Silva will risk everything to keep the woman she loves safe. (978-1-63679-087-9)

Enchanted Autumn by Ursula Klein. When Elizabeth comes to Salem, Massachusetts, to study the witch trials, she never expects to find love—or an actual witch…and Hazel might just turn out to be both. (978-1-63679-104-3)

Escorted by Renee Roman. When fantasy meets reality, will escort Ryan Lewis be able to walk away from a chance at forever with her new client Dani? (978-1-63679-039-8)

Her Heart's Desire by Anne Shade. Two women. One choice. Will Eve and Lynette be able to overcome their doubts and fears to embrace their deepest desire? (978-1-63679-102-9)

My Secret Valentine by Julie Cannon, Erin Dutton, & Anne Shade. Winning the heart of your secret Valentine? These award-winning authors agree, there is no better way to fall in love. (978-1-63679-071-8)

Perilous Obsession by Carsen Taite. When reporter Macy Moran becomes consumed with solving a cold case, will her quest for the truth bring her closer to Detective Beck Ramsey or will her obsession with finding a murderer rob her of a chance at true love? (978-1-63679-009-1)

Reading Her by Amanda Radley. Lauren and Allegra learn love and happiness are right where they least expect it. There's just one problem: Lauren has a secret she cannot tell anyone, and Allegra knows she's hiding something. (978-1-63679-075-6)

The Willing by Lyn Hemphill. Kitty Wilson doesn't know how, but she can bring people back from the dead as long as someone is willing to take their place and keep the universe in balance. (978-1-63679-083-1)

Three Left Turns to Nowhere by Nathan Burgoine, J. Marshall Freeman, & Jeffrey Ricker. Three strangers heading to a convention in Toronto are stranded in rural Ontario, where a small town with a subtle kind of magic leads each to discover what he's been searching for. (978-1-63679-050-3)

Watching Over Her by Ronica Black. As they face the snowstorm of the century, and the looming threat of a stalker, Riley and Zoey just might find love in the most unexpected of places. (978-1-63679-100-5)

#shedeservedit by Greg Herren. When his gay best friend, and high school football star, is murdered, Alex Wheeler is a suspect and must find the truth to clear himself. (978-1-63555-996-5)

Always by Kris Bryant. When a pushy American private investigator shows up demanding to meet the woman in Camila's artwork, instead of introducing her to her great-grandmother, Camila decides to lead her on a wild goose chase all over Italy. (978-1-63679-027-5)

Exes and O's by Joy Argento. Ali and Madison really only have one thing in common. The girl who broke their heart may be the only one who can put it back together. (978-1-63679-017-6)

One Verse Multi by Sander Santiago. Life was good: promotion, friends, falling in love, discovering that the multi-verse is on a fast track to collision—wait, what? Good thing Martin King works for a company that can fix the problem, right…um…right? (978-1-63679-069-5)

Paris Rules by Jaime Maddox. Carly Becker has been searching for the perfect woman all her life, but no one ever seems to be just right until Paige Waterford checks all her boxes, except the most important one—she's married. (978-1-63679-077-0)

Shadow Dancers by Suzie Clarke. In this third and final book in the Moon Shadow series, Rachel must find a way to become the hunter and not the hunted, and this time she will meet Ehsee Yumiko head-on. (978-1-63555-829-6)

The Kiss by C.A. Popovich. When her wife refuses their divorce and begins to stalk her, threatening her life, Kate realizes to protect her new love, Leslie, she has to let her go, even if it breaks her heart. (978-1-63679-079-4)

The Wedding Setup by Charlotte Greene. When Ryann, a big-time New York executive, goes to Colorado to help out with her best friend's wedding, she never expects to fall for the maid of honor. (978-1-63679-033-6)

Velocity by Gun Brooke. Holly and Claire work toward an uncertain future preparing for an alien space mission, and only one thing is for certain, they will have to risk their lives, and their hearts, to discover the truth. (978-1-63555-983-5)

Wildflower Words by Sam Ledel. Lida Jones treks West with her father in search of a better life on the rapidly developing American frontier, but finds home when she meets Hazel Thompson. (978-1-63679-055-8)

A Fairer Tomorrow by Kathleen Knowles. For Maddie Weeks and Gerry Stern, the Second World War brought them together, but the end of the war might rip them apart. (978-1-63555-874-6)

Holiday Hearts by Diana Day-Admire and Lyn Cole. Opposites attract during Christmastime chaos in Kansas City. (978-1-63679-128-9)

Changing Majors by Ana Hartnett Reichardt. Beyond a love, beyond a coming-out, Bailey Sullivan discovers what lies beyond the shame and self-doubt imposed on her by traditional Southern ideals. (978-1-63679-081-7)

Fresh Grave in Grand Canyon by Lee Patton. The age-old Grand Canyon becomes more and more ominous as a group of volunteers fight to survive alone in nature and uncover a murderer among them. (978-1-63679-047-3)

Highland Whirl by Anna Larner. Opposites attract in the Scottish Highlands, when feisty Alice Campbell falls for city-girl-about-town Roxanne Barns. (978-1-63555-892-0)

Humbug by Amanda Radley. With the corporate Christmas party in jeopardy, CEO Rosalind Caldwell hires Christmas Girl Ellie Pearce as her personal assistant. The only problem is, Ellie isn't a PA, has never planned a party, and develops a ridiculous crush on her totally intimidating new boss. (978-1-63555-965-1)

On the Rocks by Georgia Beers. Schoolteacher Vanessa Martini makes no apologies for her dating checklist, and newly single mom Grace Chapman ticks all Vanessa's Do Not Date boxes. Of course, they're never going to fall in love. (978-1-63555-989-7)

Song of Serenity by Brey Willows. Arguing with the Muse of music and justice is complicated, falling in love with her even more so. (978-1-63679-015-2)

The Christmas Proposal by Lisa Moreau. Stranded together in a Christmas village on a snowy mountain, Grace and Bridget face their past and question their dreams for the future. (978-1-63555-648-3)

The Infinite Summer by Morgan Lee Miller. While spending the summer with her dad in a small beach town, Remi Brenner falls for Harper Hebert and accidentally finds herself tangled up in an intense restaurant rivalry between her famous stepmom and her first love. (978-1-63555-969-9)

Wisdom by Jesse J. Thoma. When Sophia and Reggie are chosen for the governor's new community design team and tasked with tackling substance abuse and mental health issues, battle lines are drawn even as sparks fly. (978-1-63555-886-9)

A Convenient Arrangement by Aurora Rey and Jaime Clevenger. Cuffing season has come for lesbians, and for Jess Archer and Cody Dawson, their convenient arrangement becomes anything but. (978-1-63555-818-0)

An Alaskan Wedding by Nance Sparks. The last thing either Andrea or Riley expects is to bump into the one who broke her heart fifteen years ago, but when they meet at the welcome party, their feelings come rushing back. (978-1-63679-053-4)

Beulah Lodge by Cathy Dunnell. It's 1874, and newly engaged Ruth Mallowes is set on marriage and life as a missionary...until she falls in love with the housemaid at Beulah Lodge. (978-1-63679-007-7)

Gia's Gems by Toni Logan. When Lindsey Speyer discovers that popular travel columnist Gia Williams is a complete fake and threatens to expose her, blackmail has never been so sexy. (978-1-63555-917-0)

Holiday Wishes & Mistletoe Kisses by M. Ullrich. Four holidays, four couples, four chances to make their wishes come true. (978-1-63555-760-2)

Love By Proxy by Dena Blake. Tess has a secret crush on her best friend, Sophie, so the last thing she wants is to help Sophie fall in love with someone else, but how can she stand in the way of her happiness? (978-1-63555-973-6)

Loyalty, Love, & Vermouth by Eric Peterson. A comic valentine to a gay man's family of choice, including the ones with cold noses and four paws. (978-1-63555-997-2)

Marry Me by Melissa Brayden. Allison Hale attempts to plan the wedding of the century to a man who could save her family's business, if only she wasn't falling for her wedding planner, Megan Kinkaid. (978-1-63555-932-3)

Pathway to Love by Radclyffe. Courtney Valentine is looking for a woman exactly like Ben—smart, sexy, and not in the market for anything serious. All she has to do is convince Ben that sex-without-strings is the perfect pathway to pleasure. (978-1-63679-110-4)

Sweet Surprise by Jenny Frame. Flora and Mac never thought they'd ever see each other again, but when Mac opens up her barber shop right next to Flora's sweet shop, their connection comes roaring back. (978-1-63679-001-5)

The Edge of Yesterday by CJ Birch. Easton Gray is sent from the future to save humanity from technological disaster. When she's forced to target the woman she's falling in love with, can Easton do what's needed to save humanity? (978-1-63679-025-1)

The Scout and the Scoundrel by Barbara Ann Wright. With unexpected danger surrounding them, Zara and Roni are stuck between duty and survival, with little room for exploring their feelings, especially love. (978-1-63555-978-1)